SECOND IN
COMMAND

What Reviewers Say About VK Powell's Work

Take Your Time

"The last book in the Pine Cone Romance series was excellent, and I reckon VK Powell wrote the perfect book to round up the series. ...If these are the sex scenes VK Powell can write, then I have been missing out and I will definitely be checking out more because WOW! All in all... Fantastic! 5 stars"—*Les Reveur*

Captain's Choice

"VK Powell is the mistress of police romances and this one is another classic 'will she won't she' story of lost loves reunited by chance. Well written, lots of great sex and excellent sexual tension, great character building and use of the setting, this was a thoroughly enjoyable read."—*Lesbian Reading Room*

Side Effects

"[A] touching contemporary tale of two wounded souls hoping to find lasting love and redemption together. ...Powell ably plots a plausible and suspenseful story, leading readers to fall in love with the characters she's created."—*Publishers Weekly*

To Protect and Serve

"If you like cop novels, or even television cop shows with women as full partners with male officers...this is the book for you. It's got drama, excitement, conflict, and even some fairly hot lesbian sex. The writer is a retired cop, so she really writes from a place of authenticity. As a result, you have a realistic quality to the writing that puts me in mind of early Joseph Wambaugh."—Teresa DeCrescenzo, *Lesbian News*

"*To Protect and Serve* drew me in from the very first page with characters that captivated in their complexity. Powell writes with authority using the lingo and capturing the thoughts of the law enforcers who make the ultimate sacrifice in the fight against crime. What's more impressive is the command this debut author has of portraying a full gamut of emotion, from angst to elation, through dialogue and narrative. The images are vivid, the action is believable, and the police procedurals are authentic. ...VK Powell had me invested in the story of these women, heart, mind, body and soul. Along with danger and tension, Powell's well-developed erotic scenes sizzle and sate."—*Story Circle Book Reviews*

If you like cop novels, or even television cop shows with women as full partners with male officers...this is the book for you. It's got drama, excitement, conflict, and even some fairly hot lesbian sex. The writer is a retired cop, so she really writes from a place of authenticity. As a result, you have a realistic quality to the writing that puts me in mind of early Joseph Wambaugh, before his writing became formulaic...in a serious and at the same time rollicking and frolicking sexually novel, the good guys—or gals in this case—win out and good triumphs over evil. And the right girl ends up with the right girl."—*Rainbow Reviews*

"*To Protect and Serve* drew me in from the very first page with characters that captivated in their complexity. Powell writes with authority using the lingo and capturing the thoughts of the law enforcers who make the ultimate sacrifice in the fight against crime."—*Just About Write*

Suspect Passions

"From the first chapter of *Suspect Passions* Powell builds erotic scenes which sear the page. She definitely takes her readers for a walk on the wild side! Her characters, however, are also women we care about. They are bright, witty, and strong. The combination of great sex and great characters make *Suspect Passions* a must read."—*Just About Write*

Fever

"VK Powell has given her fans an exciting read. The plot of *Fever* is filled with twists, turns, and 'seat of your pants' danger. ...*Fever* gives readers both great characters and erotic scenes along with insight into life in the African bush."—*Just About Write*

Justifiable Risk

"This story takes some unusual twists and at one point, I was convinced that I knew 'who did it' only to find out that I was wrong. VK Powell knows crime drama, she kept me guessing until the end, and I was not disappointed at the outcome. And that's not to slight VK Powell's knack for romance. …Readers who appreciate mysteries with a touch of drama and intense erotic moments will enjoy *Justifiable Risk*."—*Queer Magazine*

"*Justifiable Risk* is an exciting, seat of your pants read. It's also has some very hot sex scenes. Powell really shines, however, in showing the inner growth of Greer and Eva as they each deal with their personal issues. This is a very strong, multifaceted book.—*Just About Write*

Exit Wounds

"Powell's prose is no-nonsense and all business. It gets in and gets the job done, a few well-placed phrases sparkling in your memory and some trenchant observations about life in general and a cop's life in particular sticking to your psyche long after they've gone. After five books, Powell knows what her audience wants, and she delivers those goods with solid assurance. But be careful you don't get hooked. You only get six hits, then the supply's gone, and you'll be jonesin' for the next installment. It never pays to be at the mercy of a cop."—*Out in Print*

"Fascinating and complicated characters materialize, morph, and sometimes disappear testing the passionate yet nascent love of the book's focal pair. I was so totally glued to and amazed by the intricate layers that continued to materialize like an active volcano…dangerous and deadly until the last mystery is revealed. This book goes into my super special category. Please don't miss it."—*Rainbow Book Reviews*

About Face

"Powell excels at depicting complex, emotionally vulnerable characters who connect in a believable fashion and enjoy some genuinely hot erotic moments."—*Publishers Weekly*

Deception

"In *Deception* VK Powell takes some difficult social issues and portrays them with intelligence and empathy. …Well-written, enjoyable storyline, excellent use of location to add colour to the background, and extremely well drawn characters. VK Powell has created a great sense of life on the streets in an excellent crime/mystery with a turbulent but charming romance."—*Lesbian Reading Room*

Visit us at www.boldstrokesbooks.com

By the Author

SECOND IN COMMAND

by

VK Powell

2018

ISBN 13: 978-1-63555-185-3

This Trade Paperback Original Is Published By
Bold Strokes Books, Inc.
P.O. Box 249
Valley Falls, NY 12185

First Edition: December 2018

Credits
Editor: Cindy Cresap
Production Design: Susan Ramundo
Cover Design By Sheri (hindsightgraphics@gmail.com)

Acknowledgments

I've been blessed to pursue two careers that brought me great satisfaction. The first, law enforcement, allowed me to help people and to work for the advancement of women in a profession that often overlooked them. In the second, I parlay that career into stories of survival, the struggle to balance love and livelihood, and the fight between good and evil. To Len Barot, Sandy Lowe, and all the other wonderful folks at Bold Strokes Books—thank you for giving me and so many other authors the chance to tell our stories.

To Cindy Cresap, many thanks for your extra time and attention on this project. Your fresh perspective and insights were invaluable. The steady doses of humor didn't hurt either.

To my beta readers—D. Jackson Leigh and Jenny Harmon— you guys are the best! This book is so much better for your efforts. I am truly grateful.

And last, but never least, to all the readers who support and encourage my writing, thank you for buying my books, sending emails, giving shout-outs on social media, and showing up for events. Let's keep doing this!

CHAPTER ONE

Lieutenant Jazz Perry closed the door of her patrol car on the top level of the Bellemeade parking deck and walked to the edge overlooking downtown Greensboro. Without the steady beat from nearby clubs echoing between the buildings and beckoning patrons, the sidewalks were quiet and deserted. Cloud cover of the day had lifted, leaving the night air chilly and exhilarating. Nothing beat the feeling of being on top of the world, but nothing reminded her more of how alone she was either. Her position as second in command to a district captain was her ideal job, but in these quiet, solitary times she longed for more than the satisfaction of a career.

She wiped a hand across her face, and the cool air momentarily revived her. Lack of sleep and an overdose of marital bliss. That's why she was so pensive bordering on morose. The hectic activity of early night shift had waned, and boredom and fatigue were setting in. After spending the day furniture shopping with Bennett and Kerstin, she'd gotten little rest.

Jazz hated shopping but wouldn't dampen Bennett's happiness by refusing their invitation. Being around two women who were obviously in love, had just gotten married, and couldn't keep their hands off each other had stirred Jazz's desire to seriously date again instead of just playing the field. She wanted to belong to someone special and have a family someday, but moping about it wouldn't make it so. She scanned Elm Street one last time and started back to her vehicle.

"All units, be on the lookout for a possible lost child in the Aycock neighborhood. Communications has received two calls of a young girl wandering down the sidewalk alone."

She stuffed her problems down. Other people needed help with theirs. The dispatcher repeated the alert as Jazz wound her vehicle down the exit ramp. Her stomach churned. She'd been that child—running away from some group home or foster parent, roaming unfamiliar neighborhoods, and looking for a way to escape the family du jour. She prayed this child wasn't doing the same.

Jazz stopped at the intersection of Elm and Bellemeade and listened for anything unusual. The Aycock Historic District was adjacent to downtown, so a determined kid could've easily made it this far. Nothing moved, and only the occasional whir of an industrial heating unit disturbed the quiet.

She stepped away from the motor noises of the car and heard vicious growling and pounding feet. The sounds ricocheted off the buildings which made pinpointing the direction difficult. Behind her? She drove through the alley beside the parking deck onto Greene Street. About a hundred feet to her left, a grayish dog chased a child, pumping her arms like a distance runner, down the middle of the street. Jazz sped toward them, horn blowing, and slid to a stop beside the child. The dog retreated, but the child kept running.

Jazz pulled alongside again. "Stop. I'm here to help." The little girl looked at her with wide eyes and kept running. "Seriously. Stop." Jazz parked and ran after her, caught up easily, and matched her pace. "So, where are we heading?"

The girl waved at her to go away and tried to speak, but was breathless.

"You might as well stop, because I'm going to stick with you until the end, wherever that is." She looked back, hoping to reassure the girl. "The dog is gone, by the way."

The girl stopped, placed her hands on her knees, and bent over pulling for breath. "Thought...he was...going to...eat me." Her torn jeans and scuffed tennis shoes with broken laces could've been those of an active kid or a child who had to make due, but the stained gray sweatshirt she tugged on as she puffed for air clued Jazz it was the latter.

"You're safe now." Under the streetlights, Jazz stepped closer for a better look. The girl was still terrified, searching behind them constantly. Blond bangs covered a scrape on her forehead that had begun to swell, blood stained the rips in the knees of her jeans, and dried blood and dirt caked the palm of her right hand.

"Safe from the dog maybe."

The child mumbled the words, but Jazz heard them. What was this kid going through? Jazz knew from her own experience and from dealing with other children on the job not to ask directly. "So, respect. You're fast."

"I run a lot."

The comment triggered a familiar ache and a fierce protective streak in Jazz. Nothing was worse than being a child and feeling unsafe and afraid. "How about a break? My car is warm and dog free." She nodded toward her vehicle behind them in the street. The girl shook her head unconvincingly. "Can I give you a lift home?"

"Don't have one."

"Where are you staying?"

"Not sure."

If she pushed too hard, the girl would shut down, but she had to ask certain questions in order to help her. "You don't have a home?"

"Been in three. Not sure where I'm staying tonight." The girl scuffed her shoe against the sidewalk, obviously frustrated.

"It's all right. We'll figure it out. How old are you?"

"Eleven."

Jazz guided her gently toward the police car, hoping she wouldn't bolt. Eleven-year-olds liked their independence, and this one appeared more headstrong than most, like Jazz had been at that age. "What's your name?"

"Shea. Shea Spencer."

"I'm Jazz. Can we sit? You wore me out." She opened the front passenger door. "Ever been inside a police cruiser?" The minute she asked the question, she regretted it.

"Plenty of times. No big." Shea climbed in and propped her feet on the dash.

Jazz breathed a little easier to have Shea corralled for the time being. Before she got in, she keyed her walkie-talkie. "Car 101,

I've located the child downtown. Will advise transport location on arrival." She settled beside Shea and stared out the window, letting her take the lead.

"Knew where I was until the dog came after me. Lost track of the turns."

"Do you have your folks' phone number?"

"It's just my dad, and he got a new number yesterday. Don't know it yet." Shea stared at her shoes, occasionally fiddling with her loose strings or glancing at the police computer.

"Okay. I'll drive around a bit to see if anything looks familiar. We at least need to let him know where you are. I'm sure he's worried."

"Doubt it."

Shea was quiet, shaking her head at each house, while Jazz cruised the streets in the Aycock Historic District. Either Shea really didn't know what her new home looked like or she simply didn't want to go back. They circled through the area for over an hour with no luck.

"Anything look familiar at all?"

"Nope."

Jazz eyed the knot that had blossomed on Shea's forehead and the cut to her hand. "How do you feel?"

"Okay, except for a little headache." Shea wouldn't look at Jazz, instead scratching at the dried blood in her palm.

"Would you mind if I take you to the hospital for a quick checkup? You've got a nasty bump on your head, scraped knees, and that cut might need stitches."

"Probably not a good idea."

"Why?" In her last foster home before the Carlyles, Jazz had experienced severe abdominal pain, but she'd kept it to herself for two days, fearing her guardians and the doctors. The next day her appendix had burst at school, and the teacher called an ambulance, resulting in emergency surgery and a month of restrictions at home. "Are you afraid of your dad, doctors, or something else?" Shea didn't answer. "Never mind. I get it."

Shea finally glanced at her with a scowl that said probably not. "All three."

"I understand. Been there. Done that."

"No way."

"I was eleven once." She waited until Shea gave her a tentative nod. "Went into foster care at four. At least you have a dad who cares about you."

"Sometimes. Not sure which is worse…him or foster parents. Been round and round with both a few times."

"Sorry, pal. How about a quick stop at the hospital first, then we'll figure this out? I promise." On the drive, Jazz struggled between questioning Shea about her father or giving her a few minutes of quiet safety.

"Sorry, Jazz." Shea pulled a string on the knee of her jeans and watched it unravel.

"For?"

"Causing trouble. Cops have better things to do."

She lightly touched Shea's shoulder. "Hey, I don't have anything better to do. I'm here just for you." Shea smiled, and Jazz thought how quickly a kind word and a glimmer of hope could transform a child's face and possibly her outlook on life. Shea seemed to relax, so Jazz tried one more time to get some answers. "So, why are you on your own so late?"

"Needed some air I guess."

"You can level with me, Shea. Is there a reason you don't want to be home?"

"Not my home. I don't belong there…or anywhere really." She stared out the window again, clearly finished talking about the situation she'd escaped.

Jazz lived with the same feeling of not quite fitting in every day but never shared it. No one would understand, especially after all she'd been through and where she'd ended up. She parked in front of the emergency room door and turned to Shea. "The nurses will ask some of the same questions. If we don't get answers—"

"A group home or foster family for me, if they can't find my dad. End of shift for you. Big deal."

"You understand we're trying to help, right?"

"Then find me a *good* home."

Jazz pulled out a business card, scribbled her cell number on the back, and handed it to Shea. "In case we're separated tonight or you just want to talk anytime, call me."

Shea looked at the card and tucked it into her back jeans pocket. She pushed open the car door and shuffled through the automatic doors to the ER, a lost child heading toward another letdown.

After the check-in process, which revealed little new information, the nurse paged the hospital's on-duty social worker. A woman Jazz had never seen motioned Shea toward an interview room off the waiting area.

"Will you be here when I come out?" Shea asked.

"Sure. I'm going for a coffee, but I'll be back." She stretched her fist toward Shea. "Pound this." When Shea fist-bumped her, Jazz added, "Help the lady out, okay?" Shea didn't answer, and the door closed behind her.

"Emory Blake, how can I help?" She held her cell between her shoulder and ear as she locked the condo door and headed toward her car.

"It's Sheri."

Her coworker never called unless she'd screwed something up or heard some juicy gossip. "What's up?"

"Just heard the hospital is officially opening bids to privatize all CPS adoption responsibilities, not just the hard-to-place ones."

Emory chilled at the thought of losing her job to some for-profit company with inexperienced caseworkers and how the change would affect the children they served. "When?"

"My source says the announcement has already been drawn up. It's just a matter of timing for the release." Sheri's voice held a hint of smugness. She handled the hard-to-place cases as she called them for the private US Adoption Agency and had been lobbying for a full takeover. Emory wasn't sure why she was so keen on the idea.

"At least we know more than we did yesterday. I'm dropping by the office in a few minutes, and if you're still there, we'll chat more. And thanks for the call, Sheri."

After the short drive, Emory pulled into the hospital parking garage and took the elevator to the main level. She hefted her briefcase shoulder strap across her body and dug inside for change for a cup of tea but stalled at the canteen entrance when she spotted Jazz Perry in front of a snack machine with an upset teenager and another officer. The girl's face was blotchy from crying, and her right arm sported a cast and sling. Emory edged closer to the door and watched the exchange.

"At least the doctor gave you a decent color cast," Jazz said

The girl nodded. "Yeah, she was nice."

"Skateboarding is serious business. I bet you're good, am I right?"

The girl shrugged. "I was doing a 360 flip with a group of boys, and I was the only one who made it…before the crash."

Jazz and the girl fist-bumped. "In honor of your mad skills, anything you want from the snack machines is on me. Name it."

"Could I have an Almond Joy and a Coke?"

"Coming up." Jazz fed the machines and handed the items to the girl as the other officer headed toward the door. When they were alone, Jazz bent to make eye contact with her. "Don't give up on something you enjoy because it's hard or you get a few bumps and scrapes. Get back on that board as soon as you can and show it who's boss."

"I will and thanks for the stash."

The last time Emory saw Jazz she'd been a teenager. Now she was a police officer handing out sage advice and treats like a mother hen. She'd often wondered what kind of woman Jazz would become, and if this was any indication, she was at least a kind one. And she'd transformed from a lanky athletic teenager to a handsome woman with a bit more weight and muscle. Emory swallowed hard but kept staring as she fumbled with her handful of coins. The change slipped through her fingers and scattered across the floor, several coins rolling to a stop beside Jazz's patent leather shoe. "Damn it," she muttered under her breath.

"First time a woman has thrown coins at me. Dollar bills make an impression too."

Jazz's black uniform and dark hair cut an imposing figure, but the streak of white near her left ear, a broad smile, and her comment added some needed levity. Emory almost swooned and forced her gaze back to Jazz's mouth. "Sorry."

Emory pulled her wrap tighter around her shoulders. The extra pounds she'd packed on during her depression months were certain to turn Jazz off. She bent to pick up the change at the same time Jazz leaned forward, and they bumped heads. Emory jerked away too fast, her heavy briefcase twisted behind her, and yanked her with it.

Jazz moved quickly, steadying Emory before she fell into a table and chairs.

Jazz's hands rested on the love handles at her waist, and Emory stiffened. Her skin flushed when she met Jazz's stare. "I'm so clumsy." Jazz's hands were firm and strong as they supported her, and Emory felt buoyant. How ridiculous. She was letting a fleeting past interest distort reality. Jazz had simply kept her from falling.

"No problem. Accidents happen." Jazz gently guided her to a chair, relieved her of her briefcase, and placed it beside her. "No wonder you're off balance with this monstrosity strapped across your body. What's in there, the history of the world?"

Emory shook her head.

"Coffee?"

Emory shook her head again.

"Tea?"

Emory nodded.

"Sugar, cream?"

"Black." Jazz's touch had her unable to string together a sentence. She hadn't been this affected by a woman since…well, never. Not even Jean had—no, she wouldn't compare Jazz to her ex in any way for any reason.

Jazz brought Emory's tea to the table and placed it in front of her. "Mind if I join you?"

"Yes…I mean no, of course not." She raised her cup toward Jazz before taking a sip. "Thanks, I needed this." Jazz scanned her once and then again, making Emory more self-conscious. She tugged at her scarf and closed it over her full breasts. Why had she worn a V-neck sweater today? She'd grabbed the first thing that matched her pants, her favorite blouses overflowing the laundry bin.

"Hey, I know you," Jazz said.

"We met, a very long time ago. I've been acquainted with your family for years." Thank God. Full sentences that made sense. "Your grandmother, mother, and I were on the board of several charities, including the hospital until I moved to Winston-Salem years ago. Now that I'm back, they'll probably talk me into it again. Very persuasive."

"You do know them."

"Norma and Gayle are wonderful women and a godsend to the community. I also knew your grandfather and father. Both great police officers."

Jazz looked away, a shadow of sadness momentarily darkening her face. And then Emory saw the same distant, almost pained look, she'd observed in eighteen-year-old Jazz. "I don't remember G-Pa very well. He was killed in the line of duty before I was adopted, but you're right about Papa. He was with us until Ben and I were nineteen and loved being a cop. Wish we all could've had more time with him."

Note to self, never bring up dead relatives to a woman you're attracted to. "I'm sorry."

"Not at all. I love hearing and talking about them. By the way, I'm Jasmine Perry, Jazz, in case you've forgotten."

Jazz extended her hand across the table, and Emory considered not taking it. Would she feel the same jumble of emotions she'd experienced earlier? But not shaking hands would make a bigger statement. Emory took Jazz's hand and was drawn back to those golden brown eyes. "I haven't forgotten you." Her body warmed again. She was being foolish. Jazz tugged the strands of hair near her left ear, and Emory thought the tell was adorable. "And I'm Emory Blake in case you've forgotten."

Jazz held her hand a few seconds longer before she said, "I haven't forgotten either."

Emory sipped her tea and let Jazz's statement register. She started to ask why and what Jazz remembered but wasn't sure she wanted to know the answer. "So, you're a lieutenant?"

"At the new Fairview Station."

"Bennett's lieutenant? How's that going?"

"Couldn't be better. Ben absolutely loves the autonomy of running the show at Fairview Station, and I enjoy being her 2IC, second-in-command."

"Interesting," Emory said. "No problem taking orders from your sister?"

"We've always had a special connection, maybe because we're not blood relatives. Who knows why things work?"

Sibling power struggles weren't always easy to navigate, and Emory admired Jazz's and Bennett's ability to work theirs out, especially in a field that challenged women on every level.

"You might've heard, Ben got married recently to Kerstin Anthony, her teenage sweetheart and the station's architect. They moved down the street from the family home, as we Carlyles are prone to do. Populating Fisher Park seems to be one of our missions." She paused. "That's probably way more information than you wanted about the Carlyle clan."

"Not at all." Emory started to touch Jazz, to reassure her that she was interested but pulled back. She wanted to flirt with her, to find out if their obvious chemistry would last through an entire conversation, but she shouldn't. Jazz was just being friendly. Besides, Emory wasn't in Jazz's dating league—young, lean, sporty women who were easy conquests—if the hospital gossip could be believed. Emory was approaching fifty, ate the wrong kinds of foods, abhorred any activity that produced sweat, except for sex, and had never been easy.

Jazz fiddled with her cup lid. "Do you come here often?"

Emory laughed despite her anxiety. Jazz was nervous too, and the thought eased her own edginess. "I'm a social worker with child protective services assigned to the hospital. Until a few months ago, I was in Winston-Salem, but I'm glad to be back in Greensboro. It's home." Volunteering too much personal information sounded desperate. "I just came by to pick up a few things from the office to review for tomorrow. Why are you here? I don't mean why. You're a police officer, of course you'll be at the hospital from time to time. Strange we haven't run into each other before, but I have just returned to the city. I've seen Bennett a couple of times." She was rambling. "I mean what brought you in today, last night, whatever." Emory blew out a long breath. She was a bundle of nerves around Jazz, while the reserved young woman she'd met as a teenager had grown into a more self-confident adult.

"Brought in an eleven-year-old who was roaming downtown about three thirty." Jazz studied her coffee cup, rolling it back and forth in her hands on the table.

"You liked her."

"And you're perceptive. I guess she reminded me of myself years ago, alone, scared, unsure where I was going, and having no choice in any of it." Jazz took a sip of coffee. "Sorry, that was deep. Anyway, your counterpart is talking to her. The kid wouldn't give me any information about where she came from, but she's probably in the system. She mentioned her dad and foster parents, so I'm not sure which she's running from tonight. Could you check on her for me?"

She wanted to say yes, anything for you, but her mind finally took over from her hormones. "I'm sorry, Jazz, but we have guidelines about interfering in each other's cases. Sheri is a competent caseworker. The girl will be fine."

"I get it, like jurisdictional or squad boundaries with cops."

Emory gave her an appreciative smile and glanced at her watch. If she left now, she'd have just enough time to check with Sheri before she went home, but Emory didn't want to leave. This was the first adult conversation she and Jazz had ever had. But that's all it would ever be, conversations about work possibly leading to a professional friendship. "I should get going."

Jazz stood and pulled out Emory's chair. "I'm sort of glad you threw change at me. Would you like to maybe…have lunch…or another tea sometime? If you want. No pressure. At all. I mean I'd understand if you—"

"Stop." Emory reached toward Jazz's forearm, experienced a tingle of expectation, and withdrew. "You don't have to do this." She licked her lips involuntarily. She should move. After an extended pause, she stepped away, her body pulsing.

Jazz captured Emory's hand and held it briefly before releasing. "I've enjoyed talking with you, Emory." She paused, as if weighing her next comment. "You said you were just picking up something, so, you're not working today?"

Emory's pulse pounded in her ears. She was either imagining things or Jazz's focus had become more personal. "I can't believe this is happening." When Jazz looked confused, Emory realized she'd spoken aloud. "What are you asking?"

"Have breakfast with me?"

"I don't date coworkers."

"That's a stretch. We might be work associates, hardly co-workers, so no rules broken. Besides, it's not really a date. Just have breakfast with me. I'd like to pick your brain about your job. Come on, Emory, what do you have to lose except a couple of hours on Sunday morning with an old friend? And you get a free breakfast."

A non-date with Jasmine Perry still meant time alone with her. She'd never imagined it would happen, and if she said no, the opportunity would probably vanish forever. Her doubts raised too many conflicting feelings. Avoiding the situation worked. "I'm sure I'll see you around the hospital again, and we can talk then. I really have to go." She grabbed her briefcase and hurried from the canteen.

❖

Jazz watched Emory practically run from the snack room on incredibly high heels. Jazz loved heels on a woman who rocked them so effortlessly like Emory Blake. She regretted scaring her away but enjoyed the view of her retreating backside wrapped in tight jeans. Had she come on too strong?

She'd sensed Emory looking at her from the doorway before she turned around. Women ogling her wasn't new, but Emory's stare was different, more inquisitive than wolfish. And *not* staring at Emory's sweater-draped breasts and shapely body wasn't an option. Emory was, in a word, beautiful.

Jazz had acknowledged the pull between them, making the bold move to take Emory's hand, but it seemed right at the time.

They'd known each other remotely for years, perhaps that added to the feeling of familiarity, but when she asked Emory to breakfast, she'd panicked. Jazz had seen that shell-shocked look on some suspects she'd interviewed.

Emory Blake had a woman's body—full-figured, soft angles, and enough meat on her bones to keep a lanky woman like Jazz warm at night—but dressed as if she was uncomfortable with her size. Jazz found it a refreshing change from the skinny, gym-addicted women she usually dated. There was an age difference between them, possibly as much as fifteen years, but that didn't worry her either. She'd often gone for older women, preferring their maturity and leisurely style of lovemaking.

Emory didn't strike her as a fling sort of girl, but there was something tangibly arousing about her. Maybe she preferred slow wooing to more overt moves, and Jazz warmed at the thought. She'd had her share of casual relationships and wanted something different. She liked Emory, and the telltale eye contact, licking of lips, and rapid heartbeat said Emory was just as interested, but she'd blown off Jazz's invitation. Why?

She let the image of touching Emory settle and stir her interest as she headed back to the interview room where she'd left Shea. The social worker sat at the table pounding on her laptop like it had offended her, but Shea was gone. "Where's Shea?"

"Probably back home by now."

"Where's home?"

"Pretty close to where you found her."

Jazz didn't like the clipped answers that lacked emotion or any concern for Shea. "Excuse me, but would you mind giving me some actual information."

The woman looked up from her laptop for the first time. "Sorry, Officer. Shea had a US Adoption Agency business card in her pocket with Karen Patrick's private number on it."

"Is that supposed to mean something to me?"

"Ms. Patrick is the director and a counselor for the USAA, the private organization that handles Shea's case. I called Ms. Patrick, and she had Shea picked up. She's fine."

"Home? With her birth family or a foster family?" It seemed odd that an adoption agency would work a child's case if she had family, but Shea admitted she'd been back and forth.

"Can't say."

"Can't or won't?" Jazz's temper rose but she tamped it down. She wouldn't get any information if she became confrontational. "Did Shea tell you why she ran away?"

"She wasn't very forthcoming, which is typical for her. She's done this before when she was unhappy."

"Unhappy? That's all you see? An unhappy child who runs away from her father in the middle of the night for no reason?" Her temper was getting the best of her. She'd wanted to talk to Shea before she left, but more than that, she wanted to know she was all right and being cared for. Jazz had been the kid shuffled through the system, a square peg that didn't fit into the round organizational holes, and she knew the frustration and sense of worthlessness it produced. She didn't want to see the same thing happen to Shea.

"This kid has been in and out of the system for a while and has been nothing but trouble. She'll be lucky to get a chance with a decent family after the revolving door with her dad."

"Maybe it's time to consider a more permanent placement if the dad isn't capable."

The woman closed her computer and started to leave. "Trying to tell me how to do my job, Officer?"

"Just suggesting a closer look based on today's events," Jazz said.

"You know as well as I do that family always gets the benefit of the doubt. Now, if you'll excuse me, I need to file some paperwork before my shift ends."

Jazz blocked the doorway and forced the woman to make eye contact. "You better hope nothing bad happens to her, or I'll be looking to you for answers. I need one of your business cards." She waited until the woman reluctantly complied. She glanced at the name. "Thank you, Sheri McGuire. I'll be seeing you."

CHAPTER TWO

Emory hurried to the former supply closet that now served as the social workers' office and unlocked the door. The old desk occupied most of the space leaving barely enough room for her to squeeze past the sides. Two straight-back chairs bunched closely together in front of the desk, and a single file cabinet stopped the door from opening fully. The only nod to a tolerable work space was a single-cup coffee and tea maker on top of the cabinet.

Emory placed her briefcase in one of the side chairs and put in a fresh tea pod. Maybe she could blame her jitters with Jazz on too much caffeine or her sluggish thinking on too little. She leaned against the wall and replayed their encounter.

Jazz still intrigued her after all these years. She'd been acquainted with the Carlyle family professionally, but hadn't met Jazz until she was eighteen, just before she went away to college. She'd been gorgeous then too, athletic, vigorous, with just a hint of lingering childhood shyness. Emory had tamped down her attraction, feeling creepy even acknowledging it because of their fourteen-year age difference, her profession, and her personal boundaries. But now they were both adults, and Jazz had asked her out, sort of. And she refused. Why? Before she could enumerate all the reasons, Sheri burst into the room waving her arms.

"I really hate when police officers try to do our jobs for us. Don't you?" Her high-pitched voice was an octave above normal. She didn't wait for an answer. "That Jazz Perry always has a hard-on for anything child-related. This makes the third or fourth time her name has popped up in one of my cases, but the first time I've encountered her face-to-face. She *actually* challenged my competence. Can you imagine?" She must've realized Emory wasn't responding because she stopped and scrubbed her hand through thick black hair that stuck out at the ends like a frayed electrical cord. "Do you know her?"

"She's just interested in the child's welfare, same as us."

"So now you're taking their side?"

"I was under the impression we were on the same side."

"Oh, whatever, Emory. You're such a…a regimented idealist." She packed her briefcase and headed for the door.

"I'm not sure that's even a real thing. So, what happened with the girl?"

"Like I told the cop, a USAA rep picked her up. She's probably back with her dad already. Shea Spencer is a revolving-door case, four years back and forth between her dad and foster homes. You know the type. I'm going home unless you have further questions. I'll file my report tomorrow, if you have no objections, Ms. Stickler-for-Details."

Emory spoke as Sheri walked away. "It would be best if you filed the report while the details are still fresh in your mind."

"Like I could forget. Report me."

"Which USAA counselor came for the girl?"

Sheri spun around and squared off with Emory. "What's your problem with USAA? Every time we have a chance to shift some of our workload to them, you have a meltdown."

Emory refused to back down from Sheri's bullying or from her beliefs. "I have concerns about a company that profits by using children as a commodity."

"There you go with your idealism again. Go home. You're off, and I'm out."

"Any more news about the contract bids?" Emory called to her as she left.

Sheri slammed the door without answering, and Emory sat on the edge of the desk and sipped her tea. She started to call Jazz but didn't have her number. She'd already told Jazz she couldn't interfere with a coworker's case. CPS had rules for a reason, and if she violated one, she'd be on a slippery slope. Besides, she wouldn't be able to reassure Jazz that Shea would be fine as a cog in the USAA wheel when she doubted it herself. She wasn't a very good liar.

❖

On her way home from night shift, Jazz located the phone number of the US Adoption Agency and called to check on Shea. Whoever picked her up and transported her home should still be awake, but the call went to voice mail. After the greeting, she left her name and contact details, asking for a face-to-face, but feeling no better about Shea's situation than when she'd picked her up on the street several hours ago.

Jazz parked in front of the Carlyle home in Fisher Park, looked up at the two-story dwelling with a wraparound porch, and warmth spread through her. This was the only home she remembered, having lost her real mother to a stroke when Jazz was four. Most of the things she knew about herself, life, and how to treat others she'd learned in this place.

She bounded up the creaky stairs of the traditional home two at a time, past the childhood photos of Simon, Bennett, Dylan, and Jazz lining the walls. She, G-ma, and Mama occupied only three of the five upstairs bedrooms now that Bennett had relocated with Kerstin down the street and Dylan had taken Ben's place in the cottage out back. Jazz remained in the family home, passing her turn in the cottage to Dylan, who needed "room to grow."

She shucked her uniform while the shower temperature regulated, eager to be clean, fed, and asleep after getting little rest the day before. She considered skipping the customary Sunday brunch, but needed to feel reconnected with family after finding Shea.

As she showered, she thought about Emory—her wavy auburn hair that Jazz itched to run her fingers through and her green eyes that threatened to divine Jazz's deepest secrets. After years of being chased by more assertive women, the slow seduction of shy Emory Blake surprisingly appealed to her.

"Hey, you eating with us?" Bennett stood outside the shower tapping on the steamy glass.

"What the hell, Ben?"

"I knocked on your bedroom door. You must've been seriously gone. Wait. Were you thinking about a woman? You weren't giving yourself a hand—"

"No!"

"Good, because I don't want that image in my head over breakfast. Get downstairs before we all starve to death." Bennett turned to leave but called back over her shoulder. "And I want details about the woman who has you so distracted that you forget about food." The sound of her laughter followed her down the stairs.

She couldn't hide anything from Bennett. They were the same age and had grown up together since she was eight. Papa and Mama Carlyle and Bennett had given her the first opportunities to make choices in her life—a bedroom of her own or sharing with Bennett; public school with the rest of the Carlyle kids or a year of private tutoring to catch up on courses; adoption or not; assuming the Carlyle surname or keeping her own. They'd given her a voice, a life, and made her the successful woman she was today. She couldn't hide anything from them, anything except her nagging desire for more.

She pulled a pair of sweats from her dresser, and a doubled envelope fell to the floor. Her breath caught as she bent to pick it up. She carefully unfolded the paper and stared at the Celtic love knot necklace and handwritten note which read: *Two hearts united are stronger than steel.* She skimmed her fingers over the smooth interlaced swirls as if she could pull some feeling or memory from them. The necklace had belonged to her mother, and Jazz kept it safely tucked away, afraid she'd lose it at work. The words returned to her often, and she wondered if she'd ever feel that connected to another person. She refolded the envelope and pushed it to the back of the drawer under her clothes before heading downstairs. When she reached the bottom, her cell vibrated in her pocket. "Hello?"

"Jazz, it's Shea, Shea Spencer from this morning."

"Yeah, how could I forget. You gave me quite a workout." She raised a finger at Dylan and sat on the bottom step, determined to give Shea all the time she needed. She was reaching out, and Jazz wouldn't turn away. Too many people had done that to her. "Sorry I didn't see you before you left. When I went back, you were already gone. Are you all right?"

"I'm in a group home again."

Jazz scrubbed her fist through her hair. Damn it. "Did they say why?"

"Because I ran, I guess, and they couldn't find my dad."

Under the guise of discipline, the system often punished children who didn't play by the rules. "I'm so sorry, Shea."

"At least it's not juvie, right?"

"You haven't done anything wrong." Jazz's heart ached at Shea's cynical response. She'd apparently been through a lot in her young life and needed encouragement not more punishment. "Where's your dad?"

"Like I told you earlier, don't remember where we were before I took off."

She hesitated, but finally asked, "Why did you run, Shea?"

"Same old, same old. Bunch of guys drinking and…" Her voice trailed off, and Jazz thought she heard a stifled sob.

"Do they ever hurt you, anything like that? Be honest with me."

"Nah, nothing like that. They just get high and act stupid, send me out for food, make me wait on them. You know, the usual stuff, but nothing freaky."

Jazz believed Shea and breathed a little easier. "What are you doing now?"

"Hiding in a closet with a cell I borrowed. My counselor is meeting with the home people about what to do with me next." Shea covered the phone, and Jazz heard a strained whisper. "*I'm coming in a sec.* Guess I better go. Can I call again?"

"Of course, you can. In the meantime, I'll see if I can help." What could she do? The guidelines for placing children in foster and group homes were exact and strictly followed, and usually a last resort if a family member was an option. She had no idea what kind of situation Shea was running from, but the system's one size fits all method was also less than ideal. It lacked flexibility and rarely worked for everyone, and she wasn't giving up. She slid her phone back into her pocket as Simon stuck his head around the corner and glared.

When she entered the sunroom at the back of the house that served as their huge dining space, the family stood around the long refectory table behind their usual chairs with Jazz's place on G-ma's left vacant. Chafing dishes rested in hollows worn into the dark walnut wood of the table keeping the food warm. A sideboard held beverages and a few desserts.

"Good, everybody's here. Let's eat," G-ma said, taking her place at one end of the table and Simon, the eldest child, at the other. Everybody else filled in.

Mama sat across from Jazz with Dylan, the youngest, to her right, followed by Bennett and now Kerstin. To Simon's right was his son, Ryan; wife, Stephanie; and twin daughter Riley, next to Jazz. She found comfort in visually placing each member of the family in his or her place around the table. It made her feel that everything in her world was right, at least for one meal.

"So, what's going on with everybody?" Mama started the meal with the usual question, and everybody was expected to participate, even the kids.

"We're starting pre-algebra this year in school," Ryan said. "Who thought twelve-year-olds needed algebra and geometry, but it's kind of cool."

Riley wrinkled her nose. "Yuck. We're studying the human body. I'm going to be a doctor like Aunt Dylan."

"Yes." Dylan pumped her fist in the air. "That's my girl. Hope you don't change your mind in your third year of residency. It's challenging."

Mama gave her a sideways glance. "She's allowed to change her mind any time she wants. Last week, she wanted to be a police officer like Ben and Jazz, and the week before a firefighter like her dad, so don't get your hopes up. Everything okay at the hospital?"

Dylan, the spitting image of a young Bennett, looked more weary than usual and slipped a piece of bacon in her mouth before answering. "Just long days without much off time, exactly what I signed on for." She shrugged.

Bennett gave Dylan a concerned look, always in tune to her younger sister's moods. "You sure?"

"Medical residency is always demanding, and I don't get to spend as much time with all of you as I'd like. That's all, really. Over to you."

Bennett nodded. "Thanks to Jazz and my beautiful wife, our house is almost fully furnished. We were out most of yesterday store hopping for the final bits and pieces. The only thing missing is a pool table for the basement." She glanced at Kerstin.

"Don't you mean a home theater and wet bar?"

Ben laughed. "Yeah, that too. Who says we can't have it all, babe?"

"Is that everything then?" Simon asked.

G-ma cleared her throat. "I call on the newest member of the family, Kerstin Anthony-Carlyle." She waved her hand toward Kerstin. "Sorry, I just wanted to say that again."

"I love it. Thanks, G-ma." Kerstin turned to answer Simon's question. "Except for the attached garage which will eventually be converted into my office. Ben has graciously agreed that I need workspace more than she needs a place to store her toys."

Bennett leaned over and kissed Kerstin on the cheek. "Relocation is a priority, before she grows too attached to our guest bedroom. We might want it for something else one day."

"I sure hope it's a nursery," G-ma said. "I'm not getting any younger, you know."

"And Riley and Ryan would be great babysitters," Stephanie added, tousling the strawberry-blond hair of her children on either side.

"Uh-uh. Hard pass," Ryan said.

"Count me in, Aunt Kerstin," Riley said. "It would be great training for my future career in pediatrics." She gave Dylan an adoring smile, and Dylan winked back.

Kerstin cupped Bennett's hand on top of the table and gave her a smile. "We both want children, but I'd like to establish my business first. We're thinking a couple of years at the most."

"The sooner the better, but since you'll be carrying her...or him, I'll let you decide."

Jazz's skin tingled as she watched the exchange between Bennett and Kerstin. *That* was what she wanted—to love someone and raise children with her. Maybe the desire had always existed but was masked by her past and the whole dating and building a career thing.

"How's Ma Rolls doing, G-ma?" Simon asked, pouring everybody seconds of their beverages.

"The food truck business is booming in Greensboro. Gayle and I could become a franchise."

Ma shook her head vigorously. "Not in this lifetime, Norma Carlyle. We've got our hands full, but everything is good. We feed the hungry during the week and the homeless on the weekends."

"Giving back," Simon said almost wistfully. "Like the Carlyles before us."

Stephanie squeezed Simon's hand and then passed the breadbasket to Jazz. "What's up in your world, Jasmine?"

Her face heated. Stephanie caught her daydreaming about her future with a wife and children. She took a drink of water to stall. How could she talk about the memorable events of her week without mentioning Emory?

"Yes, do tell, Jasmine," Bennett teased her.

"Well, this morning I found an eleven-year-old wandering downtown alone after three o'clock. She didn't remember the last place she'd spent the night with her father."

"Poor child." Mama placed her hand over her heart. "Will she be okay?" To the Carlyles, family, children, and service to the community meant everything. Papa and Mama had served as foster parents for years until Papa died in the line of duty. Mama often said she was out of balance without him, no more yin for her yang.

"I hope so. She's in the system and back in a group home. I'll follow up."

"Anything else you need to tell us, Jazz?" Bennett prodded, and Kerstin nudged her.

"Leave the woman be, Ben. She'll tell us when she's ready."

The adults turned their attention to her. She was shier than Bennett and Dylan and preferred to keep her private life private until she had real news to share, but the targeted stares ended any hope of that today. They wanted her to find someone special and settle down. Could they somehow sense the emptiness she carried inside despite her attempts to conceal it and theirs to fill it with love?

G-ma covered Jazz's right hand with hers. "Have you met someone, honey?"

Jazz couldn't meet her eyes. "Maybe. It's too soon to know, but I like her."

Everybody offered words of encouragement before quickly returning to their food. They knew she didn't like unnecessary attention. No one asked who the woman was, and Jazz was grateful. She wasn't ready to say Emory's name aloud or to share that she'd felt something a little different with her for fear of jinxing things.

She glanced across the table at Bennett who raised her juice glass in an air toast. Jazz finished breakfast quickly, pushed her chair back, and started for the stairs before turning back to the family. "I love you guys."

On the way to bed, she checked her phone for a message from the USAA counselor. Nothing. She'd locate the office and go by while she was on duty tonight. One way or the other she'd find out about Shea and, as a bonus, possibly see Emory again.

Chapter Three

Emory sat at the small kitchen table in her one-bedroom apartment and sipped tea while reading the morning paper. She enjoyed feeling the medium in her hands, whether newspaper, magazine, or book, and liked the sharp smell of ink on paper. She lifted her teacup with the other and took a long sip. Her favorite Twinings wasn't producing the needed boost to begin her day. Her eyelids flagged from spending most of the night cleaning and doing laundry. She ignored the internal voice suggesting a future visit from Jazz Perry might've been her incentive.

She gave her open-plan space a critical once-over. Would Jazz like the place? The mishmash décor didn't really suit her palate, but she'd taken the first furnished apartment she found in a decent neighborhood close to work when she moved back to Greensboro. Her priority had been getting away from Jean quickly. One day she'd find a real home, not her parents' or brother's, not a lover's, but hers, and possibly a cat. If Jazz ever visited, maybe she'd understand that the jumble of styles was temporary and not reflective of her tastes... if she ever visited.

The turn her conversation with Jazz had taken still didn't seem real. Jazz found her attractive and interesting enough to want to spend more time with her. A brief flutter of excitement quickly vanished. Jean had once thought she was attractive and interesting too, and that had ended badly. She wasn't about to set herself up for more heartbreak. The first time around had almost killed her. She tossed the paper aside and collected her briefcase.

On her way to the front door, she plucked her keys from the hall table and gave herself a rare appraisal in the mirror. Her cheeks flushed with a healthy glow, her eyes sparkled, the blouse exposed a hint of cleavage, and her lips were almost too red for lipstick. From the waist up, she wasn't bad. Below the waist, not so healthy or tempting. Fortunately, this mirror was too short for the big picture. She closed the door behind her, refusing to consider how Jazz Perry might view her ample hips and rounded backside.

Jazz could have any woman she wanted, and Emory had more important things to do than fret over an invitation that might or might not have been an actual date and one that Jazz would probably never repeat. She was anxious to get to the hospital and inquire about the latest scuttlebutt surrounding privatization. She wanted to ferret out fact from fiction. If the department was changing, she had decisions to make about her future. And if her job was in jeopardy, she needed to know sooner rather than later. Her personal life was in shambles. She couldn't afford for her professional life to follow the same path.

❖

Jazz pulled into the Fairview Station lot after night shift and parked beside Bennett's vehicle. She'd started arriving later and leaving earlier since her marriage, which made perfect sense, but why even earlier today? As Jazz keyed in the pass code to the side door, she remembered her admission at brunch yesterday. Ben wouldn't let that go.

She waved to the records staff as she passed through the public space and punched the code into the secure police area. Bennett was at her desk, feet resting on the edge, talking in soft tones on the phone when Jazz entered.

"Okay, babe, got to go. My lieutenant is here. Love you."

"You could've spent another thirty minutes with her this morning instead of coming in to harass me," Jazz kidded her as she took a seat in front of the desk.

"Yeah, but thirty minutes would've turned into sixty. We never seem to have enough time." Jazz forced a smile, and Bennett's expression said she knew the reason. "You'll get your happy ever after, don't worry. So, how was your shift?"

"Slow. I could hardly keep my eyes open, but as usual, now I'm wide-awake."

"Well, you're off for a few days. Make the most of them. Anything for the chief's staff conference this morning?"

"He should probably pass along to the mayor that some of the residents of Claremont Court are planning to attend the next council meeting. They've heard the city is considering reopening the landfill off Phillips Avenue."

Bennett made a note in her phone. "Thanks. Anything else?"

Jazz shook her head. "Things are running smoothly at Fairview Station, boss."

"Cut the boss crap." Bennett put her feet on the floor and leaned across the desk. "How are things with my sister? Also running smoothly?"

"Yeah, I'm good." Jazz fidgeted with her car keys.

"Jazz, look at me."

She glanced up but quickly looked away. "I told you, I'm fine."

"But you haven't convinced me. Want to talk about your new woman?"

Jazz concentrated on counting the keys in her hand. "She's not my woman. I asked her to breakfast yesterday, and she turned me down. Ran like I was contagious. I'm losing my touch."

"I seriously doubt that. Look at yourself, dude. Wait. *You* asked *her* out?"

She'd said too much. Bennett read her actions, expressions, and even the words she didn't say too well and often came up with the right conclusions. "Yeah."

"So, you like her enough to put yourself out there."

"Yeah."

"You're killing me, Jazz. We talk about everything except… you *really* like her, but you just met her, right?"

Jazz nodded and finally connected with Bennett's concerned stare. She loved being so well known by another person, most of the time. "Sort of just met. It's complicated."

"How can you sort of just meet someone?"

"Come on, Ben. It's probably just a case of third shift hornies, but I didn't get that got-to-jump-your-bones-right-now feeling. With her it's more like a spark." Jazz twisted the coarse strands of hair over her ear. "I sound like an idiot. I'm blaming it on lack of sleep."

Bennett came around the desk and sat beside her. Bennett had a knack for knowing when she needed distance and when a bit less space made her more comfortable. "You have good instincts. Follow them."

Maybe her earlier assessment had been on point. Emory had seemed scared when she asked her out. What if she'd been hurt and was still healing, or didn't want to get involved, or already was? Jazz winced at the possibility of Emory being unavailable. "Nothing ventured?"

"Exactly." Bennett leaned back.

Jazz breathed deeply and stood to leave. She'd dodged the other question she could almost see in Bennett's eyes. "Think I'll shower and change clothes before finishing my shift summary. Then I might have lunch."

"You don't want to tell me who she is, do you?"

Bennett's respect for Jazz's privacy gave her room to define what she'd found however she chose in her own time. "Not just yet. Okay?"

"Absolutely. Do you remember the advice you gave me about Kerstin?"

"Not specifically, but I'm sure it was brilliant."

Bennett laughed. "It kind of was. You told me to follow her lead. Maybe you should do the same. Keep asking so she knows you're interested but not in a stalkerish way. And don't give up too easily if she plays hard to get. This is new territory for you." Bennett gave her shoulder a squeeze before grabbing her briefcase. "I should get to the chief's staff conference."

"Thanks, sis." She walked toward the locker room already imagining how to ask Emory to join her for lunch without spooking her.

❖

Emory closed the computer program she'd been working on and glanced at the cold cup of tea beside the keyboard. Her plan to troll the hospital halls for outsourcing rumors had blown up with the stack of reports in her inbox. Three hours later, she dug her small shoulder bag from her briefcase, slipped her feet back into her heels, and headed toward the door. Lunch and then information.

She turned automatically through the maze of hallways toward the exit while checking her phone for messages and friends' latest Facebook posts. The doors swished open ahead of her, and she tucked her phone into the side of her purse. A group of young children headed toward the entrance as she came out, and she sidestepped to avoid a collision, bumping into someone else instead. "I'm sorry."

"We have to stop meeting like this."

Jazz's deep, teasing tone rippled through Emory, and she fumbled for a clever response. "I...yes...sorry."

"Are you okay? We banged into each other pretty good." Jazz scanned her up and down before settling on her mouth and rekindling the heat from yesterday. "I'm pretty solid."

Emory's mind was stuck on the banging into each other image and spoke before censoring. "I'll say."

"So, you're okay?" Jazz cupped Emory's elbow and guided her away from the entrance.

"Fine. Should watch where I'm going. Lunch, actually. Thanks." She blathered unrelated thoughts that made no sense. Why had seeing Jazz again, yesterday and today, reduced her to a puddle of nerves and excitement?

"Lunch, huh?" Jazz stuffed her hands in her jeans pockets and rocked back and forth like a kid about to make a confession. "Mind if I join you?"

God, she loved that shy streak of Jazz's. "What?" Was Jazz asking her out again?

"If you're going to lunch, mind if I tag along? Remember I said I have questions about your work? Add the US Adoption Agency to the list."

So, not a date. Emory tried to relax and shift into work mode but couldn't hide a twinge of disappointment. "I don't have much time."

"I can be very succinct." Jazz pointed toward a tiny bronze vehicle parked in the circular drive. "We can take my car and talk on the way. It'll save time."

"Sports car." Everything about Jazz pushed her fantasy buttons but also brought out her insecurities. Sports cars were too low to the ground, the seats too small, and she felt like Mrs. Jumbo hefting herself out of them. Still, she allowed Jazz to steer her toward the shiny vehicle shaped like a roller skate.

"It's a 1978 Datsun 280Z that belonged to my dad. I don't really drive it much, but it's paid for, so that works." She opened the passenger door and held Emory's hand while she struggled to settle gracefully. "Where would you like to go?"

When Jazz closed the door, Emory tracked her past the long nose of the car. What was there about a handsome, androgynous woman in a white shirt, jeans, and a leather jacket that turned her to putty? The only thing missing—she stifled a gasp as Jazz slid behind the wheel and she caught a glimpse of her shiny black boots.

"Well?"

"Oh my…" Emory manually cranked down the window to get some fresh air and tried to focus on the question. She was an intelligent, mature woman. Time to act like one. "Oh yes, lunch. How about Iron Hen on Cridland? It's close, and the food is always good."

"I love that place." Jazz turned the key, and the engine rumbled to life. She gently shifted into gear and pulled out of the driveway.

Emory twisted sideways to watch Jazz. No point pretending. She enjoyed looking at her, and if their time together was limited, she planned to make the most of it. "You have questions." Jazz smiled as if Emory was the most beautiful woman she'd ever seen, and her fingers steadily worked a few strands of hair into a tight twist. Jazz was nervous. Good, at least she wasn't alone. "We're wasting valuable time, Lieutenant?"

With Jazz's mind occupied forming questions, Emory was free to watch her movements and the nuances of her expressions. Jazz rested her hand atop the gearshift and drummed lean fingers to a silent beat. When she changed gears, those slender fingers came dangerously close to Emory's thigh. Jazz guided the steering wheel with her left knee, and her thigh muscles bunched visibly beneath the stretchy jean fabric. Emory never wanted to touch a woman so badly but instead swiped at a strand of hair that had fallen from her French braid.

Jazz tilted her head to the left and released the hair she'd worked into a tangle before asking, "Did CPS handle all Shea Spencer's foster placements?"

The pointed question shattered Emory's visual caressing of Jazz's body. "No."

"Did USAA?"

"No."

"This is going to be a very long conversation if you keep giving one-word answers."

"Something wrong with long conversations?" Emory couldn't stop flirting with Jazz, even though she had no chance of developing a relationship with her. A girl could dream.

"I'm worried about Shea."

The sincerity in Jazz's tone snapped Emory out of lust mind. "I'm sorry. I know you're concerned, but as I told you, I can't interfere with Sheri's case. We do confer on difficult ones, but only when asked. And I haven't been involved in any of Shea's placements so far. All I know is that she bounces back and forth between her father and other accommodation. I'm not sure what the situation is with her father, but apparently, it's not bad enough to warrant Shea's removal. And if it did—"

"You couldn't tell me. I'm afraid her father might be into drugs. Something she said, but I respect your boundaries. So, what do you know about USAA?" Jazz parked in the lot beside Iron Hen and started to get out. "Hold that thought." She came around to the passenger's side, opened the door, and waited for Emory.

She swung her legs out of the vehicle and tugged at her tight skirt that had ridden to mid-thigh. Her knees were above the level of the seat, making a graceful exit unlikely. She grabbed the doorframe to pull herself out, but Jazz offered her hand instead.

"Let me," Jazz said.

When Emory smiled her thanks, she caught Jazz gazing at her exposed thigh. She liked Jazz looking at her and the pink tinge it brought to her cheeks. And Jazz helping her out of the vehicle was a simple gesture, but Emory enjoyed the physical contact and the intimacy it implied. "Up, Mrs. Jumbo," Emory said as she pushed with her legs.

"Why did you say that?" Jazz asked.

"Isn't it obvious? I'm a little heavy in the caboose, like an elephant."

Jazz stared at her backside until Emory started to feel self-conscious. "You're not heavy, Emory. You're perfectly proportioned. Besides, Mrs. Jumbo was a loving mother, very sweet and caring, but if anybody teased or bullied Dumbo, she became a protective lioness. I can't imagine anything more beautiful."

Jazz's kind words were probably intended to make Emory feel better, but she laughed to deflect some of the energy sparking between them. "We're still talking about an elephant, right?"

"I don't think so." She guided Emory to a corner table in the restaurant and handed her a menu. "Lunch is on me since I sort of kidnapped you. And by the way, you look great."

Emory blushed and only managed to respond with a weak smile.

"You don't take compliments well, do you?"

"This is just a business suit." She focused on her clothes instead of her body.

"It might be just a pin-striped business suit with just a scoop-neck blouse, but it's how you wear them that make them special. You're fashionable but not flashy. I get the feeling you dress to please yourself not anyone else."

"Are you a fashion critic in your spare time?" Emory tried to direct the conversation away from herself, uncomfortable with anyone's prolonged appraisal, especially Jazz's.

"Hardly. I just know what I like."

"And you've had lots of experience with women? Women's clothes, I mean."

"I enjoy looking at beautiful things, and you're definit—"

"Please stop." Emory took a sip of water as her blush deepened.

"Sorry, I embarrassed you. I'm only telling you what I see."

"Thanks." Emory signaled the waiter to keep from meeting Jazz's stare. She'd wandered off topic and into Emory's vulnerability minefield. The last thing she wanted to talk about or have anyone else notice was her body.

They ordered and ate while Emory answered Jazz's basic questions about the adoption process. "That's just a brief overview of what we do, but I'm afraid my information about USAA is limited to what I've read online or heard from Sheri. She handles the outside adoption cases."

"All of them?"

"She was hired for the position so the current staff could focus on a backlog of abuse, neglect, and endangerment cases. The turn-around time on any child-related case is very short, so we needed help with adoptions, especially older children seeking permanent homes."

Jazz studied her across the table for several seconds before leaning forward. "Why social work, specifically children's services, as a career?"

Emory placed her fork across her plate and pushed the half-eaten pear salad aside. "Seemed like a good fit after caring for my younger brother while my mother worked two jobs. I learned children can be both vulnerable and manipulative while trying to cope with their circumstances. They'll try your patience, push boundaries, and step on every nerve, but they all deserve a chance at a decent life. I found it challenging and rewarding. The college courses were easy, and I had essentially already done the practical work. The hard part is what I do now, fighting a constant battle with the administration, and sometimes lawmakers, for the resources to do the job properly."

"You're passionate about your work."

Jazz's sincerity filled Emory with the appreciation and understanding she seldom received from supervisors or parents. How could a woman she barely knew get how deeply she cared about her career when others she'd known longer couldn't?

"We both want the same thing, just go about it differently. I've been known to play fast and loose with the rules to help a child."

Jazz's admission surprised Emory. People who disregarded protocol threatened the system as well as the children and foster parents. "You do realize flaunting the rules isn't really a good thing, right?"

"As my sister explained when she gave me the most recent verbal reprimand." After a quick repentant look, Jazz asked, "Has your job put you off children entirely?"

Emory adjusted to the quick change of subject and carefully formed her answer before plowing into personal territory. "Not at all. I love children. My work has only strengthened that, and I happen to think I'm very good at what I do."

"I'm sure you are. So…children of your own someday?"

The bright, expectant look in Jazz's eyes contrasted drastically with the disappointment Emory felt. Another tick in the why-this-can-never-work column. "I need to get back to work."

Jazz glanced at her watch. "Jeez, it's almost one."

Emory took a final sip of water and waited for Jazz to pay before preceding her to the car. She'd been so attuned to Jazz that the time had passed quickly. How would it feel to have someone like Jazz in her life full time? Someone handsome and chivalrous who was still unpretentious and honest? But Emory didn't want just anyone who fit that mold; she wanted impossibly unattainable Jazz Perry. Facts were facts.

Jazz drove back to the hospital slowly, her hand occasionally brushing the side of Emory's leg when she shifted gears. "Sorry. I never realized how tight this space was."

"It's all right. I'm sure I take up more room than your usual passenger."

"Don't do that."

"Do what?"

"Put yourself down like that because I'm going to call you on it every time."

Emory swallowed hard and blinked back tears. She searched for something to say, but words failed. How could she thank Jazz for doing something she seldom did for herself?

Jazz stopped in front of the hospital and came around to help Emory out. "Thanks for letting me kidnap you and pick your brain."

"Sorry I wasn't more helpful. I plan to find out more about USAA. There are rumors that the state is taking bids for outsourcing some CPS services, and as a prestigious national adoption agency, USAA will probably be a frontrunner."

"I left a message for their Greensboro director slash counselor to check on Shea but haven't heard back yet. Maybe we can compare notes later?"

Emory nodded. "Thank you for lunch…and everything else."

"My pleasure. See you soon."

Emory felt Jazz watching as she walked toward the hospital entrance. She placed one foot directly in front of the other, mimicking the runway model stroll. The trick gave her gait extra bounce and her backside an added twist. She wanted Jazz to look at her, to imagine caressing her, and to desire that touch as much as she did.

When the entrance doors slid shut behind her blocking Jazz's view, Emory slumped against the nearest wall. What was she doing to herself? To Jazz? The first answer was easy—working herself into a frenzied fantasy that would never come true. A few nights of masturbation to memories of her brief time with Jazz was all she could hope for. In her mind, she was setting Jazz up with desires and expectations she had no interest in filling. Totally unfair. With such unrealistic hopes, they couldn't possibly establish even a decent friendship. She needed a break from her flesh-and-blood dream girlfriend and a cold dose of reality.

CHAPTER FOUR

Emory parked at the Y downtown after work on Tuesday and stared at the red and beige brick building. Was this a mistake? Diane would be here soon, so she needed to decide quickly. Stay or leave? Tell Di about Jazz or not? Face the truth or hide behind the fantasy? Fantasy. Decision made. She cranked the car, but before she could back out of the space, Diane tapped on her window and crawled in beside her.

"Jeez, you scared the crap out of me, Di." Purple-spiked hair on a forty-year-old was enough to give some people pause, but on Di it was a nice addition to her exuberant personality and a perfect contrast to her grounded, realistic side.

"Were you going to jet?" Her best friend eyeballed her hard and brushed wispy bangs out of her eyes.

"No."

"You were totally jetting, so your news must be seriously low-key."

Emory shook her head but stopped short of rolling her eyes. "You realize that just because you teach teenagers doesn't mean you have to talk like them, right?"

"They like teaching me something too, and I feel lit."

"A lit forty-year-old doesn't sound so good. They probably laugh behind your back because you're using everything in the wrong context." No matter what she said, Diane's indomitable spirit couldn't be dampened. That was one of the reasons they'd become friends in college and gotten closer when their mutual friend, Jean, dumped Emory. "Okay, but when we're together could you at least attempt to speak adult?"

"Maybe. What's up? Are we actually considering sweat-producing exercises again? Not that I have anything against working out if I can do it horizontally. That shit is GOAT."

"Do I even want to know what that means?"

"Greatest of all time, but you're deflecting. Why are we here? Quick, before we're seen and can't dash." Diane rubbed her hands together, stared at Emory for a second, and went straight for the kill. "Snap! You've met someone. Girl, tell me all about her."

Hopefully, Diane was the only one who read her so easily. If Jazz had seen the lust in her eyes, she was in deep trouble. "Sort of...met again is more accurate."

"What's her name? Where did you met, again? What does she do? Is she hot? Is she totally into you? Tell me everything. Like now."

Emory glanced around the empty parking lot. They were too early for the class, so they could still abort. "I'm thinking we take this conversation to an adult establishment."

"No wonder we're best friends. Where?"

"Smith & Edge?"

"Perfect. I'm right behind you."

Diane was in her car pulling out of the parking lot before Emory readjusted her seat belt and started the engine. No moss. The woman was constantly in motion, which probably explained her size-six figure since college. But if anyone dissed Emory about her weight, Diane flew hot, *and* she'd agreed to spin class again. She was a perfect friend in so many ways.

When Emory walked into the bar, Diane had two dirty vodka martinis waiting at a table away from the noisy games section so they could talk. "Thanks. I so need this." She took a couple of sips and waited for the heat and first tingles of a buzz. "Life saver."

"Hundo-P, my new aesthetic." When Emory rolled her eyes, she added, "Hundred percent my new vibe." She took another sip and traced a bead of condensation down the stem of her glass. Diane's version of patience, but it didn't last. "Seriously, Em?"

"All right. Do you remember Jasmine Perry? Jazz?"

Diane shook her head and fished a loose olive from the bottom of her martini glass with a toothpick. She popped it in her mouth and chewed a few times before her jaw dropped. "Wait." She shoved her hand toward Emory before she could respond, took a big gulp of her drink, and then leaned across the table. "Isn't she Gayle and Bryce Carlyle's adopted daughter?"

"Uh-huh."

"Didn't I meet her and her siblings years ago at a high school basketball charity event for the Children's Cancer Society you dragged me to?"

"Good memory."

"I only remember because you bought dinner at B. Christopher's afterward. You'd just started volunteering, and Gayle and Norma were mentoring you. So…you're dating Gayle's *daughter*?" Diane's voice rose on the last word.

Patrons at the pool tables turned toward them, and Emory waved her hands as if she could disperse the words echoing toward everybody else in the room. "Could we please not share this conversation with the entire downtown population?"

Di whispered conspiratorially. "I'm right."

Emory's body heated as she recalled sitting across from Jazz at lunch and Jazz's gaze on her. She fanned herself with a napkin. "I'm not dating her. We just bumped into each other after all these years and chatted."

"I'm sensing more to the story." Diane signaled the bartender for two more drinks.

"We just talked. I probably shouldn't have another drink. You know what they say, 'one martini, two martini, three martini, floor.'"

"And I always say, when in doubt, Uber about. It might take several of these before I get the whole story out of you. Come on. First question, is she still adorably handsome? I recall she already had that I'm-going-to-be-a-butch look." Di slid her chair closer and wiggled her eyebrows. "Tell me every little detail."

Emory play-pushed her away as the bartender placed two fresh martinis in front of them. "You're incorrigible and you're cut off. I need these." She pulled both drinks closer and encircled them in her arms. "So…I ran into Jazz in the hospital canteen Sunday morning and…"

"And?" Di eased one of the drinks away from her and took a sip. "Is she hot or has she gotten flabby and snaggletoothed with age?"

Emory circled the rim of her glass with the tip of her finger.

"Does she make you all gooey in your hinter regions? Come on. I'm dying here."

"Hinter regions, Di? Is that part of your new teen vocabulary?"

"Hardly, just answer the question."

"Yes, to the hot factor and the other thing, and I'm not sure what to do about it."

"Just remember she's not eighteen any more, and you're not an inexperienced thirty-two-year-old. Has she asked you out?"

"Not exactly. We had tea in the canteen Sunday and lunch Monday." Di straightened beside her, and Emory could almost see the transformation from kidder and teen slang aficionado to mature, grounded friend, which is exactly what Emory needed.

"Sort of sounds like dating to me, Em, or at least a warm-up."

"She had questions about adoptions. We didn't discuss anything personal, except…"

"Except?"

Diane rubbed her back in small circles, a technique that normally soothed her, but right now the little kindness only fueled Emory's embarrassment. She couldn't meet her gaze.

"Wait. Did she make a joke about your size? If she did, I'll so cancel the bitch."

Emory laughed despite her discomfort. "No, I did. I referred to myself as Mrs. Jumbo." Diane gave her a questioning look. "You know, Dumbo's mother. An elephant."

"Em, you didn't."

She nodded.

"And what did she say?"

"That's the part that totally shocked me, Di. She called me on it, told me I was perfectly proportioned, and then schooled me on what a great mother Mrs. Jumbo was."

Diane fist pumped the air. "Yes! I like this woman." She toasted her glass to the side of Emory's and added, "You now have my permission to date her."

"But—"

"I see." Diane knew Emory better than she knew herself sometimes. "*She* isn't the problem. Em, you're the only one who sees someone unattractive when they look at you. You're a beautiful, Rubenesque woman who designs her own clothes and carries herself with poise and grace. Heads turn when you walk in a room. You're seriously on fleek, girl. Not to channel Oprah, but until you accept yourself, you won't let anyone close again. BTW, fuck Jean Dunlap for what she did to you. She is *so* dead to me."

"I love you so hard right now. And for the record, I don't design clothes, I just throw together what works for me." Emory struggled with the rest, but if she wanted a true reality check, she had to put everything out there. "It's not only Jazz's looks or that she's a total body goddess. I'm fourteen years older. I don't do flings, which are probably her staple. I've only had one relationship, and we know how that ended. Jazz drives a sports car for goodness sake. She was adopted and she's a cop, which can be a potentially troublesome combination. And she wants children."

Diane finished her second martini and stared at Emory. "You've already talked about having children?"

"No, we talked about work and adoptions. Then she asked the kid question."

"What did you say?"

"What should I say? I can't handle my own screwed-up life, so how could I possibly raise a child? I'd be a totally insecure, overprotective mother? Or I've had a hysterectomy and can't have children?" If she didn't get involved with Jazz, they'd never have that conversation. The next sip of her drink was especially bitter, and the thought of walking away from Jazz left another sour feeling. Diane raised her hand to order another round, but Emory said, "No."

"Fine. If I can't drink, I must dispense wisdom. Let's recap. You're passing on this woman because she's younger, attractive, has a decent job, understands your work, drives a sports car, and may want children? Have I left anything out? Oh yes, and she's had a lot of sex so she probably knows how to please you. Could it be your standards are a bit too high?"

"She hasn't just had a lot of sex, she's an opportunist."

"Meaning what in Em-speak?"

"Gossip around the hospital is she'll sleep with anyone who's available and chases her long enough."

"*Anyone?*"

"Well, maybe not all of them. She's bypassed a few," Emory admitted.

"So…she's a selective opportunist, which probably describes most humans who ever dated or had sex, except you of course. You're the exception to every dating rule."

Emory shifted in her chair. Diane was shooting holes in her excuses as quickly as she threw them out. "Never mind. It's not about me."

Diane touched her forehead to Emory's. "Oh contraire, my lovely friend. Life and love should be primarily about you, or it can never be about anyone else."

"Okay, that's a little deep for me after two martinis."

"And maybe a little too true?"

"Time to summon your Uber. I can walk from here and pick up my car in the morning, then I'll swing by and get you. Working girls' car pool." Emory tapped open the app and plugged in her location and, after a quick stop at the restroom, they headed outside to wait. She tucked Di into the back seat when the car arrived. "I love you, Di. Thanks for listening."

"Always, Em." She kissed Emory lightly on the lips before closing the door and lowering her window. "Remember my gift of advice. I may be slightly tipsy, but I speak the truth. And one more thing. Flip the script. Dick and dash, as the kids say."

"Do I want to know what that means?"

"Sex her up and leave, sister. No strings."

The car started to pull away, but Emory called, "Stop. I forgot something." She dug a pen from her purse, motioned for Diane's hand, and scribbled a phone number on her palm. "Don't say I never gave you anything."

"Is this—"

"The nurse's phone number you've been gagging for. Use it wisely. Her name is Jane, and she's a friend, so play nice." Diane yelled, "And we *are* going to spin classes, starting next week." Emory waved as the vehicle left the lot.

On the walk home, Diane's words tumbled around inside scratching at something old and buried. She'd managed the family home and her baby brother while her mother worked and had chosen a career requiring more sacrifices of time and energy. Maybe Diane was right and it was time to put herself first. Did she even know how?

Chapter Five

Jazz rolled to the opposite side of the bed and sighed as the unused sheets cooled her naked body. Her sex throbbed, and she rubbed her thighs together. She'd come in her sleep to a dream of Emory rocking a pair of red high heels, a thigh-high skirt, and a scoop-necked blouse that revealed her creamy, generous breasts. "Jeez."

She threw the covers back and stared at the ceiling fan while her skin chilled and dimpled. Emory had caught her staring the other day, but Jazz didn't care. Emory needed to know she was attractive and desirable. She'd ignited a slow burn inside Jazz along with a desire to know more.

A light tap sounded at her bedroom door, and she quickly covered herself. "Yeah?"

"Honey, do you want breakfast?"

Mama's soft voice so soon after an orgasm reminded Jazz of the first time she'd been caught with her hand in her pants. They'd had a long talk about sex with emphasis on respecting your body and your partner's wishes. She blushed and pulled the covers tighter. "Be right down. Thanks." When the first squeaky stair registered Mama's descent, Jazz hopped in the shower, suddenly feeling like she hadn't eaten in days. She was downstairs five minutes later.

"Good morning." She kissed G-ma and Mama before settling at the long bar with a plate of food Mama pushed in front of her. They were prepping for the Ma Rolls food truck run and eating at the same time. "Can I help with that?"

"Enjoy your breakfast. We're almost done, honey," Mama said.

"You must've been tired after that last shift," G-ma said. "We've only seen evidence of you since Monday."

"I guess." She stuffed a strip of bacon in her mouth. "W…wait. It's Tuesday, right?"

Mama shook her head. "Wednesday, and Norma and I are off to a committee meeting at the hospital before the lunch run."

"Hospital?" Jazz tried to moderate her sudden interest. "What kind of meeting?"

"The Greensboro Hoppers charity baseball game for kids is coming up soon, and we need to finalize plans." G-ma wrapped a line of sandwiches as fast as Mama made them and tucked them into a Tupperware container to keep them fresh.

"Who's on this particular committee?" She reached for a coffee and slowly mixed in the cream and sweetener to avoid making eye contact. G-ma and Mama didn't miss much where their children were concerned.

"The usual suspects," Mama said, "The two of us, a couple of nurses from the pediatric ward, a pediatrician, oh, and Emory. She's back in town so we railroaded her into helping because we were shorthanded this year. She's always so good with people."

"Emory." G-ma and Mama stopped their preparations and stared at her, obviously detecting something in the tone of Jazz's voice. Before they could call her on it, she asked, "Didn't she come around when I was in high school? Is she the same Emory?" She knew damn well she was but needed to lead them away from the scent before they got a whiff or they'd never give up, like good bloodhounds.

"Yes, Emory Blake. She's a wonderful woman, always working so hard for children, giving her personal time to good causes. It's sad what happened with that woman—" G-ma stopped when Mama gave her a sharp head shake.

Jazz dropped her fork in her plate too hard and leaned toward them. "What happened?"

G-ma pretended to be too engrossed in sandwich wrapping to answer.

"It's a private matter, honey, and not our place to say." Mama patted Jazz's arm. "Some stories need to come from the source in their own way at the right time." She snapped the lid on a Tupperware container and nodded to G-ma. "We better get moving or we'll be late." She kissed Jazz on the cheek, and G-ma waved distractedly as they hurried out the back door.

"Well, that wasn't weird at all." She scarfed down the rest of her breakfast while clicking through all the sad things that could've happened to Emory, hoping none of them were true.

Jazz placed her dishes in the dishwasher, tucked her T-shirt in, and grabbed her coat before heading to the car. She stopped by a bakery and cleaned out their pastry section on the way to the station, planning her day as she drove. The USAA counselor hadn't responded to her three messages, and Shea hadn't called again either. Time to do some digging.

When she pulled into the Fairview Station lot, Bennett was coming out and waited for her under the awning. "Leaving, boss? This is early even for you. A nooner with the wife?"

"Cute. What are you doing here on your off day, besides fattening up the staff?" She nodded toward the box of pastries in Jazz's hand.

"Research and I was bored. Only so much food and trash TV before the coma sets in." She wondered if Bennett knew about Emory's past, but the question would lead to a conversation Jazz wasn't ready to have.

"Any more news about the kid you found the other night?" When Jazz shook her head, Bennett added, "Just be careful."

"I won't go down that road again." The last time she'd gotten involved in a child custody case, Bennett issued a verbal warning for skirting CPS and departmental procedures. A repeat violation required a written reprimand that wouldn't help her career.

Bennett shook her head and trotted toward her car. "I'd stay and keep you company, but Kerstin's—"

"La-la-la-la-la," Jazz sang and turned toward the keypad.

She dropped off the box of goodies with the records staff and chatted before keying through to the secure area. The facilities manager's mop bucket sat outside the men's restroom as she passed, but Louis wasn't whistling like usual. Jazz turned around and went back. "Louis, you okay in there?"

He came out dragging the mop behind him. "Fine, Lieutenant." His upbeat whistling wasn't the only thing missing. Louis's eyes had lost some of their sparkle, and his shoulders rolled forward, making the usually proud, former military man look defeated.

"Leave that and come to the office with me."

"I don't want to keep you from your work."

"Then you're in luck. I'm off today." Jazz unlocked the inner door and waved him inside. "Want a pastry? I just dropped a whole box off in records."

"No, thank you. I'm not hungry."

Jazz motioned toward the two chairs in front of her desk. He waited for her to sit and then settled his tall frame next to her. "What's wrong, Louis?"

He pulled a handkerchief from his back pocket and wiped his hands over and over. "Nothing you need to be concerned about, ma'am."

"What have I told you about that ma'am business? I'm Jazz, and of course I'm concerned. You're part of the Fairview Station family, and we take care of our own. What's going on?"

"It's nothing you can fix, Jazz. My wife and I are just feeling a bit lonely these days. Our children are off at college, and we miss having them around." Tears pooled in his eyes. "Being parents was always our greatest joy in life."

Jazz's throat tightened. "Didn't you apply to be foster parents several months back?" What she would've given for parents like Louis and Denise before she met the Carlyles.

Louis nodded. "Haven't heard anything, so I figured we weren't accepted."

Jazz couldn't imagine better parents than Louis and Denise. He'd worked multiple jobs so she could stay home and care for their own children. Now there was a big hole in their lives. She knew one little girl that could fill that hole, if the system weren't so slow and bogged down with paperwork. "Would it be all right if I looked into this for you?"

Louis stood and shoved his hand toward her. "Thank you, Jazz. We'd appreciate anything you can do. There has to be a child somewhere who needs us as much as we need him or her."

"I'm certain of it, Louis." Louis and Denise owned their own home, had plenty of room for a child, were financially stable, and had passed a rigorous background check before Louis's employment as caretaker of the substation. That alone should account for something.

Her research into USAA slipped to second on her to-do list. She needed information from CPS to help Louis and Denise, which just might help Shea in the long run. Jazz could get what she needed from any social worker, but now she had a valid reason to contact Emory again. She pulled up the office number she'd entered in her phone from Sheri McGuire's business card.

"Child Protective Services. McGuire."

"Emory Blake, please." The other end of the line went silent. "Hello?" She waited several seconds and started to hang up.

"This is Emory Blake."

"Emory, it's Jazz." The line quieted again. "Hello? Is something wrong with the phone?"

"No, I'm here, just surprised to hear from you."

Jazz couldn't tell from the tone of Emory's voice if hearing from her was a good thing or not, but with a coworker in the same space, it probably wasn't the right time to clarify. "Could I come see you?"

"When?"

"Now or at least very soon." The silence returned. "Emory, I lost you again."

"Still here."

"Then I'll be right over." Jazz started to disconnect.

"Don't. I can't see you now. I'm in court all afternoon. We just took a break, and I'm headed back."

"Have dinner with me?" This time Jazz heard a sharp intake of breath before the line went quiet. Maybe Emory thought Jazz was asking her on a date again and panicked. "Please, Emory, it's important. I need your help."

"My help?"

"Yes, and it's too complicated to get into on the phone."

"So…this is work-related?"

"Absolutely." The honest answer was yes and no, but making wide circles around Emory before she closed in seemed like the best strategy. She didn't want to spook her again.

"Can you meet me at Koshary on Elm Street at six thirty?" Emory asked.

"I'd be glad to pick you up. Whatever works best for you."

"Thanks, but I need to walk." Emory paused before adding, "Guess I'll see you later."

"Emory, would you check your files before you leave for a foster parent application for Louis and Denise Robinson?" She provided Louis's details from his employment application. "If you have anything, please bring it."

There was a long pause before Emory said, "Is this about an active police or CPS case, or are you fishing?"

Emory had pushed back on details about Shea's case and now this. Was she such a stickler for the rules that she couldn't separate the spirit from the letter of the law? "If you have an application, I'd like to know, because it could help us both. Do what you think is right." She started to hang up, a prickle of irritation starting to bloom, but couldn't resist adding, "I'm looking forward to seeing you again."

On the short walk from her Wafco Mills apartment to Elm Street, Emory replayed the phone call with Jazz. Her initial surprise at hearing Jazz's voice again had vanished, leaving her more than a little excited and almost speechless at another invitation. She'd tried for a gracious response that didn't come across as too aloof or too eager.

Now she stood outside the restaurant giving herself a pep talk. She could share another meal with Jazz because she'd made it clear this was work. The folded papers inside her purse confirmed it, though she hadn't yet decided if she'd share them. So, why had she taken an hour to choose the equivalent of a little black dress that gathered at the waist and flared slightly over her hips and a pair of matching tights? Why had she agonized over which pashmina best complemented her hair and the dress? Work. She repeated the word over and over as she reached for the door handle.

"Wow." Jazz's hand covered hers on the handle. "Let me get that. You look...wow." She pulled the door open and followed Emory inside.

"Hi," Emory squeaked out of her rapidly closing throat. Jazz robbed her breath dressed totally in black with her unruly dark hair. Her rugged but tailored image would fit in anywhere. Emory suppressed a surge of excitement. She didn't have to be obvious about her attraction. "You look...hot." Emory slapped her hand over her mouth. So much for being discreet. "Did I say that out loud?"

Jazz grinned and the overhead lighting illuminated the pink blush of her cheeks. "Thanks. Shall we sit?" She motioned to a table near the front window but off to the side that afforded them privacy. "Is this okay?" When Emory nodded, Jazz pulled out her chair and waited for her to sit before taking the chair closest to her. "Thanks for this."

"For?" Emory asked distractedly, taking in the dimly lit restaurant with white linen tablecloths and candles. She should've chosen somewhere else. Koshary's Egyptian and Mediterranean cuisine was always excellent, the staff was efficient and courteous, and they didn't serve alcohol, eliminating the temptation to calm her nerves with a drink. But it felt intimate, like a date destination instead of a place to talk business.

Jazz waited until Emory looked at her before answering. "Joining me for dinner."

"You did say it was important."

"That can wait. Let's enjoy our meal. I'm sure you've had a hectic day in court." She handed Emory a menu along with a smile.

Jazz was thinking about Emory's comfort, but she wasn't comfortable. Jazz's fingers brushed hers as she passed the menu, and she was entirely too close for Emory to relax. She inhaled a deep breath and with it a combination of island fresh and woodsy musk that branded itself as Jazz's signature fragrance. She twisted her napkin in her lap. Jazz was a colleague, and they were here for business. Nothing more.

Emory scanned the menu, stalling more than reading, because she always got the same thing. "Have you eaten here before?" Good, a complete, neutral sentence without innuendo.

"Not recently. What's good?"

"Everything." She turned to Jazz and gave her an exaggerated appraisal. "What kind of appetite do you have?" Damn it. Suggestive AF, as Diane would say. "I mean, what kind of meat do you prefer?" Again, not perfect.

Jazz propped her elbow on the table, rested her chin, and leaned closer. "I have no idea what you'll say next, but I can hardly wait."

Emory shook her head. "My filter misfires around you for some reason. And I probably shouldn't have admitted that either, but it's true."

"I like a woman who tells the truth. So…back to my appetite." She winked, but when Emory started to speak, stopped her. "Wait. Surprise me." She signaled to the waiter. "If you wouldn't mind, order for both of us?"

Emory accepted the challenge, enjoying the idea of overseeing even one thing about Jazz Perry. "I'll have lamb chops and salad, and the lieutenant will have a Koshary salad with filet mignon. And two waters, please."

When the waiter left, Jazz nodded her approval. "Lieutenant plus filet mignon. So, you pegged me as a red-meat-eating warrior. I like this game. How do I like my steak cooked?"

Emory made a show of studying Jazz again, and this time concentrated on the shadows that alternated with the gleam in her eyes. Jazz had been deeply hurt. Was it her adoption, an ordeal that frequently left scars, or something else? Emory's heart ached. She wanted to tease out the pain so Jazz could have a full, happy life. She shook herself. *Not my job.* "I'm sorry, what was the question?"

"Steak?"

"Oh, right. Medium rare. Grilled. Four minutes each side. Seals in the flavor."

"Good guess. And how do you know if the meat is done?"

Emory reached for Jazz's hand. "May I?" When Jazz nodded, Emory made a circle with Jazz's middle finger and thumb. "Press against the ball of your thumb. When your steak has the same soft, springy feel, it's medium rare." She cupped Jazz's hand for several seconds longer, enjoying the heat and brushing her fingertips lightly across her palm. Touching her was a big mistake. She wanted to slide her fingers up the back of Jazz's neck, fist a handful of hair, and bring their lips slowly together. "So—sorry." She pulled away and glanced out the window.

"Don't be."

Emory started to explain, but the waiter brought their meals and saved her from making an even bigger fool of herself. Jazz dove into her filet mignon, and Emory lost her appetite watching Jazz chew and lick her lips. Emory pushed her food around the plate, nibbling, but not really tasting anything. Why was it so hard to relax and enjoy herself with Jazz? The logical part of her brain provided an answer: because this was work and the two did not mix.

Jazz's phone buzzed and she slid it from her back pocket and glanced down. "Sorry, I'm expecting an important text."

While Jazz checked her phone, Emory waited for her to explain, but she didn't. Maybe it was work, or Jazz's girlfriend, or someone she was meeting later for another rendezvous. Emory's mind spun through several more possible scenarios that inexplicably soured her mood. When Jazz placed her knife and fork across her empty plate, Emory asked in her business voice, "Do you want to tell me what prompted this invitation?"

Jazz gave her a questioning look, probably trying to figure out why she suddenly sounded so formal. "Louis and Denise Robinson applied to be foster parents, and it appears their application has bogged down in the system somewhere. I wanted to check on it for them."

Emory shook her head. "I can't discuss this with you, Jazz. If they have questions, they need to contact the administrative office.

It's not my domain." Jazz leaned closer, and Emory got another whiff of her tantalizing cologne.

"But if you put in a good word, it might speed up the process. The police department did a thorough background check on him before we hired him at the substation. They'd be great parents, might be the answer to Shea's prayers, and permanent closure of one of your, what did Sheri call it, hard-to-place cases."

Emory flinched. "I never use that terminology."

"Please, Emory, give the Robinsons and Shea a chance."

"You certainly are persistent, Jazz Perry." This was not her area, and she should stay well out of it. "Fine, I'll look into it tomorrow."

"Thank you." Jazz wrapped her hands around her water glass. "I also wanted to ask about Shea." Emory started to object, but Jazz raised her hand. "It's an active case, and I'm worried about her. She called me the first night she went back to the group home, but nothing since. Can you at least tell me if she's been placed yet? And maybe something about her father?"

Emory didn't admit she'd been following the case without Sheri's knowledge because of Jazz's interest. Exchanging information with law enforcement was customary, but Emory was pretty sure Jazz's curiosity was more personal than professional. She debated with herself a few seconds longer before saying, "No, she's still at the group home."

"Can you tell me—"

"No."

"You didn't let me finish."

"It doesn't matter. I wouldn't ask you to violate the police department's confidentiality restrictions to satisfy my curiosity about a case. Please don't ask me to. I've already told you more than I should. And besides, I know cops. If I told you who Shea's father was, you'd launch a full-on investigation until you found him…and then who knows what would happen?"

"Isn't that what we want, to find him and settle her custody once and for all?"

She pressed her lips together and gave Jazz a hard stare.

Jazz raised her hands in surrender. "Okay. I know better than to argue with that look, but I will find him with or without your help." The waiter brought the check, and Jazz grabbed it.

"You bought my lunch the other day. I've got this one," Emory said.

"I asked you out. Besides, I want to." Jazz paid and held Emory's chair as she rose. "May I walk you home? It must be close since you wouldn't let me pick you up."

Emory pushed through the door to the street and pulled her pashmina around her. "That's really not necessary. Good night." She started walking, but Jazz kept step beside her.

"It might not be necessary, but it's the right thing to do." She grinned when Emory smiled and shook her head. "When the Carlyle girls started dating, Papa and Mama sat us down and had *the talk*. When they found out Bennett, Dylan, and I were all lesbians, they used the same speech they'd used with Simon about girls, so I'm thinking they got off easy. Papa's contributions were to always treat a lady with respect and never let her walk home alone."

Emory needed to leave Jazz outside the restaurant and clear her head, but she wanted Jazz with her, and not because it was the right thing to do, but because Jazz wanted to be with her a while longer. "All right."

"So, where are we headed?"

"I've rented a small apartment at Wafco Mills for the time being."

Jazz glanced at her before directing her around a raised section of sidewalk. "For the time being?"

"Thanks. Yeah, it's temporary, until I get over…" Did she really want to bring up Jean and the horrible way she'd dumped her? She'd lost her first and only lover that day and never fully recovered.

"You don't have to tell me. I'm not prying into your personal life, just talking."

If Jazz asked questions, it meant she cared or was at least interested, but chatting about her ex was not appropriate conversation with a colleague. Emory wanted to be sure they'd permanently crossed the boundary into personal territory before they had the ex-girlfriend discussion. "It's a long story. Maybe another time?"

Jazz nodded and launched into tales of her bike patrol downtown when she first joined the force and about making her own path in school and the department with Bennett as a sister.

"Was it difficult, following in Bennett's footsteps so to speak?"

"It wasn't like that. I had the benefit of my birth mother's last name, so nobody knew Ben and I were sisters or that I was even part of the Carlyle family unless we told them. And Bennett was a bit of a screw-up in high school, her words not mine, while I was the quiet, serious one, which made doing our own things easier."

A streetlight lit Jazz's face as they walked, and Emory saw the shadows in her eyes again. "Do you mind if I ask a question… about your adoption? I don't often get to talk to someone who's been through the system and come out the other side quite so successfully."

"Okay." Jazz's subdued tone indicated she was willing but not necessarily anxious to dwell on the topic.

Emory wanted to know everything about her experience, good and bad, but she went straight to the bottom line. "Are you happy?"

"Wow. Again, not what I expected, Ms. Blake. You constantly surprise me."

"Is that a bad thing?"

Jazz took Emory's hand and tucked it into the crook of her arm as they walked. "Not at all. I thought you'd want a retrospective on the system since you're so focused on maintaining its integrity."

If only. Jazz's lips tightened and the pressure on Emory's arm increased. Maybe Jazz needed support or at least the comfort of touch before answering. "Like you told me, you don't have to talk about this if it's uncomfortable." She pulled Jazz closer to emphasize her point and then didn't move away.

"I should probably say aloud what bothers me." She looked toward the sky as if asking for strength. "I was totally blessed and so happy to have the Carlyles adopt me. They were the perfect fit for me in every way, and I have no regrets."

"But…"

"I want, no I need, to belong to someone special, to have a partner and a family of my own. I'm not taking anything away from the Carlyles because they made me a part of their family in every possible way, but some things you can only do for yourself." She stopped walking and turned to Emory. "I hope that doesn't make me sound desperate or ungrateful."

"No, not at all." Jazz's willingness to be so vulnerable, combined with the conversation she'd had with Diane and the baggage she still carried from her relationship with Jean, made Emory feel ashamed and a total coward.

"Does it make sense?"

"It makes perfect sense, and I admire your courage for talking about it. Belonging is one of those things like self-concept, which you already know I have a problem with, that can't be provided by someone else." She stopped in front of her door and took out the keys. "This is me."

"Saved. One more block and I might've told you all my faults. Thank you for accepting my invitation, the pleasure of your company, and for looking into the Robinson application."

Jazz lifted the keys from Emory's hand and brushed against her to unlock the door. She was afraid Jazz could hear the rapid pounding of her heart and feel her heat rising. "You're...welcome."

Jazz pushed the door open and stood back so Emory could enter. "I'd really like to see you again, Emory. Would you do me the honor of going on a real date with me? I'm running out of professional reasons to see you." She smiled down at Emory, her expression open and sincere.

"I...but..." She fumbled for an excuse, something that made sense and didn't sound as insecure as she felt. "We should probably stick with work, keeps the boundaries clear."

"And if I want to blur the boundaries? Please?"

Jazz whispered the last word, and Emory caved. "Okay."

"Okay? Really? Thank you." Jazz bent her head and kissed Emory's cheek. "Thank you so much. How about Friday unless you already have plans?"

"Friday would be great."

"What time should I pick you up?"

"Six thirty."

"I won't be late." Jazz's eyes that earlier had been dim with sadness now sparked golden brown with possibility.

"What should I wear?"

Jazz waved her hand toward Emory. "Look at you. Wear whatever you want and you'll be the most beautiful woman in the room. See you Friday." She kissed Emory's cheek again and backed slowly away, holding eye contact until she almost stumbled over a shrub.

Emory closed the door and dropped into a chair, her thoughts and emotions in chaos. A real date with Jazz. No work agenda. Was she ready for this?

❖

Jazz ran the mile and a half home from Wafco Mills, high on her evening with Emory and the sense of being steadily drawn together. Everything about Emory was appealing—her voluptuous body, her poise and style, and the way her eyes tracked every move Jazz made with pure desire. Even Emory's reluctance to provide the information Jazz wanted was a turn-on because she stood by her principles. Jazz wouldn't call what she felt for Emory instant chemistry, but she was definitely interested.

She bolted up the front porch steps, reached for the screen door handle, and pulled slowly to keep the squeaky hinges from waking the family.

"Hold up, Lieutenant." Dylan's voice pierced the quiet, and Jazz jerked back.

"Are you trying to get shot, Doc?" Jazz released the handle of her weapon in the small of her back and joined her sister on the porch swing.

"Not very observant for a cop. Preoccupied?" Dylan nudged her shoulder and withdrew quickly. "Yuck, you're wet. Exercise or sex sweat?"

"Shush." Jazz motioned for her to keep her voice down. "Running."

"Somebody chasing you?"

"No, I just needed—"

"To burn off sexual energy. You might as well fess up. I know my sisters. Who is she?"

Jazz wouldn't look at Dylan. "I'm not talking about this. Why are you hanging out on the porch in the middle of the night? Living in the cottage getting boring already? Remember, you wanted the solitude."

"Just got home from my shift at the hospital and wanted to wind down. Nothing better than this swing for relaxing and being close to the family without being with the family. And yes, I still love the cottage. Thanks again for passing your turn so I could move in. You still like being in the big house with the folks?"

Jazz nodded. "I love family. You know that."

"So do I, but I need some space right now. The family has always been there for me, and with my residency coming to an end, I just need to be more independent."

"I get it. Anyone interesting on your radar that you need all this independence for?" Jazz asked.

"I don't even have time to check the radar, much less act on what I find." Dylan laughed. "I only have another week of supervision before they cut me loose, and then maybe I'll think about women again. In the meantime, I'm getting carpal tunnel."

"TMI. Let me know when you're ready to date because I know a couple of decent cops who'd love to go out with you."

Dylan shook her head, and her wavy dark hair shifted across her shoulders. "No disrespect, but after growing up with cops and what happened with G-pa and Papa, that's the last thing I want in a partner. One of us on weird shifts dealing with crazies is quite enough, not to mention the daily threat of death."

"I won't tell G-ma, Mama, or Bennett you said that."

"Thanks. I value my life." She leaned over and kissed Jazz on the cheek. "Okay, if you're not dishing about your love life, I'm going to bed."

"I don't want to jinx it."

"She must be pretty special and she'd be lucky to get you. I love you, Jazz." She bounded off the porch, waved, and walked around the side of the house toward the cottage.

Emory was special, but why? Maybe being the chaser instead of the chasee was the turn-on for Jazz. She wasn't desperate to jump Emory but she was certainly attracted to her. Was that a bad thing? Too early to tell. She pushed her feet against the porch floor and relaxed into the rhythmic sway of the swing until her eyelids flagged. As she headed upstairs to bed, the same phrase repeated in her mind. Too early to tell.

CHAPTER SIX

Jazz was almost home after an uneventful night shift when her cell phone rang. "Hello."

"Lieutenant Perry?" an unfamiliar female voice asked.

"Yes, this is Jazz Perry. How can I help?"

"You left several messages. I'm Karen Patrick with the US Adoption Agency. I apologize for taking so long to get back with you, but I've been out of state, and you said you wanted a face-to-face. The question should probably be, how can I help you, Lieutenant?"

Ms. Patrick sounded professional, but her low-pitched tone was also kind of hot. Jazz was still on an adrenaline high from the last fight call and shook her head to refocus.

"Lieutenant Perry? You still there?"

"Yes, sorry. I was hoping for some information on one of your clients, Shea Spencer, an eleven-year-old who—"

"Ran away last weekend. Aren't you the officer who found her?"

"Yes, but—"

"I can't tell you how grateful we are for your help. Unfortunately, she's still in a group home, but I'm determined to find her father or placement soon. She's going to be just fine."

Professional or not, Karen Patrick wasn't blowing Jazz off so easily with a sultry voice and a quick thank you. "Is there any chance we could talk in person? I'd like to know more about your agency." Maybe appealing to her pride would be the ticket to a face-to-face.

"Well…I'm headed to the hospital now to pick up some paperwork from last night. My office computer is being replaced, and I need the files ASAP. Can you meet me there?"

"How about the canteen? I'll buy you a world-class vending machine brew."

Ms. Patrick laughed and a deep, throaty sound filtered through to Jazz. "I have a better idea. Why don't I stop by Green Bean at Golden Gate and get us a real coffee? What's your pleasure?"

If Karen wasn't flirting, Jazz was more tired than she thought. "Flat white."

"See you in fifteen. I'm coming from the gym, so don't expect business attire." She disconnected before Jazz could reply.

Jazz darted onto Wendover Avenue eastbound and pulled in front of the ER five minutes later. A steady stream of hospital personnel changing shifts crowded the parking lots and hallways. Jazz spoke to the regular night shift folks as they made their way out and nodded at the less familiar morning group.

She settled at a table in the canteen, and a few minutes later the elevator chimed and a woman dressed in bright workout gear stepped off. Jazz tried not to stare, but the woman demanded attention—clothes clinging to her like gift wrap, squared shoulders, searching her surroundings with more intensity than many police officers. Jazz stood as the woman approached.

"Good morning, I'm Karen Patrick." She studied Jazz's face as if trying to commit her to memory, placed the coffee carrier on the table, and offered her hand. "Lieutenant Perry?"

Jazz returned the firm handshake. "Yes, I'm Jazz Perry." Up close, Karen Patrick's eyes were almost hypnotic, still scanning but never losing focus. Tiny laugh lines at the corners of her mouth hinted at an age her body didn't broadcast.

"Mind if I sit?"

"Please." Jazz pulled out a chair and waited for her to settle before sliding it back in. She caught a whiff of an exotic fragrance mingled with recent sweat. "Thanks for meeting me and for the coffee, Ms. Patrick."

"It's Karen, please."

"Karen." She was attractive, and Jazz was single and intrigued. She got the feeling Karen would be uncomplicated and ready for anything—like so many other women she'd dated—nothing like the one staring at her from the doorway. She withdrew her hand from the back of Karen's chair.

Emory was stunning in a business suit jacket that gathered at her waist accenting her breasts, minimizing her midsection, and flaring slightly over her hips. She was beautiful, and Jazz started to tell her so, but Emory's rosy cheeks paled as she glared at Karen Patrick. "Em...Emory."

"Jazz." The word sounded strained as if Emory forced it out.

"Would you like to join us?"

"You're busy." She studied Jazz a few more seconds before turning without further comment and disappearing down the corridor.

Jazz dropped into the chair across from Karen, unsure what had just happened.

"Girlfriend?" Karen asked.

"Friend. I think." Emory had only recently agreed to go on a date with her, and Jazz wasn't sure how to categorize their relationship. "Maybe more, not sure yet."

"Sounds complicated." Karen slid a coffee toward Jazz. "I don't do complicated. Life is too short. Why limit yourself when so many options are available?"

Jazz took a sip of coffee, hoping to clear some of the brain fog. Maybe she was dulled by exhaustion or in sensory overload. If she listened with her hormones, Karen's comments sounded flirty and sexual. If she listened with her head, they were just substantive enough to still be professional. "Are we talking about work or something else?"

Karen leaned back and breathed deeply. "I believe my philosophy is sound in any case. But you look tired, Jazz. Maybe we should have this discussion when you're rested."

"I've waited long enough. I'd like some information about Shea Spencer."

"You said you wanted to talk about the agency."

"I want both. Actually, I'd like to see Shea."

"Why, may I ask?"

"Let's just say she made an impression on me, and I want to check on her," Jazz said.

"That might sound simple on the surface, but it's actually not. USAA is a private agency, and we value the confidentiality of our children, facilities, staff, and families. The only way I can confirm Shea's location or allow you to see her is if the group home has no objections."

"But I just want to make sure she's okay."

"And my word isn't good enough? Why such potent interest in this child?"

Jazz briefly considered spilling her life story to Karen, but her priority was fulfilling a promise she made to a little girl. "I just met you. Your company may well be everything you say, but I'd like to see for myself. Please make that happen."

Karen studied her for a few seconds before pulling a business card from an inside pocket in her tights and placing it on the table. She slipped Jazz's pen from her shirt pocket. "I've put my cell number on the back. I'll try to get an answer for you in a couple of days. Maybe we can help each other."

"How's that?"

"North Carolina is considering privatizing more of Child Protective Services' responsibilities. A positive recommendation from a high-ranking law enforcement professional could only help our cause. Of course, I wouldn't expect a recommendation until you've seen the operation, have a full understanding of what we do, and make your own comparison. It could take some time to convince you, but I'm prepared to put in the work if you are."

Jazz wasn't about politics and had no intention of stepping into that minefield, but she wanted more information and this looked like a perfect compromise. "Of course." Since they were on such agreeable terms, Jazz pushed her luck. "Do you have any input in the foster parent application process?"

"Why do you ask?"

She told Karen about Louis and Denise and the lack of movement on their application.

"Sounds about right for CPS. Sometimes I'm privy to potential parents, especially if they express no age preference and appear suitable for older children. Would you like me to look into their situation?"

Jazz nodded. "So, you'll get back to me?"

"Indeed, I will, Lieutenant, on both issues. I think you'll find me much more responsive than CPS." Karen smiled, and her gaze briefly settling on Jazz's mouth. "Speak soon."

Jazz pulled Karen's chair out and followed her to the elevator where she raised the flap of Jazz's left shirt pocket and tucked her business card inside. Either Karen was coming on to her, or Jazz's gaydar needed fine-tuning.

Karen stepped inside the elevator, and before the doors swished closed, she said, "It was very nice to meet you, Lieutenant Perry. I look forward to our collaboration."

Jazz stared at the closed door for several seconds. Why did she feel like Karen Patrick would be so easy to get to know? And why did Emory's reaction to seeing them together bother her? Women. It was too early, or in her case too late, to do such heavy thinking without sleep.

She pushed the elevator button to return to her car but changed her mind. Maybe she'd just look in on Emory before she left. She made her way through the hallways, tapped on the CPS office door, and pushed it open slightly. "Emory?"

"Not here yet." Sheri McGuire frowned at Jazz from behind the large desk and offered no further information. She apparently hadn't gotten over Jazz's questions about Shea's care.

"I just saw her in the hallway. Any idea when she'll be here?"

"Not my job to keep up with my coworker's comings and goings."

Jazz stepped closer. "Look, I'm sorry if I was out of line the other night. I didn't mean to imply you weren't doing your job."

"Really? Felt like that to me."

"That's not what I meant. I was looking out for the kid."

"Which suggests I wasn't."

Sheri McGuire obviously held a grudge, which made any chance of getting further information about Emory or Shea out of the question. "Again, not my intent. Have a good day."

Emory had spotted Jazz in the canteen and intended to cancel their pending date, having reconsidered overnight, but Jazz was with a woman who had a body like a model. Jazz's eyes were hazy and her skin flushed, sure signs of attraction. After their brief exchange, Emory rushed to the restroom and splashed cold water on her face to erase the image of Jazz attending to the woman the same way she had to her. Her heart ached, but her self-respect hurt more. She'd fallen for Jazz's self-deprecating manner and smooth talk too easily, and now she was paying for it.

She stared at her face in the mirror. "You don't have a chance. You should've known better." The gorgeous stranger was the kind of woman Jazz deserved. They made a perfect couple. She tried not to imagine them naked, touching each other. She splashed her face again. Jean was history, but Emory still harbored the belief she'd never be special to anyone again, especially not someone like Jazz.

She straightened her suit while her automatic jump to insecurity passed, and then she headed for the office, running a denial scenario in her mind. The woman might be a crime victim or witness, and Jazz had no real interest. But something about Jazz's expression said she was wrong. She opened the office door, and Sheri was packing her bag. "How was last night?"

"No problems. Quiet for a change."

"Any calls…or visitors this morning?"

"Nope."

"Any more scuttlebutt about privatization?"

"Not a peep. I'm out. See you tomorrow."

Emory made a cup of tea, hung her suit jacket on the back of the chair, and settled behind the desk scanning the night's entries on the computer, but her mind wandered back to Jazz and the mystery woman in the canteen. The woman's skin-hugging attire didn't scream professional, but her look and demeanor certainly did. Who was she and what did she want with Jazz? Emory read the same paragraph three times, but nothing registered. She swiveled toward the small window behind her that let in a slender rectangle of light and rested her teacup against her chest. The view of sky and clouds settled her and helped her think more clearly.

"Emory?"

She jerked and tea sloshed down the front of her blouse. "Damn." She jumped from the chair, pulling the wet, warm fabric away from her skin.

"Let's go." Jazz cupped her elbow and practically ran down the hallway to the employees' restroom and locked the door behind them. "Take it off. Quick."

Without question, Emory pulled the blouse from her skirt and shucked it over her head, not bothering with the buttons.

Jazz handed her a wet paper towel. "Blot your skin before it burns, then your bra so it won't stain." Jazz ran cold water over the blouse in the sink and rinsed it up and down.

When the shock and fear of burning wore off, Emory realized she'd stared at the computer long enough for the tea to cool a bit. She started laughing and couldn't stop.

Jazz gave her a quizzical look. "Are you in shock?"

"Not at all. Look at us. We're a comedy act. You're washing my blouse, which I could never imagine in the real world, and I'm standing half naked dabbing my breasts like a lactating mother who's had an accident."

Jazz propped against the sink, the blouse forgotten, her gaze resting on Emory's chest. "And you do have magnificent breasts."

"*What?*" The heat scorching Emory's face and chest had nothing to do with lukewarm tea and everything to do with the hungry look in Jazz's eyes.

"God, I'm so sorry," Jazz said. "That was totally inappropriate. Please forgive me." She glanced between Emory's wet blouse in the sink and her damp bra with a face almost as red as Emory's felt.

"It's all right." Emory turned to survey the damage in the mirror. "Oh, my." The silk fabric of her bra was almost transparent, highlighting her dark, puckered nipples. "This is embarrassing."

"You should never be embarrassed about your body, Emory. Trust me. Here." She handed Emory a fresh paper towel. "Hold this over your breasts while I examine your chest…for injury. You could have serious burns."

Emory took the towels but shook her head. "I'm fine. The tea wasn't hot. I guess I was more surprised than anything. I'll be okay, but I'm not so sure about my wardrobe."

Jazz turned back to the sink, squeezing and wringing the blouse until it was somewhat clean but a mass of wrinkles. "I hope you have a spare blouse somewhere."

"Actually, I do. Years of working with upset children taught me that lesson. If you'll get it from the bottom drawer of the file cabinet, I'll take this bra off and try to make it wearable with the hand dryer."

"Okay, be right back."

Emory locked the door behind Jazz and rested her back against the cool metal. Her body shivered from the arousal she'd seen in Jazz's eyes. No doubt it was lust, because she'd seen the same expression earlier when Jazz looked at the woman in the canteen. What was their connection? A light tap on the door sidetracked her thoughts.

"Here's your blouse."

She eased the door open a crack. "Thanks. You can head home. I know you've been up all night. I'm fine here."

"I'm not leaving until you're fully dressed and back in your office. I feel responsible for this whole fiasco. I'll wait at your office, if that's okay."

"Fine. I'll be out in a few minutes." She stripped off her bra and held it under the hand dryer until the garment was dry enough to wear. She wiped the tea residue off her breasts, the coarse towel fanning the desire Jazz's stare sparked. She splashed water on her face again, redressed, and squeezed the water out of her blouse before heading back. "All better."

Jazz paced the hallway in front of Emory's small office. "Again, I'm sorry."

"It was an accident." She stretched her wet blouse over one of the side chairs and moved toward her desk, wanting distance and the solid piece of furniture between them.

"Did Sheri tell you I came by earlier?" Jazz asked.

"This morning?"

"Yes, right after I saw you in the canteen."

"She didn't mention it." Why wouldn't she? Sheri was always in a hurry to leave work, so maybe she'd been in too much of a rush or maybe she'd simply forgotten. But she'd asked specifically if she'd had any calls or visitors, and Sheri said no.

"I wanted to explain who—"

"You don't owe me an explanation." The words tasted bitter as she tried to accept the truth.

"The woman was Karen Patrick, director and counselor with the US Adoption Agency."

"Oh, I see." The explanation didn't change what she'd really seen.

"What do you see?"

"You're attracted to her." She had no right to make such an observation but couldn't seem to stop. Too much had gone unsaid in her last relationship, and she wouldn't make the same mistake twice. She and Jazz had shared coffee, lunch, and a working dinner, which didn't make them soul mates, partners, or even girlfriends. Jazz was free to do as she pleased, but Emory deserved the truth.

"What?" Jazz's slightly colored cheeks and the fact she couldn't meet Emory's gaze told her everything she feared. "I won't lie. She's my type…or has been, but I'm into different now."

Emory struggled for something neutral to say so Jazz wouldn't see how disappointed she was at her admission. Jean had taught her that the right temptation could turn any woman's head. "She looks about my age." The realization comforted and confused Emory. Jazz found an older woman attractive, just not her. But the way Jazz looked at her said she *was* interested. And she wanted something different. Could that mean Emory? Why was this so complicated? "Are you seeing her again?"

Jazz's eyes grew wide and she stared at Emory as if she wasn't sure what to say.

"You are." Emory choked down the sick feeling rising in her throat. What she wanted to say and what she had to say warred inside. She hated judging anyone by their outward appearance. Those balms and barbs never considered the real person underneath. "We both want to know more about the agency, and you have to satisfy your curiosity about her. What choice do you have? Besides, we're not in a thing." She wanted to take the high road, but was she pushing Jazz into the arms of another woman?

Jazz tugged her bottom lip with her teeth. "What? But I thought we—"

"Coffee and two business-related meals, Jazz, that's all. You're a free agent. And I was going to tell you that I'd decided against our dinner date."

"But what if I—"

"I need to get back to work." Emory shuffled papers on her desk to avoid looking at Jazz. "Would you mind closing the door behind you?"

Jazz didn't move. "No."

"What?" Emory looked up, certain her dismissal would've scared Jazz from the room.

"I want to have dinner with you tomorrow night like we planned. Please, Emory? Don't let whatever just happened come between us. I don't plan to." Then she slowly started toward the door. "Think about it and let me know later."

When the door closed behind Jazz, Emory dropped her head in her hands and angrily brushed away a tear. She refused to cry over another woman who would probably choose beauty over substance and break her heart again.

Chapter Seven

Emory sliced the cooling meatloaf into meal-sized portions and placed them in containers along with a scoop of green beans and scalloped potatoes. She repeated the process until twelve meals of meatloaf and twelve of chicken lined the kitchen island in her brother's house. After labeling each with their contents, she stacked them in the freezer and loaded the remainder of the dishes in the dishwasher. The mindless activity relaxed her and gave her uninterrupted time to think. She'd repeated the ritual every month since her mother died four years ago, and every time, her brother objected, also part of the routine.

The front door slammed, and Ross called, "Something smells great. You still here, sis?"

"In the kitchen finishing up."

Ross dropped his briefcase in a kitchen chair and gave Emory a hug. He was tall and broad like their father, compared to her short, squat features of their mother, and when he hugged her, she always felt safe and loved. "What did you make this month? Wait, let me guess." He sniffed the air. "Mama's meatloaf and...I give up."

"Barbecued chicken, green beans, and scalloped potatoes. Should last you a while considering how many business meetings you have over dinner."

"Thank you, but you don't have to do this anymore. Most of the grocery stores in the area carry TV dinners that are pretty good quality, and they have deli sections with ready-made meals too. It's called progress, sis."

"I know, but are they as good as a home-cooked meal?"

"Never, but I could also have the wonderful lady who cleans for me do some light cooking. You make me feel like a charity case."

"You could never be a charity case, Ross. And besides, I enjoy cooking." Ross did financial planning and was making much more money than he knew how to spend, which was why every month she found a generous donation in her bank account from his. She'd asked him to stop, but so far, he hadn't listened, so she put the extra into savings for her forever home.

"You're early today, Em."

"Took half a day off to come by. I have plans tonight." After talking through every excuse she could think of with Diane, she'd finally called Jazz to confirm their dinner plans.

Ross studied her while he pulled a beer from the fridge, twisted the top off, and took a pull. "Date type plans?"

"I think so." She flushed and turned away to wipe the stove again.

"I love redheads. You can't hide anything. If you weren't so honest, I'd still know the truth because of that blush. Just like Mom's. Is this date someone you're seriously interested in?"

"I'm not sure." When she was around Jazz, everything inside her screamed that she was sure, but when apart, the logical and damaged parts of her urged caution. Women like Jazz didn't go for women who looked like her, at least not for the long term.

"As long as she treats you right, I'm fine with it, not like that last one. If I could get my hands on her right now I'd—"

"Stop, Ross. She's not worth the breath it'll take to finish the thought."

"Amen to that." He toasted her with his beer bottle and glanced at the kitchen clock. "You better get moving. Takes forever for you to decide what you're going to wear, not to mention showering, shaving your legs, putting on makeup, and doing your hair."

"You really do notice things, don't you?" He grinned. "You're going to make a good husband someday. Any prospects?"

He shook his head. "The only prospect I want tonight is a few more beers and the football game I taped last night." He gave her another hug and pushed her toward the front door. "Have a great time. And thank you again for the grub. Love you."

Ross was right. It took almost two hours before Emory emerged from her bathroom clean, shaved, moisturized, and makeup lightly applied for a natural look. Now for the hair. Most of the time she loved her long wavy tresses, but tonight they had a case of the frizzies. A French braid would be quick and easy, but she wore that style most days to work and tonight she wanted something different for Jazz. She settled on a braid within a braid, wove a three-strand at her crown, incorporated it into a larger weave, and then pancaked the two together for fullness. For the final touch, she pulled a few wispy strands loose to feather around her face and stood back from the mirror. "At least my hair looks good."

She checked the clock. Fifteen minutes until Jazz arrived and six outfits to try on. Less than three minutes each. If she knew where they were going, her choice would be easier, but since Jazz wanted to surprise her, this whole process was a crapshoot. She closed her eyes, spun in a circle, and pointed. When she opened her eyes, she was pointing at a spaghetti-strap gold knee-length dress with lace above the breast. The same color belt wouldn't visually divide her body into halves like a carnival balloon animal. Added bonus, the dress was comfortable and caressed her body in softness as she moved.

The final touch, perfume. She reached for her everyday brand, but then spotted the slender bottle of Chanel No. 19 Ross had given her for her birthday tucked behind the other cosmetics on her dressing table. At a hundred dollars a bottle, she used it sparingly, but tonight definitely qualified as a special occasion. The fragrance was a blend of jasmine, rose, iris, and sandalwood, all her favorites in one yummy combination. She spritzed a tiny pump in the air and walked through it on the way to the front door.

Jazz rang the bell exactly on time, and when she saw Emory, her lips parted in a tiny gasp and her eyes sparked with flecks of gold that matched Emory's dress. "Oh. My. God. You look amazing. I'm a lucky woman." She sniffed the air. "And that perfume. It's like...flowers, but more. Sorry, I'm not very good at describing girly things."

"Thank you."

Jazz produced a bouquet of three roses, white, red, and yellow, from behind her back and handed them to Emory. "I know this is probably old-fashioned, but you deserve beautiful things." She leaned in and gave Emory a quick kiss on the cheek. "Is it all right?"

"I...of course." Her pulse quickened as she breathed in the fragrant aroma. "I love roses. You're so thoughtful." She raised a finger. "Don't move while I put these in water." She raced to the kitchen, found a vase, and carefully placed each one in separately. Could Jazz be any more perfect? She took a few extra seconds to calm her heart rate before returning to the entry where Jazz still stood framed in the doorway.

Emory stopped to drink Jazz in. Her pinstriped suit gave her added height, and the silver Mandarin-collared shirt contrasted with Emory's gold dress as if they'd coordinated for prom. If Di saw the two of them, she'd say they were totes on fleek, or something similar. Emory licked her lips. "Nice outfit. Who does your clothes shopping?"

Jazz feigned shock. "How do you know I didn't pick this out?"

"Dylan?"

"Am I such a fashion dinosaur?"

Emory took Jazz's arm as they walked toward a black SUV. "I just don't see you clothes shopping beyond jeans and T-shirts."

"You're right." Jazz laughed as she opened the door, waited for Emory to climb in, and then lingered against the doorframe staring at her. "I had to go with Dylan though, to try stuff on. Does that count?" Emory grinned. "I hope I haven't lost cool points."

"Not at all. I appreciate the extra effort." And she was close to swooning at Jazz's continued gallantry—flowers, compliments, opening the car door, and just the right amount of eye contact and subtle flirting. Her insides twisted with a delicious tingle of desire.

"May I?" Jazz reached for the hem of Emory's dress and waited until she nodded. "I just wanted to feel the material. It looks so soft."

Jazz's fingers grazed the skin above Emory's knee and she sucked in a quick breath. The tingle of desire flared as she watched Jazz caress the fabric between her forefinger and thumb so close to her burning center. "Do you do anything that isn't sexy?"

"Sorry?" Jazz let the fabric fall from her fingers and smoothed the dress back over Emory's knee before she closed the door.

"Nothing." *Not helping.* Emory watched in the side mirror as Jazz walked around the vehicle and fist pumped the air like a kid on the basketball court. Emory leaned over and unlocked her door.

Jazz settled in beside her and glanced over before starting the car. "You haven't mentioned our ride."

Emory had expected the sports car but was pleasantly surprised with the larger vehicle. "Much...bigger, roomier. I hope Dylan didn't make you buy a new car as well."

"This is mine too. I call it my big-girl car." Jazz grimaced. "I didn't mean *for* big girls. I meant when I need more room for friends, stuff, whatever, like—"

"I understand the concept of big-girl cars, and I didn't take offense." Emory squeezed Jazz's hand where it rested on the gearshift and quickly released when her body heated again.

"Because I'd never do or say anything to upset you."

"I guess I can be a little sensitive on the subject."

"Trust me. I'm not like that. And now, Ms. Blake, I need you to close your eyes, please."

"What?"

"I want our dinner location to be a surprise until the last minute. Trust me?"

"In theory."

Jazz cupped her hand and pulled it onto her thigh.

Emory obediently closed her eyes, and everything disappeared except Jazz's thigh and her body heat searing the heavy wool-blend fabric and creeping up Emory's arm. She shivered from the warmth and the images it burned into her mind. Her discomfort about seeing Jazz with Karen Patrick and almost canceling their date vanished. "Talk and distract me."

"Okay, one note about work and I promise nothing else tonight. In the interest of full disclosure, Karen offered to check on Louis Robinson's foster application. If she's as unresponsive to that request as she was returning my call, I'm not going to be happy."

Emory opened her eyes and glared at Jazz. "I wish you hadn't done that. Don't you trust me to do my job or do you just enjoy circumventing the rules to get what you want? Neither of those options work for me." She pulled her hand from Jazz's.

"Em, don't. She offered to help, and I didn't want to put you in the middle."

"Karen Patrick doesn't have access to every application for foster parents, but you can bet she'll do whatever is necessary to get it now. For you. Do you know that she's trying to close my branch of CPS and put quite a few people out of work?"

Jazz stopped the car and waited until Emory looked at her. "Did it occur to you that privatization might not be the worst thing that could happen?"

Anger bolted through Emory and she blurted, "You have no idea how much damage a woman like Karen Patrick can do." Her hurt and anger fused, and she wasn't sure if she was talking professionally or personally. And right now, she didn't care.

"I'm sorry, Em. I didn't realize how much you dislike her."

"I don't even know her, just her kind. This is a bad idea. Please take me home." She looked out the window, realizing for the first time where they were. "Take me home *now*." The night with Jean in the corner booth here at Green Valley Grill flooded back. Her stomach churned. Too much was happening at once. Her career and any potential with Jazz were dissolving around her, at this place with its ghosts.

"Emory, are you all right?"

Emory shook her head. She hadn't been back to Green Valley in the three years since her breakup.

Jazz turned sideways and reached for Emory's hands.

"Don't."

"I'm so sorry, but please just have dinner with me. Let's talk this out."

"I can't be here."

"We can go somewhere else. Anywhere you want. We can have hotdogs and ice cream if it'll make you feel better. I just want to spend some time with you and forget work."

Emory concentrated on breathing in and out slowly. Jazz couldn't have known this place represented one of the biggest failures of Emory's life. The look of pure anguish on her face tempered Emory's distress and kicked her into rescue mode. "Give me a second. I'll be fine."

"We're leaving." Jazz started to crank the car again.

"No." The callous expression on Jean's face when she ended their relationship returned, and Emory made a split-second decision. "It's time to make new memories. I can't let my past or Karen Patrick spoil my life." She took a few deeper breaths. "Just stay close."

"My pleasure. If at any time you feel overwhelmed and want to leave, just say the word. I'll do whatever you need." Jazz opened the door, tucked Emory's hand into the crook of her elbow, and escorted her into the restaurant. "Table for two. Perry."

The maître d' led them toward *that* booth in the back, and Emory whispered, "Definitely not here."

"Is there something else?" The waiter diverted to a table around the corner that offered a view of the entrance. Jazz looked to Emory for approval, and when she nodded, said, "Very nice. Thank you."

The soft light, linen tablecloths and classical music, along with potted plants that cocooned diners in privacy, transformed the huge space with tall ceilings into an intimate dining experience. She had loved this place since bringing her mother here for high tea just before she died. Emory started to relax as she clung to Jazz's arm and enjoyed seeing heads turn when Jazz pulled out her chair.

"Are you sure this is okay? I don't want you to be uncomfortable, about anything."

"I'm fine. Really, Jazz. Relax." Jazz brushed her hand across Emory's shoulder as she helped remove her coat and handed it to the waiting maître d'. Her touch helped calm Emory's nerves. At least for tonight, Jazz found her attractive and wanted to spend time with her. Emory told herself to forget about Jean and Karen and focus only on the two of them. Their problems would still exist tomorrow.

"I think in honor of your courage and to create new memories, we should toast with champagne." Jazz's eyes met hers, concern swirling in their depths.

"Excellent idea. I'm sorry I overreacted, but I haven't been here in a while."

"It's okay, Em." Jazz ordered their drinks and reached across the table for Emory's hand. "I don't know how you're feeling, but you look very composed and absolutely beautiful."

Emory glanced around the room, unable to take Jazz's compliment and appreciative stare without blushing. "Thanks."

"I'm serious, Em. I wish you could see what I do when I look at you." She released Emory's hand when the waiter placed two flutes on the table and an ice bucket between them. "But stick with me and I'll convince you." The waiter popped the champagne cork and poured their glasses before Jazz gave him a quick nod, and he moved to another table. She raised her glass. "To Emory Blake, the most beautiful woman in the room, and to making new memories."

Emory hesitated but finally clinked her glass against Jazz's and took a sip. "Thank you."

Jazz waited patiently while Emory toyed with the idea of telling her about that night. Maybe purging would be a good thing. Or maybe her story would just be ammunition for further pain. Jazz's face showed only concern while her stare bathed Emory with warmth. "Jean and I had been together three years and were celebrating our anniversary, or so I thought. You've already figured out we sat at that booth in the corner. The white tapered candle on our table slowly burned halfway down while we drank wine and shared my favorite salmon dish." Her voice sounded rough and melancholy, and her throat felt raw.

"You don't have to talk about this, Em."

"I want to, sort of." She twisted her napkin in her lap. "Jean looked edible in a tuxedo with a cummerbund that matched my dark green gown, and her short blond hair was finger combed back with gel in the sexy way I loved. I couldn't wait to peel that tux off and devour her. I'd just told her that while sliding my foot up between her legs." Jazz licked her lips, and Emory asked, "Should I stop? You really don't need to hear the details. It's all just pouring out."

"Go on. I already think she's a fool."

"I'd just finished the devouring statement when the waiter placed a chocolate brownie a la mode on the table between us along with coffee and Bailey's, totally derailing further foreplay.

Jean looked at me and said, 'I'm sorry, Em, this just isn't working for me.' Her voice never changed pitch. She sipped her coffee as casually as if she'd remarked on the weather."

"What a class act," Jazz said.

"I thought she was talking about the dessert. So, I plunged my spoon into the chocolate, but the look on her face stopped me. Then she said that classic line, 'It's not you. It's me.'"

"Seriously?"

Emory nodded, the pain of that night gouging her again, only duller this time. "Then she asked me not to make a scene and to enjoy the dessert while she took a cab home. Oh, and maybe I could spend the night at our friend Diane's. She said I could pick up my stuff the following week when she was out of town. And then she apologized, threw a handful of bills on the table, and walked out of my life."

Jazz stared, her expression a cross between anger and disbelief. "You deserve so much better than that, Emory." She raised her flute again. "Good riddance, Jean."

Emory took a few seconds to let the feelings, bad followed by better, wash through her before she smiled and said, "Amen." She gave Jazz a chance to ask questions, and was relieved when she didn't. "Thank you for letting me vent. It's the only time since the night it happened that I've told anyone. I cried on poor Di's shoulder for a week, but this time I feel like I've closed that door forever." But she hadn't told the entire story. The final blow had come two weeks later, and she couldn't bear telling Jazz after the recent events with Karen.

Jazz slid her chair closer and leaned into Emory's side. "Thank you for trusting me. I know it wasn't easy."

She nodded. "Something like that chips away at your self-confidence, self-concept...all the things that make a successful relationship possible. You've probably had your heart broken as well and know what I'm talking about."

"Not since I was in college, but age doesn't make the lessons easier or the pain less. I haven't found the right person to take a chance with again. I'll know when I do."

Emory shook her head, refusing to let the entire evening be about Jean Dunlap, losses, Karen Patrick, or her job. "Here's to second chances." She sipped her champagne and fiddled with the stem of the flute. "I'm sorry about earlier, the Karen thing. Just promise you'll be careful. I don't trust her and I'm not sure why."

"I promise." Jazz tipped her glass against Emory's.

"This is really good. There's just something about champagne that says happy."

"I couldn't agree more, and—"

"Well, good evening you two." Bennett and Kerstin stopped beside their table. "Emory? You look fantastic." Bennett openly stared until Kerstin nudged her. "Oh, I'm sorry. Emory, this is my wife, Kerstin. Kerstin, Emory Blake, the best social worker CPS has ever had…and apparently Jazz's date."

While Emory and Kerstin exchanged greetings, Bennett shot Jazz what looked like an ah-ha expression. Jazz shrugged and grinned.

"You've been holding out on us, Jazz," Bennett said. She waved toward the champagne. "What's the occasion?"

Emory's stomach roiled as she waited for Jazz's response.

"Emory finally agreed to go out with me. How about you guys? What's up?" Her quick change of topic was too obvious.

Kerstin rolled her eyes at Emory. "How soon they forget. Ben and I are celebrating six months of wedded bliss. Right, darling?" She leaned in and kissed Bennett on the cheek.

"Absolutely right. The happiest six months of my life." She squeezed Jazz's shoulder and added, "They're holding our table, so we'll let you two get back to it. Nice to see you again, Emory, and I hope to see more of you in the future."

Bennett started to walk away, and Jazz grabbed her hand and whispered, "Please don't tell the rest of the family. I'm not ready for all the questions."

"No problem," Bennett said.

Kerstin made a cross over her heart with her fingers and kissed Jazz's cheek.

When Bennett and Kerstin slid into a booth across the room behind another grouping of plants, Emory took a big swig of champagne and turned her attention back to Jazz. "So…why the secrecy?"

"You *do* know my family."

"Yes, and they seem totally supportive of all their children." But maybe not of Jazz seeing her or any woman her age. "What would they think about the two of us on a date?"

"They'd think I got pretty damn lucky. And just FYI, I haven't asked my family's approval on who I date in years. They already like you, which would only add pressure if they knew we were going out. I'm just not ready to tell them."

Emory's insecurities screamed into overdrive. Jazz wasn't ready to tell her family she was dating an older woman, a social worker, a friend of the family, or her specifically? If any one of those things mattered to Jazz, this, whatever this turned out to be, was already over.

"Are you okay?"

"Sure."

Jazz looked at her skeptically. "*Sure* is one of those answers like *fine*, which basically means you're not. I'd like us to have a good time tonight, so if I upset you, I'm sorry. If I even hint to my family that I'm into you, they'll have you sharing Sunday brunch, buying a home down the street, ordering furniture, and suddenly nothing is private. I'd like to avoid that as long as possible, or at least until we get to know each other better. This *is* our first real date."

Jazz smiled at her, probably trying to make her feel better, but it wasn't working. No matter how she justified it, Jazz wanted to avoid telling her family about them. Interpretation, whatever was happening between them wouldn't be long-term. "I get it." *Stop it, Em. Dick and dash.* Diane's voice echoed like a mental bitch slap. She was getting ahead of herself. This *was* only a first date. After their disagreement in the car, Jazz might never ask her on another. She needed to relax and remember that no expectations equaled no disappointments and no pain.

Emory raised her flute. "To a fun evening." When Jazz tapped her glass, Emory added, "We might need more champagne."

The meal was delicious—salmon for Emory and, of course, red meat for Jazz—followed by crème brûlée for dessert and more champagne. Emory retold childhood stories about her and Ross, and Jazz shared some of the antics of the Carlyle clan. Except for the location, nothing else about the date reminded her of Jean.

After dinner as Emory walked toward the car, the buzz of too much alcohol dulled the bite of the night air and heightened her attraction to Jazz. Should she invite Jazz in when they got home? Would Jazz want to spend the night with her? Was Emory ready to stand naked in front of another woman and risk rejection? After only one date? Uncertainty and indecision burrowed deeper the closer they got. By the time Jazz escorted her to the front door, Emory was a total wreck.

"Thank you for a wonderful evening, Jazz, and especially for helping me erase some unpleasant memories. I've reclaimed Green Valley Grill."

"The pleasure was all mine." Jazz pushed the door open and stepped closer. "Thank you for agreeing to see me, off duty."

Jazz leaned down and kissed Emory lightly, a chaste kiss that lingered and stirred her desire. Emory took a quick breath and licked her lips, preparing for more, but changed her mind and stepped away. Jazz tried for another kiss, but Emory stopped her with a hand to her chest.

"You're a very special lady, Emory. Thank you for a wonderful evening. Good night." Jazz walked away.

Emory stood in the doorway watching her leave, torn between calling her back and letting her go. Jazz had been chivalrous and accepted her obvious uncertainty without pushing. She'd decided earlier to have sex with Jazz, but on the way home fear and insecurity made her second-guess her decision. She wanted Jazz, no doubt, but if she wasn't sure she could handle it now and later, she probably shouldn't. When would she feel comfortable enough to expose herself physically and emotionally?

CHAPTER EIGHT

The smell of fresh ground coffee and the buzz of early-morning conversations surrounded Jazz as she waited for her latte at Green Bean in Golden Gate Center. She settled at a table by the side window and took a quick sip, needing the extra caffeine. Sleep had been elusive since her emotional date with Emory on Friday. Her plans for a pleasant evening went sideways when she brought up Karen and inadvertently chose a place with unpleasant memories for Emory. While the meal and conversation went smoothly after the false start, the parting stumbled. Jazz thought Emory wanted her to kiss her, maybe more, but then she'd pulled back. Jazz hadn't pushed or questioned her. If and when they finally shared a real kiss, she wanted Emory to be sure.

Jazz felt someone standing behind her, but before she could turn around, the person grabbed her shoulders. "Lieutenant Perry, you're so tense. Something wrong?" Karen's voice was liquid velvet, sending shivers down her spine.

"It's early...and work stuff," Jazz managed.

"Nice to see you again." Karen gave Jazz's shoulders a final squeeze before taking a seat. "Sorry about the time. Mrs. Broadmoor from the group home insisted on meeting before school. She's parking the car and will be in with Shea in a minute. I wanted a chance to speak privately."

"Okay." Karen's touch left goose bumps on Jazz's skin, and when she saw her sexy casual clothes, she almost forgot this was a business meeting. Karen wore jeans and a scooped-neck sweater like a runway model, tight and flashy, accenting her assets.

"As you might've noticed, Shea is a bit defensive. We've had trouble placing her in a suitable home because she rebels, typical for a child who's shuffled from birth parent to foster family and then back through the system. I'm hoping she won't be in the home long. Please be gentle with her. She likes you."

"Of course." The door opened, and a fiftyish looking woman followed Shea into the coffee shop. She rose and greeted Shea first. "How's it going?"

"Whatever."

Jazz shook hands with Mrs. Broadmoor and received a genuine smile. "It's a pleasure to meet you, Mrs. Broadmoor. I appreciate you letting me see Shea. Would you mind if I talk to her alone for a few minutes?"

"You know the rules." Mrs. Broadmoor's voice was matter-of-fact but kind. "Anything you say to her must be said in my presence. I'm trying to establish some boundaries."

Jazz disliked the response but couldn't argue with the reason. "Okay. Shea, would you sit by me, please? Want something to drink? Hot chocolate?"

Shea glanced at Mrs. Broadmoor, waited for her to nod, and said, "Yeah. Thanks."

Karen stood and grabbed her purse. "I'll get it. Anyone else?"

Jazz turned her attention back to Shea. "So, how have you been?"

Shea wouldn't meet her gaze for several seconds and didn't answer.

"The woman asked you a question, Shea," Mrs. Broadmoor said.

"I'm fine. All good." Her clipped words were as unconvincing as her inability to make eye contact.

"Sorry I haven't been around. I've been trying to see you ever since we chatted on the phone, but as it turns out, getting an appointment with you isn't as easy as you might think."

"Yeah, right."

"Really. There are a lot of laws and rules that prevent just anyone from spending time with children."

Shea gave her a skeptical glance. "But you're a cop."

"Exactly, which means the rules apply to me twice as much. It's not because I didn't want to see you again."

Karen placed Shea's hot chocolate in front of her and said, "It's true, Shea. She's been nagging me for days to see you, but it required approval, and we had to find a convenient time for everyone."

Shea didn't reply but still looked unconvinced. Jazz wanted everyone else to leave so she could have a real conversation with Shea, but such a request would've ended the meeting. "Anything interesting happening at school?"

Shea shook her head.

"What are your favorite subjects?"

"Math, I guess. Numbers don't lie." She took a sip of her drink, but Jazz caught the sideways glare from Mrs. Broadmoor, who checked her watch.

"You playing any sports?"

"Nah, not very athletic."

Jazz laughed and nudged her shoulder. "Seriously? I've seen you run, remember? You could totally make the track team. You might like it, make friends, and be part of a team."

For the first time, Shea cracked a smile before her eyes shifted toward Mrs. Broadmoor. "Nah, it wouldn't work out." She fidgeted with her cup lid.

Mrs. Broadmoor stood and made a show of examining her watch again. "We should probably get going. Shea is due in school, and I have other responsibilities."

"I could take her if—"

"Thank you, but no." Mrs. Broadmoor shook Jazz's hand and nodded toward Karen. "I'll be in touch."

"Thank you," Karen said.

"I appreciate your time," Jazz said and then knelt in front of Shea as Mrs. Broadmoor moved toward the door. She slid another business card into her hand. "In case you lost the last one. Call if you need anything. Really, Shea. I care."

Shea threw her arms around Jazz's neck and squeezed. "Thanks." When she let go, tears pooled in her eyes and she ran to the door, and Jazz's heart broke a little more.

Mrs. Broadmoor placed her arm around Shea's shoulder and escorted her across the parking lot.

"Glad she could spare the time," Jazz said sarcastically.

Karen settled across from Jazz with a cup of coffee caged between her hands. "At least Shea has a roof over her head and food on the table."

"Yeah, at least."

"As I said earlier, Shea came with issues, and the vanishing act with her father didn't help her case. She has to do her part."

"More like her father's vanishing act. What kind of parent lets his eleven-year-old run around loose at night? He should be in jail, have his parental rights taken away, and Shea should be in a permanent home with decent people. Look at her, Karen. She's not happy."

"She will be, but it takes time." She took a sip of coffee. "In other business, you asked about the Robinsons' foster application."

"Yeah." Changing the subject wouldn't solve Shea's problem or take Jazz's mind off it for long, but if it worked out, the Robinsons might be able to help.

"The application has been on a desk for the past two weeks under a stack of more important papers. The good news is, it's been approved, and I think I can get them assigned a child very soon, at least on a trial basis." Karen leaned toward her. "How's that for results, Lieutenant?"

Jazz inhaled her exotic fragrance and was again surprised by how much she liked it. "I think they'd be a great match with Shea."

"Not so fast, Jazz. I'll see what I can do, but no promises. Anything else you need?" She casually touched Jazz's arm and pulled back. "I'm at your service."

Karen was sexy as fuck, and maybe Jazz was reading too much into her overly friendly behavior, but it felt like she was flirting. She swallowed hard and said, "I'm still interested in your agency."

Karen grinned as if sensing Jazz's discomfort and the reason for it. "Basically, the US Adoption Agency is a private company contracted by the state to manage nationwide placement of newborns with special emphasis on assigning older children permanent homes. Babies are easy to place because most parents want to raise a child from infancy. My focus has become finding homes for older children. They're often circulated between foster homes and group homes until they age out of the system. I find that egregious, don't you?"

"Absolutely."

"I believe every child deserves a happy, healthy upbringing. And I admit, I enjoy the challenge of placing hard-to-match children with deserving families. I thrive on any type of contest." She pointed at herself with her thumbs. "Classic overachiever."

"Speaking of parents, how do parents become part of your agency's database?"

"After we receive the application, we have an extensive vetting process. As a nationwide organization, we've repeatedly tested our guidelines and revised them to meet the highest standards. Our parents are usually financially viable, well-adjusted, and emotionally stable."

"Does that mean rich?" Jazz had found out the hard way that rich didn't necessarily equate with good parenting.

"Not necessarily, but money opens doors. Why such interest?" Karen cupped Jazz's hand and gave her a look that said she really wanted to know. "Is it just this girl or something else?"

"Well, I—" Before she could answer, the door opened and Emory stood framed by sunlight streaming in around her. Jazz had an immediate sense of joy followed by panic.

Emory paused in the doorway, her eyes drawn to the manicured hand resting on Jazz's and the svelte body attached to it. She started to turn around, but it was too late.

"Join us, Emory." Jazz rose to pull out a chair, but Karen Patrick didn't move. Their connection was palpable, and Emory felt sick. "Emory, you know Karen, counselor with USAA? Karen, Emory Blake, CPS."

Karen fixed Emory with an appraising gaze before offering a handshake. The same hand she'd just removed from Jazz. "Pleasure to meet you, Emory. I've heard a lot about you."

"Really?" Emory reluctantly eased into the chair on the opposite side of Jazz.

"Sheri McGuire and I work closely on older children adoptions. She mentions you from time to time."

"Yes, of course." Emory shifted her attention to Jazz, who was staring at Karen's mouth, again. "I don't want to interrupt, so I'll just get my drink to go."

"Please, stay. Let me. What would you like?"

"Hot chai tea." She waited until Karen walked away before finally making eye contact with Jazz. Her eyes were dark with emotion. "Are you all right?"

"Yeah, sure. Didn't expect to see you this morning."

"I offered to leave." After pulling away from Jazz Friday night, Emory shouldn't be surprised if she turned to another woman, but so soon.

Jazz shook her head. "I didn't mean it that way. I'm happy to see you."

Emory forced down nausea every time the image of Karen touching Jazz reemerged. "You didn't waste any time." Why did she say that? Jealous much? "Getting in touch with Ms. Patrick, I mean."

"She arranged for me to see Shea."

"And…"

"Shea is obviously not happy."

"It's a group home, Jazz. They aren't always happy places." Emory considered trying to explain about Friday night, but what could she say? That she'd freaked out, been torn between just kissing Jazz and asking her to spend the night? She couldn't put herself out there after the way their date ended and what she'd just seen. Jazz and Karen shared an obvious attraction, and Jazz deserved the freedom to explore it without complications from her. "We'll do our best to find Shea suitable placement soon." She glanced toward the counter to make sure Karen was still waiting. "Have you discussed the privatization issue yet?"

"I was about to bring it up when you came in…and distracted me. You look great, by the way. We probably need to talk later."

Was Jazz referring to Karen and what she'd seen pass between them, the privatization issue, or what happened Friday night? "Whenever you have time. You know where to find me." She kept her voice even, belying the tumble of emotions inside. She could pretend Jazz wasn't interested in Karen, but she'd been devastated by pretense before. Not again.

"Maybe you should ask Karen the questions," Jazz said. "You have a better understanding of what you need to know."

"She can't know I'm involved. Her agency is probably one of the top contenders for the contract, so I can't be seen to interfere in any way."

"Okay." Jazz grinned and winked at Emory. "I'll be your James Bond, if you'll be my Moneypenny."

Being relegated to the role of confidante and sidekick but never leading lady, Emory nodded toward Karen as she approached the table. "You've obviously found your Bond girl."

Karen placed Emory's tea in front of her and rejoined them. "Hope this is okay."

Emory grabbed the cup and stood. "It's fine. Thank you. I'll leave you to it. I have a lot of work piling up at the office." She left before either of them could object, but neither tried. On the way to her car, Emory dropped the cup in the trash bin. Unlike Jazz, she didn't want anything from Karen Patrick.

Jazz watched Emory until she disappeared around the corner, confused about their exchange and Emory's cool demeanor.

"Something I said?" Karen asked.

"More likely something I did."

"Like I said before, complicated. Are you and Ms. Blake enjoying your dance?"

"What are you talking about?"

Karen quirked her lips into a teasing grin. "She wants you." When Jazz gave her a quizzical look, Karen continued, "You're not used to being the pursuer, are you?"

Jazz shook her head.

"If you want the demure Ms. Blake, you might have to up your game."

"She's not interested."

Karen shook her head as if Jazz were totally missing the obvious. "Seriously, Lieutenant? I know women, and Ms. Blake is beyond interested, she's besotted." Jazz started to object again, but Karen raised her hand. "But that works for me. As I've said, I love competition and I'm not afraid of an invigorating chase, if you're interested." She winked. "Now, where were we?"

Jazz stared at Karen a few seconds longer, trying to decipher what she'd heard. Karen was interested in her and thought Emory was as well. That explained the mixed feelings she got from both, but it didn't clarify how she felt about either. She shelved her feelings and returned to the familiarity of work. "Your agency?"

"Why don't we go for a site visit, if you have time? You can ask questions and get a firsthand demonstration of how we operate. What do you say?"

"Why not? I'm off today." Jazz allowed Karen to tuck her hand into the crook of her arm as they walked across the parking lot. As she got into her car, she saw Emory pulling out of the lot and made eye contact briefly before she gunned the motor and pulled onto the street.

What was going on with Emory? She was running hot and cold, encouraging her to get information about the privatization contract while giving her the cold shoulder anytime she was around Karen. Maybe Karen's observation was right. Women. Would she ever understand how they operated and what they really wanted?

While Jazz followed the Mercedes coupe down Elm Street, she searched again for the reason, beyond obvious sex appeal, for her interest in Karen. She wanted to know everything about the foster care and adoption systems, and she was particularly interested in which organization provided the better option for children—Karen's or Emory's. And, if she was honest, getting the information Emory wanted played a big part as well. They stopped at a multi-story building that resembled any other business office and then proceeded to the fifth floor. Plush furniture and luxurious accent pieces that exceeded the usual government requisition populated the office and gave it a lavish feel.

While explaining the layout and operation, Karen occasionally touched Jazz's arm, nothing overt but more physical contact than a regular work associate. Karen's nearness made it hard to pretend she wasn't flirting, and Jazz's body warmed at the familiarity of being pursued.

"Nice setup. Are you publicly funded?" Jazz asked, forcing her attention back to work.

"We're required to be licensed by the state and receive a small stipend, but we're a private organization so most of our funding comes from service fees."

"So, prospective parents pay to adopt children."

"Of course. We provide a service, and customers pay, like any other company."

"Except you deal in children." Jazz felt her insides churn from the memory of her time in the system, and neither Karen's soothing tone nor her touch could calm her.

"I'd never describe our agency in that way. We're very professional, thorough, and discreet. We have counselors for every aspect of our process, specialists if you will, in the areas of newborn and older adoptions, national and international services, home evaluations, and even an onsite therapist for children or prospective parents who need a little extra care."

Karen directed Jazz into an expansive office overlooking a large church. She closed the door behind them and motioned to a leather chair in front of a sleek glass and metal desk. "Would you like coffee?"

"No thanks, I'm good." Jazz enjoyed the view of Karen's jeans-clad ass as she fixed herself a cup and then settled in the chair beside her, placing her coffee on the desk. Karen moved with the assertiveness and self-confidence of a woman used to getting her way.

She crossed her legs and edged toward Jazz, the neck of her sweater easing farther down. "I want you to be completely satisfied when you leave here today, Jazz."

"What?"

"About the agency." She knew exactly where Jazz's mind had wandered. "You have other questions?"

Jazz swallowed hard and looked away from the creamy swell of Karen's breasts. "Yes. How do you decide who gets to adopt a child?"

"We thoroughly vet everyone who applies to adopt. The process is quite grueling, with several home visits, a trial period with additional evaluations, and a couple of surprise visits after final approval. We leave nothing to chance." Karen raked her fingers through her hair and brought it forward toward her face, framing her cheekbones and eyes.

"Sounds very comprehensive. And does money factor into the final decision?" She'd raised the question before, but still wasn't satisfied with Karen's pat answer. None of Jazz's foster parents had been rich or even upper-middle class, until she landed with the Carlyles.

"Financial stability is certainly a consideration. A child has a much greater chance of succeeding in the world if she's given certain advantages. Why shouldn't we try to make that happen?"

"Because money isn't everything. A cliché, but also the truth. What a child needs most is attention and love. The material things are secondary."

Karen placed her hand over Jazz's forearm where it rested on the chair, squeezed lightly, and withdrew. "I couldn't agree more. I assure you, Jazz, we're not some moneymaking machine with no interest in the children we serve. I stake my professional integrity on each match, which is why I plan to pitch a proposal to the state to oversee all adoptions and basically replace CPS."

Jazz's arm tingled from Karen's touch, and when she looked up, Karen licked her lips. Was she trying to distract Jazz or misdirect her? Wait. Karen said something important, something Jazz needed to follow up. "Aren't you already contracted with the state?"

"Very good, Lieutenant. I thought I'd lost you for a second. We have an agreement for limited services, but I believe we could improve efficiency and cut costs if we took over the entire operation. I'm hopeful the powers-that-be agree."

The rumors were true, but the bids weren't open because Karen hadn't presented her proposal yet. What else would Emory want her to ask? Jazz didn't know enough about politics or how contracts within state agencies worked to venture much further. She'd get with Emory later and figure out a plan. Karen's eagerness to have Jazz on her side would come in handy.

"Well, guess I better get going. You have children to place, and I have to sleep." Karen offered her hand, but Jazz just waved, careful not to touch her again. Was she simply attracted to Karen? The physical sensations were familiar, but the energy felt different, like Karen was trying too hard to act like she wasn't trying. And Jazz was holding back. Maybe she'd just never questioned or resisted when a beautiful woman came on to her. Maybe it was Emory's influence in her life. Or maybe it was something entirely different she couldn't figure out.

"I look forward to seeing you again, Jazz. Don't be a stranger. We still have a lot to talk about." At the elevator door, she leaned in and kissed Jazz on the cheek and then wiped her lipstick off with her thumb. "Be safe."

Jazz walked toward her car in the parking lot reviewing the morning and her interactions with Karen and Emory. They couldn't be more different. Karen—svelte, fast, and flashy like her 280Z, and Emory—substantial, measured, and eloquent like a Rolls Royce. Her thoughts ricocheted from one to the other, but her feelings came down solidly on Emory's side, leaving her a little confused. Why these two women and why now? Was it a test—one offering the familiarity of the past and the other showing her the possibility of the future?

CHAPTER NINE

Emory's plan to talk with the staff about privatization rumors had been sidetracked all week by an unusual number of walk-ins at the hospital and off-site committee meetings. Friday was no different. She placed her third cup of tea on the side of her desk, hoping she'd get to drink this one, but her phone vibrated beside her. "This is Emory Blake."

"Emory, it's Jane. We've got another walk-in. Possible abuse. ER three."

"Have the police been notified?"

"They're interviewing the mother now and asked if you'd check by."

"On my way." She breathed deeply on the long walk to the ER to steel herself for what lay ahead. Putting her feelings in a box for the sake of her career and emotional survival wasn't ideal, but it preserved her sanity. The abuses she'd seen also kept her motivated. If she wasn't so committed to helping children and the work wasn't so gratifying, she would've switched careers years ago. She pulled the electronic notepad from under her arm and slid back the curtain surrounding the exam area.

Jane and a younger nurse stood on either side of a gurney on which a child lay motionless. Emory flinched and saw her anguish mirrored in the young nurse's eyes as they filled with tears. Jane shook her head. "Focus on the work."

"What've we got?" Emory asked.

"Ten-year-old male. Head trauma. Unconscious since arrival. X-rays indicate hematoma to the frontal lobe resulting—"

"Layman's terms if you don't mind, Jane." The impassive medical terms served to distance patient and clinician, but Emory needed plain words for her report, words that tugged on emotions, and opened hearts and pocketbooks.

"Sorry, Emory. He's got a brain bleed and clot on the front portion of the brain, probably caused by a fall or a blow to the head. Based on past X-rays, I'd vote blow."

Emory took notes from the chart to fill out the intake report and searched her records. "He's been in before." She flipped through the history. "And he's a USAA adoptee." Jane gave her a knowing glance. "Guess we'll be doing another family risk assessment...as if the risk isn't obvious from this. Anything else?"

"Not right now. All we can do is try to reduce the swelling and hope he wakes up soon." Jane addressed the younger nurse. "Monitor him and notify me of any changes." She stepped outside the curtain with Emory. "The mother is here, been in several times with other children. You should have an extensive file."

Emory nodded. "Unfortunately. Doesn't get any easier, does it?"

Jane drew a heavy breath before pulling Emory farther down the hall into an alcove. "Have you heard about the contract proposal that landed on the CEO's desk this morning?"

She looked around to make sure no one was within hearing distance. "Tell me."

"United States Adoption Agency has recommended they take over CPS adoption responsibilities. Entirely. The brief suggests an enormous cost savings, improved placement figures, and less backlog."

"You've got to be kidding. Where did you get your information?" Jane shook her head, but Emory pushed. "Is it at least reliable?"

"Completely. The person who told me has read the entire document."

She'd expected the debate to hinge on efficiency, but the USAA proposal struck at every administrator's nightmare—funding. Emory doubted all USAA's claims. "Thanks, Jane. If you hear anything else, please let me know." She started to leave but turned back. "By the way, I gave your number to my friend Diane. She should be calling soon."

"Already has. Thanks for that. Well, I better get back to it before my junior pops a cork. Not sure she's going to make it."

"Good luck." After conferring with the police officers interviewing the child's mother, Emory walked slowly back to her office, digesting the information Jane had provided. Contracting out public services, especially child protective and adoption services, was Emory's pet peeve. Some of the private agencies accepted public funds as a state licensed entity but profited under the table from rich parents desperately searching for a child while paying others to accept difficult cases to boost their numbers. In her opinion, either scenario was offensive and immoral. This recent case of abuse was bad timing for USAA. She added a check of USAA placed children who had been abused or neglected to her to-do list.

Emory's other issue with privatization was competent staff and job security. When private companies took over public services, many of them replaced experienced personnel with less qualified and cheaper in-house people. She was at the top of her pay grade and had no doubt she'd be one of the first to go. She couldn't afford to be unemployed, financially or emotionally.

She needed access to USAA's stats, and if they convinced her they could do a better job for less, perhaps she'd acquiesce and file a résumé. But if they presented a proposal based on inaccurate or padded figures, she wanted to stop them before they damaged the system, endangered more children, and brought everything CPS did into question.

When she got back to her desk, she speed-dialed Jazz's number but hung up. What could she do? And why was she Emory's first go-to person? She'd ensured their relationship would be only friends by her epic kiss-fail and by basically shoving her into Karen's arms. Why should Jazz help her or even see her again? She tried to talk herself out of the call, but Jazz cared about children as much as she did and she had unlimited access to Karen. Emory picked up her phone and redialed.

"This is Jazz."

The sound of her husky voice spun Emory into another round of fantasies—Jazz whispering to her in the dark, calling out in ecstasy, waking her in the morning. Would she ever tire of that voice?

"Hello? Is anyone there?"

"Oh, yes, hi, it's Emory. Am I disturbing you?"

"Of course not."

"Can I see you?" Her tone sounded eager, and she hoped Jazz didn't interpret it as a personal request.

"Music to my ears," Jazz said.

"It's work."

"Okay. I was about to pop open a beer to celebrate a long weekend. Care to join me?"

The invitation caught Emory off guard. Jazz didn't sound upset or even distant. "Well, where are you?"

"I'm at home right now, but I can meet you anywhere."

This conversation needed to be in person, but not at the Carlyle home. Norma and Gayle were entirely too perceptive. One inadvertent longing glance at Jazz, and they'd know exactly what she was thinking. Jazz had made it clear she wasn't ready for her family to know they were dating, and Emory certainly wasn't. "Not there. How about…maybe we…what—"

"Emory, just tell me where to meet you and I'll be there."

She looked at her watch and decided to leave work early. "My place in an hour."

"See you then." The line went dead, and Emory stared at the phone. What was she doing? She could've chosen any of the hundreds of restaurants or bars in Greensboro for a drink. Maybe she was a masochist after all.

Exactly an hour later, Jazz rang the doorbell, and Emory hesitated before answering, checking the jeans and sweatshirt she'd chosen, hoping she looked casual but not sloppy. She swung the door open too hard and banged it against the doorstop. "Sorry. Come in." Jazz took her breath away when she passed with her calm presence and that distinctive ocean-woodsy fragrance. She took her time closing the door to regain her composure. "Thank you for coming."

"It sounded important. You look nice. Casual works for you too." Jazz looked her over again causing a flash of heat.

"Thanks."

Jazz held up a bag. "I brought my own beer. You don't strike me as a fan. But I also brought you a couple of bottles of wine. Wasn't sure if you prefer red or white."

"Good call. Thanks." The gesture reminded her of Jazz's earlier comment. "So, you're off the whole weekend?" It wasn't really any of her business, but she did wonder what Jazz did in her spare time, if she was still into sports, if she dated a lot, but she didn't ask.

"I've been covering night shifts while some of our sergeants attended supervisory training, but I'll be on days again starting next week. Shame really because I love the action of night shift, but it throws my whole system out of whack. Sorry, that's probably TMI." She handed the wine to Emory, pulled a beer from the bag, screwed the top off, and inclined her head toward the sofa. "Mind?"

"Of course not. Have a seat and I'll pour some wine."

She placed Jazz's remaining beers in the fridge, uncorked the bottle of shiraz, and poured a glass. When she returned, Jazz was turning a circle in her small living space taking it in.

"Nice place. I like open concept. One bedroom?" She sounded tentative, asking neutral questions, and pulling at the patch of white hair over her ear.

She nodded. "It's small, but if I want to throw a party, I'll borrow my brother's massive house in New Irving Park." She curled her feet under her on the sofa, motioning for Jazz to sit.

"Is he older or younger? I forgot to ask before." Jazz pulled her cell from her back pocket, placed it on the coffee table, and settled across the other end of the sofa, her long legs nearly touching Emory.

"Ross is quite a bit younger and a financial advisor."

"Your only sibling, right?"

Emory nodded again, and Jazz stared at her mouth. No matter how many times Jazz looked at her, it was always like the first time—exploring and wanting. No one had ever looked at her like Jazz did, and Emory never wanted her to stop. She felt attractive and desirable under her hungry stare. "Jazz, I'm sorry about the other night, our date, and about the coffee shop. I've been giving you mixed messages and I wanted to explain—"

"No need. You have your reasons."

"You're too kind." Jazz gave her a way out, and she took it. Since she didn't fully understand her behavior yet, best not to dissect it with anyone else. "Thanks. Guess I should tell you why I wanted to see you so you can get on with your weekend." Emory took a deep breath and plowed forward before she lost her nerve. "I need USAA's operational stats."

"What?"

Emory explained what Jane had told her, what total privatization of CPS could mean to the hospital and her, and about the child Jane had treated. "After the way I've behaved recently, I have no right. And I know it's a big ask, but it's not like I can waltz in and demand the information. If you don't want—"

"I'll do it."

"Just like that?"

"Yes," Jazz said. "But why don't you just ask for a copy of the proposal?"

Emory grinned. "You're not big on politics, are you?"

Jazz pulled a face and shook her head.

"Look at it this way. If the chief of police was accepting bids to provide new weapons for the department, would he pass them around to the troops and ask for input?"

"Good point."

"If I'm to lose my livelihood, I want to be damn sure the change is better for children. All the stats probably won't be in the proposal anyway, just the broad strokes, and I need everything for comparison. Since you have a connection...access to Karen... I'm not asking you to do anything illegal or unethical—"

"You'd never." Jazz grinned and nudged Emory's foot with hers.

"Just look at the stats, if you can. She's trying to get you on her side, so she'll probably give up the information willingly."

"Back up. What do you mean I have a connection to Karen?"

Emory shook her head. "Seriously, Jazz?"

"I've tried to explain and—"

"I'm not criticizing, just making an observation." Emory took a big sip of wine, the hope of anything personal between her and Jazz fading further by the minute. "I did a lot of soul searching after Jean. In retrospect, all the signs were there, but I didn't want to see them. I know what to look for now and I pay closer attention. Please do me the courtesy of not lying. I need to be able to trust my instincts again where women are concerned."

Jazz sat up straighter and met Emory's gaze. "Okay. It's obvious Karen is attractive...but so are you."

"Don't, Jazz."

"You asked me to be honest, so let me be totally honest. I've dated women like her all my life, and I'd be lying if I said her attention wasn't flattering, but like I've told you before, I want something different." She softened as if to temper the impact of her words. "I don't know what Karen's agenda is any more than I know exactly what's going on with us, but it's her strategy that interests me, not her personally."

Emory blinked back tears that felt partly about relief along with hope. "It's obvious she wants you, and she's certainly something to look at."

Jazz placed her beer and Emory's wine on the coffee table and took Emory's hands, her eyes totally focused on her. "Looks aren't everything."

Jazz's sincerity registered with Emory, but she didn't respond. She'd heard that line too many times and seen people act exactly opposite.

"I'm just asking you not to make any snap decisions about me and Karen or me and you. I *have* to see her, to follow up about Shea and now to learn about the contract." Emory tried to pull away, but Jazz held her hands firmly. "And I *want* to see you because I think we have something special."

Emory freed her hands. "And what would that be, Jazz?"

"Well, I…"

The emotions flashing across Jazz's face painted a clear picture of her confusion. She had no more idea what was going on between them than Emory did. "That wasn't a fair question. We've only been on one date. Do what you want, Jazz, but I won't compete for you. I'd really appreciate your help with the information, but if that puts you in conflict with what you want personally, don't do it."

"Please don't shut me out, Em. Karen is about work, and you're so much more." Jazz slid closer and cupped Emory's cheek. "I've wanted to do this since the day we met. May I please kiss you? Properly kiss you?"

"I…"

Jazz waited for Emory to object, and when she didn't, she closed her mouth over Emory's. She traced Emory's lips with the tip of her tongue and probed gently for entry.

"Umm." Emory's moan ripped through her as she melted against Jazz. Her mind screamed *run*. Jazz was attracted to Karen, had admitted it seconds before. She should step back, keep things professional, but her body ached for Jazz's touch. Their kiss deepened, and she stroked her fingers through Jazz's hair to the nape of her neck, pulling to maintain their connection. "Yes." She breathed softly against Jazz's mouth, her life spinning out of control, and moved in for another kiss, but Jazz's cell vibrated across the coffee table.

Jazz rested her forehead to Emory's, her eyes glassy and unfocused, before pulling away.

"Come back." Emory reached for her, but Jazz glanced at her phone.

"I have to take this." She picked up her cell. "Hello?" She listened while Emory tried to calm the trembling that threatened to overpower her. "Yes, I can be there in ten minutes. No problem, really."

"Duty calls." Emory tried for nonchalance, but her voice sounded hoarse and needy.

"I have to go." Jazz stood beside the sofa, looking down at her.

"Of course." Emory fought the urge to pull her back down.

"I'm sorry, Em." Jazz tucked a strand of loose hair behind Emory's ear before collecting her beer bottle. "Will you be at the charity game tomorrow?"

"I better be. Norma, Gayle, and I are co-chairs of the event, and I have first shift at the main gate with the donation bucket."

Jazz walked into the kitchen area and poured the remainder of her beer down the sink before heading for the door. "I'll leave the others for next time." She hesitated before adding, "There will be a next time, right?"

Emory stood on shaky legs and followed her to the door. When Jazz reached for the knob, Emory eased her back against the door. She trailed her finger lightly across Jazz's cheek and down between her breasts before slipping lower and tugging on her belt buckle. She kissed Jazz again tenderly, and then harder, pressing their bodies together. "I'm thinking yes."

When she stepped back, Jazz pulled for breath. "Damn, woman."

"Just something to remember me by." She winked and opened the door. "Good day, Jazz, and thanks for the help. I look forward to your report…next time." She closed the door and nearly collapsed against it. Where had *that* come from? All her years of waiting and wondering culminated with their kiss, and she couldn't let Jazz leave thinking she didn't matter, regardless of the Karen factor.

She sipped her wine and relived the kiss over and over, pressing her fingers against the heat and sensitivity that lingered on her lips. It had been everything Emory imagined and more—soft and tender followed by passionate and demanding. Her body pulsed and ached.

What the hell was she doing? She told Jazz she wouldn't compete, but when they touched, logic and restraint vanished, and every dream and desire she'd fantasized about clawed its way to the surface. Jazz asked for her patience, kissed her, and meant it. Right now, that was enough.

The doorbell rang, and she ran to answer. "Did you forget—"

"Surprise." Diane raised two bottles of wine. "Oh, snap. Did you just have sex?"

"What? Of course not."

"You so did. You're flushed. Your lips are puffy. And your eyes have that glazed over look. Deets immediately." She pushed past Emory and looked around the room, craning her neck toward the bedroom. "I assume she's not still here."

"No, she's not…I mean, I haven't had sex." Emory looked everywhere but at her.

"But you've totes had something."

"Not now, Di."

"Oh, yes, most definitely now. I'm not leaving until we've finished these two bottles and you've told me every minute detail." She plopped down on the sofa.

Giving in to the inevitable, Emory filled their glasses and joined her on the sofa. After a summary, Diane stared open mouthed. "What? That's everything. I swear."

"Let's recap. Jazz kissed you first. You kissed her back and then let her leave?"

"I didn't exactly let her leave. She got a phone call and ran out."

"Who called?"

"She didn't say, and I didn't ask, but I'm thinking Karen Patrick."

"The skank you were telling me about the other day at spin class?"

Emory nodded.

"So…this woman calls, and Jazz just leaves you all hot and bothered. Not a good sign, Em. Sorry."

Emory covered her face with her hands. "Believe me, I know. But she asked me to be patient, after I told her I wasn't going to compete for her."

"Patient as in give me time to sleep with this other woman so I can decide which one of you I want kind of patience, or time to work through our mutual work thing and get away from her kind of patience?"

"I'm not exactly sure what you just said, but I'm thinking the latter."

Diane scooted closer and wrapped her arm over Emory's shoulder. "Are you sorry you kissed her?"

"Never, and if that's all I ever get—"

"Don't tell me you'll be fine with it because I totally won't. It'll suck so hard. I've never seen you so excited and glowy."

"Glowy? Is that even a word?"

"Who cares? You know what I mean. She's good for you, and you adore her. Don't just roll over and let Karen Patrick have her without a fight."

"I don't fight." Emory took another sip of wine before topping up their glasses. "Like I'd have a chance against all that anyway. Can we please talk about something else? What's happening with you?" Diane filled her in on her progress with Jane, but Emory's mind wandered. Was Jazz with Karen? What was the emergency?

❖

Jazz pounded the steering wheel with her fist as she drove. "Damn it." She tugged the seam of her jeans away from her tender flesh. "Our first real kiss. What a kiss. And I had to leave. Damn." Any fleeting concerns she had about not being sexually compatible with Emory vanished the minute their lips met. Their connection had been immediate and intense, and pulling away had caused a physical ache. Karen had been right about Emory's interest, and Jazz could work with that.

But Shea needed her, and Jazz couldn't refuse. She considered telling Emory, but didn't want to admit she was going to violate another CPS rule and put Em in a bad position. She parked at the athletic field behind the school and scoured the area for Shea. If Mrs. Broadmoor was here, Jazz would observe from a distance or make up a plausible excuse for her presence that didn't involve Shea. Jazz skirted the field toward the bleachers and took a seat near the edge.

She relaxed in the late afternoon sun and watched while the coaches set up and gave instructions for the track trials. A group of kids divided into two teams had taken their places on the field when she finally spotted Shea and waved.

Shea grinned and bent over to tie her shoelaces. She looked so small compared to the rest of the children, but she appeared excited as she jumped around warming up for the contest. At the coach's instruction, all the kids crouched in place and waited for the start. The whistle sounded, and Shea sprinted forward but behind the rest of the group.

Jazz sprang to her feet. "Go, Shea. Show them what you've got."

Shea hung back until halfway through the race and then sprinted to the front, easily defeating the others by a wide margin. She picked up her backpack and kept running across the track toward Jazz and pumped both fists in the air. "Did you see that?"

"You dusted them." She high-fived Shea and clapped her on the back.

"Yep." Shea sat with her on the bleachers. "Just wanted to know if I could do it."

"So, you're going for the team, right?"

Shea shook her head. "Mrs. B doesn't have time to come get me after practices. I asked after I saw you at the coffee shop."

Jazz started to volunteer, but that would be another violation of CPS rules. She was staring at one already by visiting Shea unsupervised and about to commit a second. "Could your coach drop you off after practices?"

"I don't know." Shea kicked the bleacher in front of them. "Practice starts right after classes and he's volunteered rides before, so maybe."

Jazz wasn't about to let Shea's temporary living situation ruin what could be a great experience for her. "Why don't I talk to the coach and see if we can work something out?"

Shea smiled up at her. "Really?"

"Absolutely. I'll check with him, but you should ask Mrs. Broadmoor. Promise?" Shea nodded, and Jazz added, "I'll call as soon as I know something."

"How can you call me?"

"I'm glad you asked." Jazz pulled the prepaid cell phone she'd picked up yesterday out of her jacket pocket and handed it to Shea. "I added my number. You should tell Mrs. B as soon as you get back. If she has a problem with you having a cell, tell her to call me. I'll make it right."

Shea turned the small phone over in her hands. "I've never had my own phone. Thanks, Jazz. You're the best."

Jazz took a deep breath before asking her next question, unsure she was ready for the answer. "So, how's it going? Truth time, Shea."

"Okay, I guess."

"You guess?"

"You know how it is in group homes. I don't know anybody, don't have friends to talk to, none of my things are there, don't know where anything is in the house, and I have to hoard food if I want a snack."

"Yeah, I remember those days too well. Some of those things will get better, but honestly, Shea, some of them never will. I'm hoping you won't be there long enough to get used to them. CPS and USAA are trying to locate your dad. Any word from him?"

She glanced up at Jazz, possibly gauging how much she really wanted to know. "They won't find him unless he wants to be found. He owes some people money I think. He called the home yesterday and said he was coming to get me, but I'm not holding my breath."

"Not great on follow-through?"

Shea shook her head. "Depends on how much he's had to drink, smoke, or snort. He used to say having me around paid the rent, but I'm not sure what he meant."

Jazz's insides seized. This was the first time Shea had mentioned her father and drugs. And knowing he used Shea as a source of government income made her sick. "Sorry, pal." Shea shrugged, and Jazz asked, "What's your dad's name?" She'd do a complete rundown on him when she returned to work. She wanted this guy located and all his parental rights revoked.

"Joshua Spencer, Josh." She fidgeted with the hem of her shirt. "What happened to your real family?"

She tried not to think about that time of her life, but Shea deserved honesty and someone who understood what she was going through. "My mom died too young." She'd woken to her mother's lifeless body beside her in bed and remained there for a day and a half before anyone checked on them. Her throat tightened and she swallowed hard. "Didn't know my dad, so I ended up in foster care at four."

"My mom died of a drug overdose," Shea said.

"Stroke."

"I thought old people had strokes."

"She was taking some medicine that wasn't right for her."

Shea leaned against her on the bleachers. "Sorry. Was it hard when you finally got a forever family?"

"Really hard." Jazz paused, the memory of those first months of trying the Carlyles' patience as fresh as if they'd happened yesterday. She'd run away several times, defied every rule, picked fights with the other kids, and basically been a nightmare. Later, she figured out she'd been testing them to see if they really wanted her and intended to keep her, even if she was a total pain. "My foster parents already had three children of their own. I didn't understand why they wanted me, but in your case, it's obvious." She stared across the athletic field letting her statement register with Shea.

"What do you mean?"

"The family who adopts you will search the entire adoption database, hundreds of kids, looking for the best possible child for them. When they choose you, it will be because they see how unique you are. Your forever family will be special, like you."

Shea's face brightened and a grin played at the corners of her mouth. "Never thought of it like that." She nodded toward the line of buses pulling into the parking lot. "Guess I better go." She gathered her book bag and turned back to Jazz. "Thanks for coming today."

"You bet. Great job on the track. Keep it up."

Jazz waited until Shea was on the bus before approaching the coach and explaining the situation to him. He'd apparently seen Shea's potential as well and eagerly added her to the list of students who needed rides. She dialed Shea's mobile and gave her the news. She shrieked so loudly Jazz had to pull the phone away from her ear.

As she walked back to her car, Jazz texted Karen. *Ask Mrs. Broadmoor to bring Shea to the charity baseball game tomorrow. See you there?*

The reply was almost immediate. *I have a surprise for you. Until tomorrow.*

Jazz drove home, her earlier frustrated mood lifted. She was helping Shea get something she wanted, possibly for the first time in her life, which made leaving an eager and excited Emory almost worth it.

CHAPTER TEN

The enthusiastic crowd lined up in both directions on Bellemeade Street at the main entrance of the Greensboro Grasshoppers stadium where Emory stood with an oversized baseball cap soliciting donations for the Cone Hospital children's Christmas party. She'd been smiling nonstop for two hours and already emptied her cap three times.

"What do we have here?" Jazz whispered in Emory's ear, her hot breath brushing the side of Emory's neck and sending delicious warmth skittering through her body.

"W—what?" Her voice cracked and she cleared her throat before turning around. Jazz was so close and looked so butch in her baseball cap that Emory forced down the urge to kiss her in front of everyone. She'd thought of nothing else since last night, except going further. She licked her lips and grinned.

"Nice." Jazz waved her hand toward Emory's bright orange Hoppers T-shirt and matching green tights. "Very nice."

"Take a good look, Perry, because this is as close as I'll get to anything that requires a ball." She play-shoved Jazz. "You're distracting me and disrupting my soliciting mojo."

Jazz grabbed her chest in mock pain. "Are you shooing me away, Ms. Blake?"

"Not really. Just flirting a bit." After their kiss, Emory was surprised how much more confident she felt around Jazz, how easy it was to tease her, and how good she felt about both.

Jazz stepped even closer, and Emory felt herself pulled into her sizzling stare. "You look so hot in that outfit. The only thing that would be better is you out of it and me—"

"Jazz, you're incorrigible." She ducked her head to hide a blush and thanked a man for his donation. If Jazz never stopped teasing and complimenting how hot she looked, it would be fine with her.

Jazz grinned and waggled her eyebrows. "Okay, I'll have mercy, but only because we're in public and my parents taught me better." She scanned the long line of people waiting to get in. "Looks like a great turnout. Have you seen Shea come through? Mrs. Broadmoor is supposed to bring her to the game."

"Not yet." Though she hadn't met Shea in person, Emory had read her file when Jazz took such an interest and was sure she'd recognize her on sight.

Jazz's phone pinged, and she pulled it from her back pocket. "Never mind. She just texted. They're already inside."

"She has her own cell phone, at eleven?"

"For your information, Ms. Blake, thirty-five percent of children aged eight to ten have phones already. I did my research before I got it." Jazz nervously tugged the hair at her temple and couldn't meet Emory's gaze.

"Jazz?"

Norma Carlyle walked toward them. "I'm just in time. By the look on my granddaughter's face, I'd say she's in trouble. I'll take over, Emory, while you sort her out."

Jazz kissed Norma's cheek. "I'll see you later, G-ma. I should probably go—"

"Oh no. You're not going anywhere just yet." Emory caught Jazz's arm and guided her into a small office where the volunteers checked in and stored personal items during their shifts.

"Thank God," Jazz said, closing the distance between them. "I've wanted to do this since the minute I saw you in that ridiculously distracting outfit." She wrapped her arms around Emory and pulled her in for a kiss.

Jazz's lips were full and wet and beckoned Emory to taste. Her heart pounded in anticipation. Her skin tingled, but she backed away. If she kissed Jazz, she'd be lost and no closer to the answers she needed. "Did you buy Shea a cell phone?" Jazz stared at the floor. "When did you give her a phone?"

"This sort of reminds me of yesterday when you pinned me against the door." Jazz eased closer, but Emory backed away again. "I know you want to kiss me. I see it in your eyes."

"How much I want to kiss you, which by the way is quite a lot, is not the issue." Jazz shrugged like a guilty kid, and Emory almost forgot her point. "When did you give her a phone?"

"She needs to know somebody cares. And she might need to call if she gets in trouble at the group home or runs away again."

"When did you give it to her, Jazz?"

"All right already. Yesterday afternoon at her track tryouts."

"So, that's where you went when you left my place?" Emory felt a wave of relief followed by more irritation.

Jazz nodded. "Shea called and asked if I could come watch her run track."

"A supervised visit I hope."

"Not exactly. And that's why I didn't tell you. I just dropped by to give her the cell and to watch her do something she likes. What's wrong with that? I'm a police officer for God's sake. If you and everybody else can't trust me with children after what I've been through and my years on the force, I need to find another profession."

Emory shook her head, not sure if Jazz was being purposely obtuse, if she really didn't understand the rules, or was blatantly ignoring them. "Tell me you at least got Mrs. Broadmoor's approval before seeing Shea and handing over a phone." Jazz suddenly found her boots mesmerizing. "Jasmine Perry?"

"You don't know what it's like, Em." Jazz reached for her, but Emory held up her hands to ward her off.

"I've worked with children all my life, so I'm very aware of how hard adjusting can be."

"But you've never *been* that child. I get her in ways you'll never understand. Can't you just trust that I know what I'm doing?"

"Just because something worked for you doesn't mean it will work, or is even right, for another child. Bypassing rules and protocols, especially when children are concerned, causes side effects, most of them not good. The caregivers feel blindsided, compromised, and undermined, and they lose control of the situation and power over decisions that affect the entire family unit. The social worker is circumvented and loses track of the process. And when a child is influenced by advice and gifts from outside sources, not the family or primary caregiver, it can result in lack of proper bonding and discipline. When those types of things happen, the system eventually falls apart and everybody loses. And that's just for starters." Jazz stared at her but didn't respond. "Do you hear what I'm saying?"

"I think half the stadium heard what you were saying, Ms. Blake."

Emory turned at the scolding voice behind her and found Karen Patrick standing in the doorway with her arms crossed over her chest. The skin-hugging jeans and Hoppers game shirt looked way too sexy on her, and she glared disapprovingly at Emory. Several other people had stopped near the door watching their exchange as well.

Karen stepped around Emory and hooked her arm through Jazz's. "I've been looking for you, Lieutenant. Shea sent me on a search and rescue mission, and just in time it seems. We have a surprise for you." She tried to pull Jazz with her, but she resisted.

"Just a second," Jazz said and then spoke to Emory. "I'm sorry if I violated some sacrosanct rule, but it made a little girl very happy. And for the record, I don't really give a damn what her so-called caregiver thinks until she starts acting like she actually cares."

"That's the difference between us, Jazz. I have to care what everybody thinks and feels, the group home staff, parents, the child, the people I work for, and you. Have you given any thought to how this could affect your career?"

"Aren't you being a little overdramatic, Emory?" Karen asked.

Emory squared off with Karen, irritated by the interruption and her possessive grip on Jazz. "I don't believe this is any of your bus—"

"What's going on?" Bennett stepped between Emory and Karen, and the room suddenly felt incredibly small. "You're drawing a crowd, and I don't think it's in the way you intended. Whose career is in jeopardy?" She glanced from Emory to Karen and finally to Jazz. "Something I need to know?"

Jazz shook her head. "Ask Ms. Blake. She has all the answers."

"Emory?" When she didn't immediately answer, Bennett turned to Karen. "I don't believe we've met. I'm Captain Bennett Carlyle, Jazz's sister, and supervisor. If there's a problem, maybe I can help."

Karen offered her hand to Bennett and practically oozed sex appeal. "Karen Patrick, US Adoption Agency. It's a pleasure to meet you. We're fine here. Jazz and I were just leaving."

Emory looked at Jazz, pleading for understanding. Karen added a component of challenge and insecurity to the situation that rattled Emory, and she needed a few more minutes to explain her point. But Jazz's hard stare told her that wasn't going to happen. She shrugged at Bennett. "Just a lively conversation about rules. Sorry for the disturbance."

"So, let's get back to the business of having fun and raising money." Bennett reached for Kerstin, who'd been watching from the doorway, and they headed toward the bleachers.

Jazz started to follow but swiveled back to Emory. "It might do you good to forget about the rules occasionally and loosen up."

Emory stared after Jazz as she cupped Karen's elbow and disappeared into the crowd. She grabbed the back of a chair and took a few minutes to steady herself. She'd done it again, pushed Jazz into Karen's arms. Maybe Jazz was right, and she needed to loosen up, but she'd seen too many children's lives adversely affected by well-meaning people who thought they knew better than the tried and tested procedures. She wasn't going to be responsible for hurting one of her charges by letting things slide, even if it cost her Jazz.

She closed the office door and followed Jazz and Karen as they made their way down the bleachers, unsure why she was torturing herself further. Watching Jazz interact with an older man and woman and then with Shea made Emory's heart ache. Jazz looked so comfortable, so content, and Shea's face came alive when Jazz paid attention to her. Children were often good judges of character, so why was Emory having such a hard time with her feelings for Jazz? Maybe Diane was right and Jazz wasn't the problem. Maybe she was.

She turned away from the scene that looked too much like a happy extended family and rejoined Norma. "Are you ready for me to take over again?"

"No, honey, I'm fine, but you can stand with me if you're at a loose end." Norma Carlyle's eyes shone with concern. "My granddaughter can be a challenge."

"Sorry?" Emory's insides tightened as she glanced at the line of patrons filing in, unable to find an appropriate response. Her scolding of Jazz in hearing range of her grandmother and sister had been a bad call. Bennett and Norma probably thought she was a total bitch.

"I couldn't hear everything, but I'm guessing that little scene was about a child."

Emory nodded.

"The only time Jazz has been in trouble with her job was over a girl who ran away from a group home. She hid the child for a day until she found a relative who agreed to take her. You better believe fur flew when Bennett found out. Gave her a serious scolding, just like any other violation. She had to, and Jazz accepted the discipline, but wouldn't acknowledge she'd done anything wrong."

"She cares deeply," Emory mumbled.

"That she does. Jazz was full of anger and grief when she first came to us. She withdrew from everyone, and we thought we'd never reach her. Anger led to defiance and she challenged everything about our lives and pushed all the boundaries. After what she put our family through, I'd say her concern for children is karma, but it goes deeper than that. She's still floundering with where she belongs in the world."

Emory was surprised that Norma apparently knew what Jazz seemed determined to hide from her adopted family. She nodded in the direction she'd last seen Jazz arm in arm with Karen. "I think she might've found her place."

Norma puffed out a breath. "That blond one? Not likely. Jazz might enjoy being chased for a while, but she'll get tired soon enough. But a woman like you—"

"Norma, no. We're not..." She stopped shy of lying to this woman who'd always been a straight shooter with her.

"I'm not implying anything, just saying Jazz needs a woman of substance who challenges her, but at the same time gives her a sense of belonging, of home. I get the impression you're a woman like that."

Norma's kind words brought tears to Emory's eyes, but what would the Carlyle family think if she *was* that woman? "Thank you for saying that, Norma, but I can't just grab a woman like Jazz and hold on. She has to choose me, and from what I've seen, that isn't likely to happen."

"Well, that certainly wasn't how I thought we'd start our day," Karen said.

"Yeah, me either." Jazz regretted her sharp comment to Emory the minute she said it. She understood Emory's need for order and control. It often made life easier, more predictable, especially after significant life events. Emory was still finding her way after losing her girlfriend, trying to keep her job, and managing a process that could have devastating results for children if handled improperly. Jazz accepted Emory's rules in principle, just not the need for such strict adherence. Still, her comment was thoughtless, born of frustration on multiple levels. No excuse.

"Hey, you okay?" Karen asked.

"Yeah." Jazz's skin tingled from Karen's hand tucked into the crook of her arm, but her whole body burned from Emory's dressing down. She didn't understand what it was like to be a child without anyone to trust, but she was certainly passionate about her beliefs, and that was appealing in a totally different way. And she was right. Jazz should've had a conversation with Mrs. Broadmoor before seeing Shea and giving her a cell phone, but bottom line, she'd do whatever she could to help Shea, with or without permission.

"What was that all about?" Karen asked. Jazz gave her the highlights, and Karen said, "Spending time with Shea will improve your mood. Trust me."

"Thanks, but I should apologize to Mrs. Broadmoor."

"Later. Shake it off, Lieutenant. We're here to have a good time." She pointed two rows down from where they stood. "There's Shea. Let's have some fun."

Jazz stopped when she saw Shea seated beside Louis and Denise Robinson. "What the—"

"Told you I had a surprise." Karen smiled and kissed her cheek. "I work quickly when motivated."

"Good to know," Jazz said as she approached the group. "This is great. You guys have been holding out on me."

Louis stood and offered his hand. "Ms. Patrick made this happen, with a little help from you I'm guessing."

Jazz nodded to Denise. "And quickly. I saw Shea yesterday, and she didn't say anything."

"Didn't know," Shea said.

"I wanted final approval for the trial period before I told you. Got it this morning and thought this would be the perfect way to let you know," Karen said.

Jazz reached for Shea's hand. Sometimes her work was rewarding, but nothing compared to seeing the smiles on Shea's and the Robinsons' faces. "Mind if I take Shea to the concession stand?"

Louis and Denise waved them away, and Louis added, "Bring lots of food, Lieutenant. Being a dad gives me an appetite." He winked and his eyes sparked with genuine joy.

Jazz led Shea up the steps through the bleachers to the concession area. "So, how are you with this new development?"

"Good." Shea grinned. "I like Louis and Denise."

"They're good people. Louis works at the substation with me."

"He said. Maybe we can visit sometime. He and Miss Denise introduced me to their grandchildren this morning, some my age. And I got a tour of the house so I know where everything is. Their place isn't huge, but it feels like a home. Does that make sense?"

"Sure does, pal."

"I've only been with them since this morning, but so far I like it."

"That's great. Did you tell them about the cell phone I gave you?"

"Yep. Was that wrong?" Shea's grin vanished and she looked up at Jazz like she expected censure or punishment.

Jazz knelt in front of her. "You did exactly right, Shea. I'm the one who messed up. Honesty is always best, and I should've talked to Mrs. Broadmoor before I saw you or gave you the phone. It's like I told you at the coffee shop, there are rules about who can see you and when, and I need to follow them like everybody else. I'm sorry I put you in the position of having to explain what I did. It was wrong. Can you forgive me?"

"Sure."

"Were the Robinsons upset when you told them?"

Shea shook her head. "Louis said if you gave me the phone, he was fine with it, and with us seeing each other whenever we wanted, as long as they know where I am. Can we eat now? I want a huge hotdog, pizza, and a drink, and ice cream later."

"You bet." They ordered everything Shea wanted, and Jazz added pretzels, popcorn, nachos, and extra drinks for the Robinsons and Karen. When they returned to their seats, she handed the carrier to Karen for distribution and settled beside Louis.

"Shea told you about the phone?" Louis and Denise nodded. "I promise not to go behind your back to see Shea in the future. I'll always ask. Those are decisions you should make. I just care about her because I know how she feels. I was orphaned early, bounced around to various foster homes for four years, taken in by the Carlyles at eight, and adopted by them just before I turned ten."

"I didn't know." Louis's expression said he totally understood. "She likes you."

"Shea has a lot of potential. I'd like to see her occasionally, if you'll let me."

Louis glanced at his wife, who smiled and nodded. "Denise and I have no objections to you seeing Shea if you let us know with a phone call or text. If the family has nothing else on, it should be fine. I know and trust you, Jazz, but we'll need to establish a routine, ground rules, and boundaries in the beginning."

"No problems from me." Jazz took a sip of drink to ease the dryness in her throat. She'd forgotten how nerve-racking talking to parents could be.

"I was impressed with Shea's honesty and courage when she told me about the phone," Louis said. "Kid didn't flinch. I get the feeling she's been through some stuff in her young life."

"Probably, but she hasn't shared any of that with me yet."

"One more thing," Louis said. "When your prepaid phone runs out, we'll get Shea a smartphone and add it to our plan. She'll send you her new number."

"Thanks, Louis."

"Hey, come sit by me," Shea called.

Louis nodded, and Jazz moved between Shea and Karen. "What's up?"

"What's that dog doing on the field?"

Jazz laughed. "That's Yogi, the Hoppers bat-fetching dog. He picks up the bats after each player and brings them to the dugout. He's a black Lab. Isn't he great?"

"I like him best of all."

"Not the game?" Jazz asked.

Shea shook her head and leaned closer. "A little slow." Her eyes twinkled, and Jazz thought she'd never seen anything more beautiful than a happy child.

"Not like track, right?" Jazz settled back in her seat, explaining what happened on the field when Shea asked and just enjoying the warm fall day. If the packed stadium was any indication, the hospital Christmas party would be fully funded this year.

When the umpire called the final out, the crowd stood and a roar echoed through the ballpark at the Hoppers' win. Shea high-fived Jazz and gave her a hug before gripping Denise's hand and pulling her up the steps.

"You did good, Ms. Patrick."

Karen leaned against her. "I try. Walk me home?"

Emory returned to Jazz's mind, never far away all afternoon. She should find her and sort out their earlier disagreement or at least apologize for her harsh comment.

"Come on. Let Ms. Blake cool down. She was pretty annoyed earlier."

"I don't know. Maybe I shouldn't give her another reason to be upset."

Karen grinned and slid her arm around Jazz's waist as they exited the ballpark. "I thought you two were just friends."

"It's complicated, and—"

"Women always are, my dear." Karen pulled Jazz closer. "Come on. We have things to discuss."

The privatization proposal. Emory wanted her to find out as much as possible, had asked her to make it her mission. "You're right."

Karen guided them south on Eugene toward Friendly and then east. "I'm just four blocks down at Governors' Court."

The cool night air on Jazz's skin made her more aware of the heated press of Karen's body against her side, the gentle strokes on her arm and down her back. The constant touching unsettled Jazz, making her wonder what Karen really wanted. Whatever it was, Jazz had a feeling sex was simply the vehicle.

They stopped in front of the three-story Governors' Court complex, and Karen pointed. "I'm on the top floor, northwest corner, great views." She motioned Jazz toward the entrance and after a short elevator ride, opened the door to a spacious living area.

"Wow, this is larger than I thought it'd be." Jazz walked toward the west side balcony and stared up at the imposing Center Pointe high-rise a block away. The north-facing balcony overlooked the back of the Cultural Arts Center and part of LeBauer Park. "I see what you mean about the views."

"I lucked out." Karen walked up behind Jazz. "Business or pleasure first?"

Jazz slid sideways and put some distance between them. "I'm here about business. This contract you mentioned, how do you plan to sell it to the state? CPS has handled adoptions forever, so it's not like you have more statistics."

"But we do have better ones. USAA has been in business for years and not just in North Carolina. Our figures support a more efficient operation and improved outcomes. Surely, you don't want to spend our time together poring over boring numbers." Karen stepped closer again. She was persistent and confident of her appeal, but Jazz's mind was still on Emory.

"Actually, I do. Emory will adamantly oppose your proposal when it's presented, and I'm not entirely convinced which organization is better for the children." She let the statement hang between them while Karen considered it. If she thought Jazz could persuade Emory to support her plan, she might be more forthcoming.

"Is that part of the reason for so much tension between you, aside from her obvious attraction?"

Jazz wasn't discussing her relationship with Emory because it just felt wrong and she was certain Emory wouldn't approve. "She stands to lose control of an operation she firmly supports and has given a large part of her life to."

"Not to mention her job."

"That too."

Karen moved to her desk, opened her laptop, and scrolled through several documents before waving Jazz over. "Emory doesn't realize what an absolutely brilliant career move it would be for her. She has a great reputation, and I'd be crazy not to offer her a position, which I might add, pays much more than the state ever could. Here." She pointed to an Excel spreadsheet. "Help yourself. I included all the supporting documentation and cost projections in the proposal. Use it as you see fit." She kissed the side of Jazz's face and stood. "In the meantime, I'm going to have a quick shower and get comfortable."

"Thanks." Jazz waited until Karen left before turning her attention to the laptop. Getting access was easier than she imagined. She glanced at the file's columns and numbers, which meant nothing to her. She had no frame of reference, but Emory would be able to decipher their meaning. Karen had said to help herself. After locating a flash drive in the top drawer, she downloaded the entire file and shoved it in her pocket. She'd just risen from the desk when Karen returned.

"Any revelations?"

Jazz stared, her mouth open. "Wow." Karen had changed from her Hoppers garb to a pair of shorts and a tank top that were quite revealing. Her hair was still wet, and her cheeks rosy from the shower. "That's some outfit."

"I hope you don't mind. These are my comfy house clothes." Karen moved closer, and Jazz backed up against the desk. "Am I being too forward? Have I misread your signals?"

"I think so." Jazz's words squeaked out.

"Surely I haven't been too subtle. I thought you liked assertive women. Am I wrong?" She stood so close that Jazz smelled the fresh scent of toothpaste, but she didn't touch her.

"You're pretty clear about what you want."

"And what do you want, Jazz? Right now?" Karen made eye contact and held, waiting for Jazz to answer.

Jazz's body ached for the release Karen offered, but her emotions were dulled by the lack of tenderness and intimacy. Emory's touch—the way she pinned Jazz against the door, trailed her finger lightly across Jazz's cheek, between her breasts and lower, and tugged playfully on her belt—had her longing for more than quick relief. Karen used her lean, strong body like a weapon, unlike Emory who saw her own curves and softness as somehow undesirable.

"Do you want me to touch you, Jazz?" Karen whispered.

Jazz captured her bottom lip between her teeth to tamp down her body's traitorous desire. If she just wanted sex, Karen was a sure thing. Emory didn't chase her and wasn't easy. The choice should be simple based on her past preferences, but she didn't just want sex any more. "This isn't a good idea." Her cell phone vibrated in her pocket, and she stepped away from Karen. "Hello."

"Lieutenant, it's Louis Robinson." His voice quivered. "I'm sorry to bother you, but—"

"What's wrong? Is it Shea?"

"Yes."

"Has she been hurt?"

"Taken."

A shock rippled through her, but Jazz remained outwardly calm, totally focused on getting all the details before acting. "What?"

"I'm not sure if she's safe. Her father came to the house right after we got home from the ballgame and insisted on taking Shea. I don't know how he found us. Maybe he followed us from the ballfield."

"Focus, Louis. What happened?"

"I tried to stop him because he looked drunk or drugged."

Hairs on the back of Jazz's neck bristled. She feared what was coming next. "And?"

"He pushed Denise down and punched me in the face."

"Are you okay? Do you need an ambulance?"

"No, we're fine, but Shea was really scared. She talked about him a little on the drive home. Said he might come around, like he'd done before when she went somewhere new. Once he took her out of a group home and to Atlanta. What if he's taken her there again? I'm rambling, but Denise and I don't know what to do." Jazz heard a muffled cough that resembled a strangled cry.

"We'll find her. Trust me."

"But what can you do if they're in Atlanta?"

"One step at a time." Jazz went into problem-solving mode. "Do you want her back...or has this put you off?" She had to know for Shea's sake as well as her own before she went any further. Louis and Denise were good people, but everybody had a breaking point.

"Of course, we want her back. She was only with us for the day, but we'd already started bonding, and I think she felt it too."

She heard Denise in the background say, "Please bring her back to us, Jazz."

She turned to Karen. "Isn't the father prohibited from taking Shea out of state?"

"There's a temporary custody order placing her in DSS custody, so he isn't allowed to just take her."

"Louis, call an officer now and file a report. Tell them you work at Fairview Station, give all the details of what happened, including the assault on you and Denise, provide them with the paperwork you have regarding custody, and get a copy of the report. File charges for the assault. I'll call communications and have them put out an alert for the dad and Shea locally, and I'll also contact a friend of mine in Atlanta once I find out more about the father."

"Thank you, Jazz. I can't tell you what this means to us."

"Stay by your phone." Jazz put her cell in her pocket and said to Karen. "Got to go."

"I heard. Shame really, I was hoping we could get better acquainted tonight, but I understand."

Jazz headed for the door. "About that. I really don't think we should—"

"Don't be so quick to make that decision. When you get tired of Emory playing hard to get, and you will get tired, I'll be waiting. Now go be a shero, Lieutenant."

Jazz took the stairs two at a time to the street with Karen's offer barely registering. She called records and asked for a complete check on Joshua Spencer on her desk within the hour. She sprinted home, got her car, and took a detour by Emory's before heading to the station. She'd want the information on the flash drive as soon as possible, but it was late, and Jazz didn't want to explain where she'd been or with whom or to revisit their earlier disagreement right now. Did Emory even care at this point? She riffled through her briefcase for a sheet of paper, folded the drive inside, and slid it under Emory's welcome mat before leaving her a text.

On her way to the substation, she reviewed the day that had started so well—the charity event with the promise of seeing Emory and Shea—but ended in a contest of sorts between Karen and Emory. Karen certainly seemed professionally capable, and her plan sounded viable, but Emory had passion for her work and was willing to sacrifice for the greater good.

On the personal side, Karen was very clear about just wanting a fling, while Emory seemed more interested in the long-term. Jazz knew nothing about Karen's past, but Emory had shared her history, but would she ever trust Jazz enough to explore their potential? When it came to what Jazz wanted personally, the choice was clearly Emory, but the professional decision was far from resolved.

She pulled into the substation lot and thought about her mother's entwined-hearts necklace and her words. *Two hearts united are stronger than steel.* Would she ever know that feeling or know herself well enough to recognize the opportunity if it came along? She prayed she would, but right now more urgent matters needed her attention.

It was well after midnight when Jazz scanned the criminal history on Joshua Spencer and dialed Travis's number. She and Travis had attended Southern Police Institute in Louisville, Kentucky, together, bonded quickly as orphans and adoptees, and kept in touch through the years. At the message prompt, she said, "Travis, it's Jazz. I know it's late, but call me when you get this. It's important. Thanks." If Josh Spencer was in Atlanta, Travis would find him or burn the city trying. He was a true Georgia bulldog, untiring and tenacious. Josh Spencer didn't stand a chance if he hoped to disappear in Travis's territory.

She reread Spencer's extensive history, which began as a teenager—petty thefts, minor assaults, marijuana possession, and finally felony assault and dealing prescription meds. The latest entry was a felony charge of possession with intent to sell and deliver cocaine, on which he'd skipped bail and his court date. His name also appeared in a drug overdose case several years earlier, possibly Shea's mother.

Jazz felt tension build in the back of her neck and across her shoulders. She worried about Shea and couldn't shake the feeling that she was in danger. She'd tried Shea's phone several times, but the calls went directly to voice mail.

Her phone vibrated on the desk, and she snatched it immediately. "Perry."

"Jazz, it's Travis. What's up, pal?"

"An eleven-year-old CPS custody case. Taken by her father, probably on the way to Atlanta. He's a seller and user. I'm afraid for the kid's safety." It was customary for them to launch right into business, leaving the pleasantries for later over a beer. "I'll buy next time, if you help me locate her." The nerves in her stomach tightened. She cared about Shea and the Robinsons. This had to work out.

"What's the father's name?"

She provided the information along with his date of birth and the references to Atlanta she'd found in his file.

"Wait. Did you say Josh Spencer?"

"Yeah, why?" Jazz heard papers shuffling on the other end of the line. "You're still at work?"

"So are you, so no judging. I have an informant who's trying to convince me this Josh character is involved in a big drug deal here in the next few days. Nothing more definite on the timeline though. We've already got a file on him. He has a few relatives and associates in the city, so I'll check those out for you, but I don't want to spook him if he's involved in this deal."

"I get wanting to nail Spencer with the drugs, but the girl has to come first."

Travis paused before answering. "She's important to you. I can hear it in your voice."

Jazz told him the story about finding Shea wandering downtown and their subsequent interactions, along with a physical description to help with the search. "She deserves a break. I finally got her in a nice home, and this jerk snatches her the same day."

"I'll look for her. You got paper on him?"

"He didn't show on his latest felony cocaine charge and he assaulted Shea's foster parents tonight. Those warrants will be signed within the hour. Whatever you can do, man, really. And keep me posted, please."

"You got it, pal. Be in touch."

CHAPTER ELEVEN

Jazz woke the next morning to pots banging in the kitchen and plates and glasses being set noisily on the table, Simon's way of getting her up in time for Sunday brunch. She dressed quickly and joined the others. "Thanks for the wake-up call, bro."

He gave her a big hug when she entered the kitchen. "Keeping you on your toes, sis. You're lucky I didn't send the twins up. They're in rare form this morning."

Jazz made the rounds giving G-ma, Mama, Stephanie, and Kerstin cheek kisses, hugging Dylan until she squealed, and play-boxing with Bennett. The twins yelled hellos from fixed positions in front of a PlayStation in the adjoining living space.

"Okay, gather around," G-ma said, placing a platter of eggs in the center of the table.

"And pause," Ryan said. "I'm winning. Yes." He did a quick spin and raced his sister to their seats.

"Are not," Riley answered.

"Am too."

Stephanie did a zip-the-lip gesture, both kids settled quietly, and everybody turned their attention to G-ma at the head at the table.

"Eat. The honeydew is especially good this morning." G-ma added a couple of slices of bacon to her plate and handed the tray to Mama on her right, which was the signal for everyone else to serve themselves and start passing.

Jazz waited as the rest of the family reached for dishes and scooped food onto their plates. When she came to live with the Carlyles, she'd been first to grab food at every meal, unaccustomed to having enough and feeling full. Now she was content to watch others eat and to interact for a while, certain there would always be more than enough to go around.

After the first few minutes of spooning followed by rounds of appreciative moans, Mama began the Sunday morning sharing. "G-ma and I sold out of everything on the food truck this week thanks to the footrace downtown. If this keeps up, we might retire sooner rather than later."

G-ma nodded and said, "And none too soon for me. I think the whole needing-something-to-keep-me-busy phase has passed."

"Maybe I'll retire from the fire department and take over the business." Simon grinned at Stephanie. "How about that, wife?"

"As long as you can support these two," she inclined her head to both sides indicating Ryan and Riley, "you can do whatever you want, husband." She leaned over and gave him a kiss.

Bennett stared at him. "Are you seriously considering that, Simon?"

He shook his head. "I love firefighting. It's just a shame to lose such a great customer base. You have to admit the business has been profitable, and unfortunately, my two aren't quite ready to be entrepreneurs."

"What about you, Steph?" Dylan asked while buttering a piece of toast.

Stephanie brushed blond bangs off her forehead and placed her coffee cup on the table slowly. "I could do that."

"What?" Simon asked.

"Really?" Kerstin looked shocked, and then suddenly everybody talked at once. "Can you do that?" "What about the kids?" "Do you know how?" "We've never talked about this." "Keep it in the family." The room finally quieted, and they all stared at Stephanie.

Jazz asked, "Is that something you'd enjoy, Steph?"

Stephanie looked at Jazz, and a broad smile brightened her face. "Thank you for asking the right question, Jazz. And yes, I believe

I would enjoy it. I've filled in for G-ma and Mama occasionally. I know the routes and many of the people. If I did the prep work at night, I could finish after I dropped the kids at school in the morning, and I'd be home before I needed to pick them up in the afternoon. The timing would be perfect."

The rest of the family continued to stare, until Simon finally said, "I had no idea you were even interested, but if that's what you want, I think you should go for it."

"Well, she can gossip with the best of us," Mama said and laughed. "We'll talk more when we've had a chance to think on it seriously. I like the idea. How about you, G-ma?"

"Fine by me. Now, speaking of gossip." She turned to Jazz. "Tell us what all the hullabaloo was about at the ballgame yesterday between you, Emory, and that blonde."

Jazz shifted uncomfortably and stirred her eggs and grits until she could meet G-ma's gaze. "Just a misunderstanding. Everything's fine."

"You're not in any trouble with Ben?"

Jazz shook her head.

"With Emory?"

"No, G-ma."

"I didn't realize you and Emory were well enough acquainted to raise your voices at each other. Something is going on."

Now everybody's attention shifted squarely to Jazz, and she squirmed in her chair. Bennett and Kerstin had seen her and Emory together at Green Valley Grill. And like it or not, G-ma always knew when anyone in the family was holding back. "We've been working together on a case, and we have different ideas about how to do things is all."

"And…" Bennett prompted her from across the table, always keeping it real.

"And we've been out a couple of times, mostly for work."

Mama slowly lowered her fork onto the side of her plate. "You're *dating* Emory?"

"Sort of, not exactly, and after yesterday, who knows." Jazz glanced around the table looking for any sign of disapproval, but all she saw was surprise. "Is that okay?"

"Depends."

Mama's voice was too matter-of-fact, not the excited tone Jazz expected when she finally announced she was seeing someone. "On what?"

"Who the blonde was, and how she's involved. Was she the reason for the scene?"

Her armpits itched as she sweated under Mama's concentrated stare. Jazz had no idea how to answer the question honestly. Emory would probably say Karen was absolutely part of the problem, but Jazz caused the situation. "Not really. I bent one of Emory's rules."

"Oh, honey," Mama said, and Bennett gave her a questioning stare.

"Gayle, you know Jazz was probably helping some child in trouble. Am I right?"

She nodded, anxious to have the spotlight off her, but G-ma wasn't finished.

"Back up. When two women go at it like you and Emory did, there's usually more to it than work and a couple of casual outings. Are you dating the blonde too?" Everybody around the table stopped eating and leaned forward waiting for her answer.

"No." She said, barely above a whisper.

"But you've slept with her," Simon said and slapped his hands on the table. "Damn, girl, you and Bennett always got more action than me." Stephanie glared at him. "Sorry, babe, but it's true."

"I haven't slept with either one of them."

From across the table, Dylan shook her head. "Really, sis? The least you could do is keep them separate. That's what I do, when I have a sex life. One on night shift, one on days or in different departments of the hospital, and never two who are on opposite sides of an issue. Makes for way less drama." She wiggled her eyebrows at Jazz and puckered her lips in a kiss.

"I repeat, I haven't had sex with either of them," Jazz blurted.

"Yuck," Riley and Ryan said at the same time and put their hands over their ears.

She thought about last night again and the opportunity she'd passed up. When Karen was around, she had a way of confusing habits of the past with hopes of the future, but Jazz had become clear on one point. The only woman she wanted to get to know better and have sex with, when the time was right, was Emory. She breathed a little easier.

G-ma turned her attention back on Jazz. "What's this blonde's name?"

"Karen Patrick. She's the director and a counselor with US Adoption Agency, and we've been working on a case together too."

"Karen Patrick. Don't believe I know her. You just be careful with both and for entirely different reasons. You hear me, honey?"

Jazz nodded and the cacophony of breakfast sounds started again. And none too soon for Jazz. Dylan reported on her final week of residency, and Kerstin shared plans to move into her new architectural office that she and Bennett had fashioned from their garage. When the room quieted again, G-ma rose signaling the end of another Carlyle family brunch.

Jazz had just finished stacking the dishes in the dishwasher when her cell pinged with a text. She retrieved her phone from the basket on the island, glanced at Emory's message, and said, "See you guys later. Love you."

❖

Emory had tossed and fought with her pillow most of the night before finally getting up and making a cup of tea. Jazz's comment yesterday tortured her as she paced. *"It might do you some good to forget about the rules occasionally and loosen up."* Was it only a professional observation or a personal one as well? Karen's arm securely tucked into Jazz's made Emory fear the latter, but either way it stung. No matter how hard she tried, she'd never be as loose as Karen, nor would she want to be. Karen pushed all of Emory's buttons at once—totally gorgeous, perfect body, affluent if her attire was any indication, and if she didn't patently sell children to the highest bidding parents, she at least profited by their placement.

Emory poured her cold tea in the sink, started the kettle again, and reached for her cell phone in the charger on the counter. Jazz's text popped up first. *Left a gift under your mat.* Cinching her robe tighter, she cracked open her front door and pulled a bulging square of folded paper from under the mat. She turned it over in her hands and pressed the outline with her fingers. A flash drive. She'd asked for Jazz's help, and she'd come through, regardless of their personal differences. She placed the small package on the counter and made another cup of tea.

Maybe Jazz had only spent time with Karen to get the information Emory needed. What lines had she crossed to do so? Emory had put her in that position, which made her complicit in whatever she'd done. She spun the paper square around with her finger while arguing with herself. What had this cost Jazz? Did she even want to know?

Emory started her laptop, slid the drive in the slot, and stared at the single folder entitled *USAA*. She expanded the folder and chose the *Proposal* file, which contained the document and several pages of statistics on an Excel spreadsheet. At first glance, the numbers appeared unremarkable, but on closer inspection, they were obviously inflated. Working with adoptions for decades had taught her that figures this high were unrealistic. Then the information on the page practically jumped out at her. She'd prepared CPS's annual report, and these numbers were identical, but side by side with the USAA figures, they painted a grim picture for the future of CPS. Karen's agenda was clear.

Emory tabbed through the entire Excel workbook, past several blank pages, before coming to a sheet buried in the back entitled *Personal*. Her finger hovered over the touchpad, her conscience warring with curiosity. Maybe this was a log or diary, or maybe the answer to all Emory's questions about USAA's operations. Was viewing the page a violation of law or at least of ethics? Could she live with herself if she looked? Or if she didn't? She clicked on the sheet and stared at what she saw.

Suddenly, how Jazz obtained this information was important because it could become public if Emory used it to discredit Karen and USAA. She checked the time and shot Jazz a text. *We need to talk ASAP.*

Jazz's response was immediate. *Agreed.*

My place, thirty minutes?

On my way.

Emory took a quick shower, pulled on a pair of jeans and sweatshirt, and dug a couple of coffee pods from under the counter where she kept them for guests. She and Jazz needed to talk and not just about the USAA information. Whether they were going to be friends or more, they had to learn to communicate better. She paced and thought about what she'd say until the doorbell rang.

She paused with her hand on the knob. The woman on the other side of the door had the potential to hurt her in ways Jean never could. Jazz already inhabited every corner of her mind and her heart and complicated every interaction, professional and personal. She didn't know how to break free, even if she wanted to. She took a calming breath and opened the door.

"Good morn—" The word caught in her throat when she saw the tight lines around Jazz's mouth and dark circles under her eyes. "What's wrong?" She forgot her own discomfort, slid her arm around Jazz's waist, and guided her to the sofa. "Are you all right?"

Jazz nodded then shook her head.

"I'm afraid you're going to have to be a little clearer, darling." She'd never seen Jazz so upset and trying so hard not to show it. "Talk to me."

"It's Shea." She grabbed Emory's hand and squeezed. "Her drug-dealing father took her from the Robinsons last night. I don't know where she is." Jazz pulled her bottom lip between her teeth and looked at the floor.

"The Robinsons?" Advice seemed unnecessary, but clarification was essential if she was to understand. "I'm lost, Jazz."

"Karen fast-tracked her placement on Friday with the Robinsons. We have alerts out in Greensboro, and a friend in Atlanta is looking for her. She could be in real danger, Em."

She pressed her lips to Jazz's hair. "Have you been working on this all night?" Jazz nodded against her shoulder, and the gesture broke Emory's heart. "You should rest."

"I slept a bit before brunch. Your text seemed urgent, so I came right over."

"We'll get to that." Emory urged Jazz down beside her on the sofa. "Relax a few minutes. We'll talk later."

"But what if Travis calls?"

"Shush. You'll hear the phone. You're no use to anyone in this condition." Jazz tensed slightly as she stretched out beside Emory, then went slack, and slowly, her breathing deepened. Emory watched the transformation of Jazz's face—the tight lines at the corners of her mouth softened, the furrow between her brows eased, and worry drifted away as sleep claimed her.

She'd never met anyone more committed to children's issues than Jazz. Her methods were sometimes questionable, but always well-intended. When Jazz cared, she did so with her whole heart. What was it like to be the object of such devotion?

She stroked Jazz's hair and wished her a deep, restorative sleep. Everything else could wait. Emory drew the blanket from the back of the sofa across them, snuggled closer, and soon fell asleep as well.

❖

Jazz's stomach growled and she unwrapped the candy slowly, the crinkling paper too noisy in the confined space. If she ate quickly, they wouldn't know. Those people. Another foster family whose name she didn't want to remember. Footsteps in the hallway. She paused. Were they coming for her? Her heart hammered too loud as she took the first bite. So good. She curled into a fetal position around the stolen treat and took another nibble. Was that a door opening? Her door? She waited but heard nothing else. She tried to eat slowly, but it was too good and she was so hungry. The floor outside her closet creaked, and she stuffed the remainder of the candy bar in her mouth.

Her foster mother jerked the closet door open and dragged her out by her feet. "There you are, you little thief. Give me that candy bar. Now."

Jazz chewed quickly, hiding her face and swallowing.

"Where is it?"

She shrugged.

The woman slapped her hard across the face, and Jazz gasped. The woman grabbed her jaw. "Spit it out." She forced her to the trash can and held her head over it. "Spit."

Jazz chewed a few more times and swallowed again before coughing a small piece of the candy into the bin. "Sorry."

"Sorry won't keep you from a serious belting." She grabbed Jazz's hand and pulled her toward the living room where a worn leather strap hung on a nail by the door. The woman's face contorted into an evil sneer as she snatched the belt and pulled it back.

"No," Jazz screamed. "Please, don't. Please..."

"Jazz, wake up."

"Don't," Jazz said. "Please."

"Shush, Jazz. It's Emory. You were dreaming."

Jazz forced her eyes open. Her knees were curled into her chest and her arms clutched them tightly against her. She was wet with sweat and her heart pounded. "Dreaming?"

"Yes, darling. You're safe." Emory pressed against her back and brushed her damp hair off her forehead. "Are you okay?"

"I will be, eventually." She swung her legs from the sofa onto the floor and reached for her phone. Nothing from Travis or the PD yet.

"You were trembling." She rubbed her hand up and down Jazz's back, and the soothing strokes began to calm her. "Want to talk about it?"

"You're smart. Figure it out." The fear and defiance of that earlier time were so clear in her tone that Jazz flinched. She'd come too close to feeling the leather strap across her back again. She turned toward Emory. "I'm sorry. You don't deserve that." Emory smiled but didn't respond, the warmth in her eyes holding Jazz captive. "My four years with foster parents, before the Carlyles, weren't good ones. You know, the usual stuff."

"I'm so sorry, Jazz."

She stood, not sure what else to say about her display. "Sorry I fell asleep on your sofa." She walked to the large windows overlooking a community courtyard. The sun was just topping the horizon. "And apparently spent the night."

"Fortunately, my sofa is big enough for two and quite comfy."

"I wanted our first night together to be very different, smoother, less drama."

Emory didn't look at her as she folded the blanket over the back of the sofa. "We've got time. Could I interest you in some coffee or breakfast?"

"Coffee would be great. Mind if I use your bathroom?"

"Of course. I think there might be a spare toothbrush in the cabinet."

Jazz closed the door behind her, stared at her reflection in the mirror, and winced. Her eyes were dark and eerily blank, an expression she'd perfected as a child that had served her well when showing emotion made her feel weak and vulnerable. She'd hoped those days were over. What did Emory think of her display? She splashed water on her face and brushed her teeth.

Meeting Shea and sharing some of her own experiences had resurrected her nightmares, which only made her more determined that Shea would travel a different path. She washed her face with the frigid water again and returned to the kitchen and the heavenly smell of fresh-brewed coffee. Emory offered her a cup, and she sat at the kitchen peninsula. "Thanks."

"Feel better?" Emory joined her but didn't press for conversation.

Jazz nodded, sipped her coffee, and hoped the lingering feeling of vulnerability she'd awoken with would soon dissipate. "Before we talk about why you asked me over, I owe you another apology. I'm sorry for what I said at the ballpark…about you needing to lighten up."

"My mother used to say the truth is welcome in heaven."

"Maybe, but how and when I said it probably isn't. I was frustrated and upset, which is not an excuse for bad behavior. Can you forgive me?"

"Of course."

"That was too easy," Jazz said.

Emory rubbed her back again and lowered her voice. "We all say things we shouldn't when we're upset."

"I'll do better. Promise. I want us to be able to talk to each other about anything." She took another sip of coffee and wondered if she'd ever share everything that happened to her in foster care. Emory was probably one of the few people who'd understand. Maybe someday.

"I want that too." Emory hesitated, fiddling with the handle of her cup. "There's one more piece of old business I'd like to clear up too. It's about Jean." Jazz nodded, and she continued. "Two weeks after the scene at Green Valley Grill, I ran into Jean…with her new girlfriend." Jazz started to comment, but Emory held up her hand. "I need to say this all at once. She was with a woman who looked like she'd stepped out of the pages of a fashion magazine, basically everything I wasn't and will never be."

"I'm sorry, Em."

Emory shook her head. "I'm over it, or at least the Jean part. But Karen, with her gorgeous looks, brings some of that insecurity up for me again, which is probably why I have such negative reactions to her. I don't want to be so petty, but it's how I feel."

"And you have a right to your feelings, Em, but you don't need to be insecure, not about me. I'm sorry if I've made things worse. I'd never hurt you on purpose."

Emory caressed the side of Jazz's face and stared into her eyes. "I know you wouldn't. I just wanted you to know. And I'm working through the insecurity part. It's a slow process."

"Good thing I'm a patient woman. And can I just say again how crazy Jean was for letting you go, but I'm good with that." She took Emory's hand and kissed her palm. "Totally good with it." She loved being so close to Emory, feeling their connection and sharing their secrets. "What else do we need to talk about?"

"Well…" Emory seemed to be weighing her options before settling. "The USAA stats, if you're ready."

"I need a distraction, and we need a plan."

"Thanks for getting those to me so quickly."

"No problem. I assume you found something helpful," Jazz said.

Emory spread several printed pages across the island. "I need a second opinion." She pointed to the last page and pursed her lips but didn't say anything while Jazz examined it.

The Excel sheet labeled *Personal* contained four columns entitled *Names*, *$To*, *$From*, and *For*. The *From* column amounts were significantly higher than the *To* column and much more frequent. "What do you think this means?"

"I'm not sure," Emory said.

"Speculate. We have to start somewhere."

"It looks like Karen is paying some parents to take certain children and accepting money from parents for others."

Jazz scanned to the last entry, which indicated Louis Robinson had received five thousand dollars. Under the *For* column, Shea's name appeared with the initials *HTP*. Emory might not have made the connection since she just learned about the Robinson placement Karen had pushed through late Friday. Louis didn't strike Jazz as the kind of person who'd do anything underhanded or illegal. "What do you think these letters mean?" Jazz pointed to the *HTP* and *NB* beside names in the *For* columns.

"If I had to guess, hard to place and newborn. This looks really bad, Jazz."

"Until you put names together with actual adoptions or placements, we won't know anything for sure."

"This payment scheme is why her stats are so high. They're way out of proportion to the CPS numbers. If she's taking money to place kids—"

"Let's not jump to conclusions before we have all the facts. USAA is a private agency that takes fees for services. That's not illegal. And by your own admission, you might be a tad prejudiced against Karen."

"And you might be a tad prejudiced in her favor." Emory paused, took a sip of tea, and asked, "Did you go home with her Saturday night after the ballgame?"

"Yes." Jazz's emotions were still on edge and she blurted the truth.

"Did you…sleep with her? Not that it's any of my business."

"No."

"No, it's none of my business, or no you didn't sleep with her."

Jazz scooted her stool closer and wrapped her arm around Emory's shoulder. "She tried to persuade me that having sex with her was a good idea. I wasn't convinced."

Emory smiled and her eyes twinkled as if Jazz had given her a gift. "That's very good news indeed. And why, may I ask, weren't you convinced? She's a looker."

"She's definitely something to look at, but you're something to see. There's a big difference."

"How so?"

Emory was fishing for compliments, but she deserved them, and Jazz was happy to oblige. "The adage about beauty being skin deep comes to mind. If I peeled all the glitz from Karen Patrick's exterior, I get the feeling she wouldn't be all that. But you, Emory Blake, are authentic through and through. The more layers I peel, the more interesting things I discover about you." She kissed Emory's lips lightly. "Can I stop yet?"

"Never." Emory kissed her back, the air between them growing thick. "Does that mean you're finished with her?"

Jazz reluctantly pulled away. "Not entirely. I still want to figure out her game. It can't be as simple as wanting to sleep with me and get me on her side of the privatization issue."

"Whatever she's up to, I don't like it. She's a scorched-earth type of woman. She'll try to seduce you again. You know that, right?"

She nodded.

Emory's smile faded, and she clutched her teacup in both hands.

"That doesn't mean I'll give in, Em. I just need to know why she's so determined."

"Promise me you'll be careful, whether we have a relationship or not, I worry for you."

"I promise and—" The ringing phone cut her off, and she snatched it from the counter. "Perry."

"Jazz, it's Travis."

"What news?"

"You know, just another wild night in Hotlanta. Look, pal, I've sandwiched my search for your missing kid between crazies the last twenty-four hours, but I wanted to update you."

Jazz pantomimed writing in air, and Emory pushed a pen and notepad toward her. "Go."

"I've eliminated some of Joshua Spencer's relatives as possibly harboring the child. Left them all with a strong warning about being an accessory to kidnapping. I have two more to check out, one is an older brother Josh is supposedly close to, and an ex-girlfriend. Nothing definitive yet, but I'm hopeful. Anything on your end?"

"Not one sighting." Jazz dropped the pen on the counter, frustrated with the lack of results. "Thanks for what you're doing, Travis. Find this kid so we can get her back to the Robinsons and put her worthless dad in jail."

"I'll be in touch."

The line went dead, and Jazz turned to Emory. "You heard?"

Emory nodded. "I'm sorry, Jazz. I give Ms. Patrick credit. She gets results, but I can't help wondering if they're always legal. Any idea how Shea's placement happened so quickly?"

Jazz wavered between pride for facilitating the Robinson-Spencer match and discomfort at going behind Emory's back, but it was time to come clean. "I might've had something to do with it. I vouched for Louis and asked Karen to find out why it was taking so long for them to get a placement. Shea needed a good home. They seemed like a nice fit. Karen agreed...she was handling Shea's case, not CPS." She saw the hurt in Emory's eyes before she glanced back at the list of figures.

Emory slid her finger down the column to the final entry, Louis Robinson's name. "And this?"

"I had no idea, but at least we have a place to start. Louis will tell me if he was paid."

Emory looked at the wall clock. "Guess I better hit the shower. Work awaits." She started to get up, but Jazz stopped her.

"Thanks for earlier…the nightmare…and for letting me sleep. It helped." Embarrassment flushed her skin and she looked at the floor.

"I'm glad." She kissed Jazz firmly on the lips and pulled back breathless. "Now go before you make me late." She playfully shoved Jazz toward the front door. "I'll start working on that list today. Keep me updated about Shea? And remember what I said about Karen. Be careful."

Jazz stepped into the cool morning air and breathed it in. Her body hummed with warmth from being so close and comforted by Emory. Every moment she spent with her was a gift. She wanted more—time, kisses, and a chance for something substantial—but Karen Patrick and her privatization proposal were causing problems. The sooner she and Emory sorted the issue, the sooner they'd be free to pursue whatever came next.

Chapter Twelve

Jazz spent the day driving through the neighborhood Shea had run from, checking all the seedy hotels in town that catered to the drug trade, and following up tips from the Crime Stoppers media blasts. When she finally started toward home, she was more frustrated and worried about Shea and no closer to finding her. How could a kid just disappear without a trace? She pulled into the driveway and her phone rang.

"Jazz, it's Travis. You might want to get to Atlanta ASAP. We're planning a drug raid tonight, and I have information your kidnapped child is in the house."

"When are you going in?"

"After midnight when everybody is stoned out of their minds. Can you make it?"

Jazz checked her watch. "I'll catch the next flight. And thanks, Travis. I owe you."

Two hours later, she stepped out of the airport terminal in Atlanta. At six feet tall and always wearing a baseball cap to cover his partially balding head, Travis was easy to spot over most of the people waiting for travelers.

He waved as she walked toward him and pulled her into a hug. "Damn, you're a sight for sore eyes, girl. It's been a while."

"How's it going?" Jazz slung her backpack into the back seat of the Hummer. "Obviously APD pays much better than GPD, or have you finally gone over to the dark side?" At SPI, they'd planned the perfect faux drug heist so they could retire to the Bahamas, like homicide cops planned the perfect murder.

"Asset forfeiture vehicle, the only way we can afford undercover cars. You look the same, maybe a bit grayer in that skunk streak of yours."

"Ha, ha. Are we all set for the raid?"

"Of course."

"And where did you get your information about the girl?" Her pulse raced with the prospect of going on a narcotics raid for the first time in years and possibly finding Shea and returning her to the Robinsons.

Travis grunted. "Same old Jazz, straight to business. My informant has been reliable in the past, so I'm hopeful, but you know how these things go. We've got a couple of hours before we head out. Something to eat?"

"Sounds perfect."

Travis filled her in on the narcotics case and the players involved in the operation while he drove. "We've been working with DEA, so it's a pretty big deal." He pulled in front of an overnight café that resembled an old Airstream travel trailer and glanced at Jazz. "Wipe that skeptical look off your face. You're going to love this place."

Travis was right. Jazz pushed her empty plate aside thirty minutes later, pulled her coffee cup closer, and leaned back in the booth. "Found a wife yet, Travis? I'm anxious for some godchildren to spoil."

"Trying to nail down a little filly by the name of Cynthia. You?"

Jazz felt the familiar tumble inside when she thought about Emory. "Not really."

"Your face says you're holding out on me. Who is she?" Jazz couldn't look at Travis. "Or is it more than one?" She stared out the café window. "It is. You dog."

"I'm not really dating, dating anyone."

Travis waited until the waitress topped up their cups from a fresh pot of coffee. "But you're sleeping with more than one, right? Come on, pal. I'm on restricted rations."

Jazz laughed but it sounded more like a nervous cough. "No, I'm not sleeping with either of them. It's complicated."

"Since when aren't women complicated. What's the problem?"

"I'm really interested in this lady, Emory, who is beautiful, full-figured, erotic, but a little insecure. And there's this other woman, Karen, who's lean, sexy, and assertive, that I have to work closely with on a case."

"Ah, I get it. Competition."

"Not really. I want to see if Emory and I can have something real, but working with Karen is complicating things. I did mention she's assertive and that pushes Emory's buttons."

"No problem. Fuck one and marry the other and get me some godchildren."

"I'm certain fucking one would exclude marrying the other. They're on opposite sides of a privatization issue and basically hate each other," Jazz said. "Besides, I only want Emory."

"Then go for it, pal. Don't let a one-night stand keep you from getting your happily ever after, no matter how tempting this Karen is." Travis nudged her foot and made eye contact. "Take it from a guy who's been there and done that." She nodded. "So, where do you stand on the privatization issue? Is that going to be a problem with your woman?"

"I'm not sure yet. There are pros and cons to each." She didn't relay her recent conversation with Emory about the stats, which had pushed her more into Emory's camp.

Travis slid the check off the end of the table and nodded toward the door. "I'll meet you at the car after I pay and hit the head."

Jazz stood outside the diner staring at the Atlanta skyline and considering what she'd told Travis about Emory. It was the first time she'd admitted aloud that she wanted to explore her relationship with Emory, to see if they could have a future, and it felt good, right even.

Travis burst through the café door. "Gotta bolt. They've just finished the briefing, and we're due in position in fifteen minutes."

Jazz raced Travis to their vehicle. "What's our assignment?"

"Securing the front door after the entry team gets inside. Hope you brought your vest."

Jazz reached into her bag on the back seat and pulled out her heavy flak jacket, ripped the Velcro flaps down that read POLICE, and strapped the vest around her. She slapped the front metal plate. "Good to go."

Travis stopped behind a warehouse, two blocks from the raid location, and killed the headlights. The rest of the team mingled waiting for the go order. A group of four officers, probably the leaders of each team, huddled over the hood of an SUV. Travis motioned for her to follow. "Guys," he nodded toward her, "this is Lieutenant Jazz Perry from North Carolina. She's here to take the girl home, if she's in there."

The commanding officer shook her hand and pointed to the photograph of the outside of the target building and the raid plan, confirming she knew her assignment. "Any questions?" These officers knew what was expected of them and how to deliver. The excitement of pending battle thickened the air. "Let's do this."

Jazz followed Travis into one of two large black vans, the first carrying the larger entry team, and theirs the security and search teams. She breathed deeply as they started to move, repeating her ritual during high-risk situations of ticking off the things she wanted to do before she died. Her priority was always the same, get married and raise lots of children.

The van screeched to a stop, and the doors slammed violently open. Jazz's vision tunneled on the entry team sprinting toward the front door of a single-story home. A loud crash echoed down the quiet street, and officers rushed inside to a chorus of *Police, search warrant*. Jazz ran beside Travis, and they flanked the door after the search team entry.

"Gets the blood flowing, am I right?" Travis asked.

Jazz nodded, unable to speak until her heart rate and breathing settled. The yells from inside indicated the officers had located several occupants but no drugs. "Doesn't sound good."

"You know how it goes. They stash dope everywhere. We'll be guarding this door for hours until they're finished. Never give up."

Jazz wasn't giving up until they'd searched every inch of the house and the officers came out with eleven-year-old Shea Spencer. She didn't have to wait long.

"No kid in there," one of the entry team said when he stepped outside and shucked off his armor-plated vest.

"Are you sure?" He cut her a how-dare-you-question-me glare. "No disrespect, but the informant said she was here."

"And informants never lie or get it wrong? You might want to question the loudmouth, Jeremy, who says he lives here, and his last name is the same as your wanted person and the kid." The officer walked back to the van, slung his vest inside, and sat in the doorway.

Travis held up a finger toward her and dialed his cell. "What the fuck, dude? Where's the kid? You said she'd be here." Travis listened and finally replied. "Thanks for nothing. You won't get paid today or maybe ever again." He slid his phone into the side of his vest. "He said Josh left with the girl about an hour ago in a van carrying dope north."

"Perfect. What better way to disguise a drug run than by having a child along."

"Exactly," Travis said. "He gave a description of the van. I'll put out an alert as soon as I check with the on-scene commander."

"Let's talk to this Jeremy Spencer," Jazz said.

Spencer was one of three kneeling on the floor of the residence with his hands cuffed behind his back. "You Jeremy?" Travis asked the skinniest man.

"I got nothing to say."

Jazz stepped into his body space and towered over him. "You got anything to say about being charged with accessory to kidnapping?"

"Bullshit, that kid is my flesh and blood, and she's with her old man. You got nothing."

"We'll see about that," Travis said. "You could help yourself out of these drug charges."

"Nothing to say."

Jazz nodded but wasn't really paying attention anymore. "Let's go, Travis." Her purpose for being here was over. She checked her phone and had several missed calls and texts from Ben and Emory. She texted Ben first. *Will be late to work. In Atlanta.*

A few seconds later, her phone rang. "Yes, Ben?"

"What the hell are you doing in Atlanta?"

Two uniformed Atlanta officers relieved Jazz and Travis on the door, and she walked away for some privacy. "Right now, I'm on a drug raid."

"*What*?" Jazz heard Kerstin ask in the background if everything was all right. "Why didn't I know about this?"

"It was last minute, and it's not work related...not GPD work." Which was a stretch.

"You're on a drug raid. In another state. You're a police officer. And my guess is you're looking for Shea Spencer. I'm thinking it's work related. Are you okay?" Bennett sounded more concerned than upset.

"I'm fine, Ben. Can I explain later? And before you ask, I paid for my own ticket and I'm off the clock."

"I don't care about any of that. I'd just appreciate a heads up when my sister is putting herself in harm's way out of state. Is that too much to ask? Did you tell anyone?"

Bennett was right. She should've at least told someone in case things went wrong. "No. Sorry. When Travis called, I left in a hurry."

"When will you be home?"

"As soon as I get a car to the airport and book a return flight."

"Okay, and, Jazz, we need to talk when you get back."

Jazz hung up, wondering if Bennett had figured out why she and Emory were arguing at the ballpark too. If so, she would have more than one reason to reprimand her.

She checked the rest of her messages. Emory's text read, *We need another meet, away from work. Let me know when you're free.*

CHAPTER THIRTEEN

The next afternoon, Jazz made herself and Ben a cup of coffee and started toward the office. Emory's text last night had sounded urgent, but Ben expected her first thing. The choice made her even more anxious than the consequences of her recent actions. She passed one of the records staff on the way and said, "When Louis comes in, please ask him to see me in the captain's office." Bennett's voice echoed down the halls as she greeted folks on her way in, and Jazz settled in front of Ben's desk, placing her coffee in the center.

"Good afternoon, Lieutenant." Bennett's formal address indicated the tone of the meeting.

"Captain."

"Thanks for the coffee."

"Sure. Look, Ben, I can explain about Atlanta."

"I certainly hope so." She leaned back in her chair and waited while Jazz filled her in on Shea's last-minute placement on Friday and the events of Saturday.

"So, you see why I had to go when Travis called." She twisted her hair and finally met Bennett's stare.

"Louis is part of the Fairview Station family, and you were trying to help, on your own time and at your own expense. That's not the problem. My objection is that you didn't let anyone know where you were or what you were doing. That's also about family, Jazz. You can't imagine the grilling G-ma and Mama gave me. We were worried." Bennett looked at her, and Jazz felt her concern and hurt.

"I can imagine. And you're right. I'm sorry."

"Don't do it again. And as I'm sure you know, what you were doing was totally police business, so don't try to blow smoke up my ass." Bennett took a sip of coffee. "Did you find Shea?"

"Can I fill you in when Louis gets here so I only have to say it once?"

Bennett nodded. "Next item of business. What the holy hell was happening between you, Emory, and that Patrick woman at the ballpark Saturday? I didn't want to grill you in front of the family at brunch."

"Thanks for that, but it was just a misunderstanding." Jazz hung her head. She didn't want to admit violating CPS and department policy, nor did she want to put Bennett in the middle of her woman drama.

"It must've been serious to get Emory that worked up. You said that you bent one of her rules. Please tell me you didn't break another one. She's rabid about guidelines…" Bennett paused and gave Jazz a quizzical stare. "Or was it personal?"

Jazz blew out a long breath. No sense putting off the inevitable. "Both." Bennett's fingers turned white as she clutched her coffee mug. "I'm sorry, Ben." She admitted seeing Shea without supervision or permission, buying her a cell phone, and apologizing to Mrs. Broadmoor and the Robinsons. "Guess you'll have to write me up again."

"Damn it, Jazz. CPS regulations exist for the protection of children. When you're trying to help, that's not always easy to see. We've had this conversation before. You put me in a difficult position. As your sister, I understand why you do what you do and I love you for it, but as your commanding officer, I can't condone the violations."

"I know, Ben. Do what you have to."

Bennett rolled her cup between her hands. "If Mrs. Broadmoor, the Robinsons, or USAA don't press the issue, I'll let you go with a written warning, but it will go in your file this time."

Jazz nodded.

"I need a verbal acknowledgment, Lieutenant."

"Understood, Captain."

Bennett took several sips of coffee and shifted forward in her seat. "So, now about the personal side of the issue. You and Emory, you and Karen, or both?"

"You sound like Travis. He reckons I should sleep with one and marry the other."

"So?"

"I don't want to sleep with Karen, but she is persistent, and that's causing problems with Emory. I was with Karen when Louis called, and she was very disappointed when I left."

"Were you? Disappointed?" Ben asked.

"More relieved. I feel different with Emory, more...something. When I'm with her, I'm excited, comfortable, and totally confused at the same time. I want to have sex with her but I want it to be at the right time, in the right place, and for the right reasons." She lifted her hands in the air and let them drop in her lap. "What is that about?"

Ben grinned but didn't respond.

"Well?"

"I can't answer that for you, but I have faith in you."

Jazz shook her head. "That's as lame as the advice I gave you about Kerstin. Totally useless."

A light knock sounded, and Louis stood in the doorway. "Bad time, Captain?"

"Not at all. Come in, Louis." Bennett motioned toward the chair next to Jazz.

Louis sat and clasped his hands in his lap. "You have news about Shea?"

"I flew to Atlanta last night on information she might be in a house there with her father." Jazz left out the drug part, not wanting to worry Louis more. "Unfortunately, they'd already left, apparently driving back this way."

"You didn't see her." His anguish made Louis's voice gruff. "You don't know if she's okay. I really like that little girl. She's special."

"I talked to Josh's brother, Jeremy, but he wasn't very helpful. The guy who gave us the information originally said she looked healthy." Jazz tried to sound upbeat. "We've got an alert out nationwide. I'll let you know as soon as I hear anything."

"Thank you, Lieutenant. And thank you for going to Atlanta. I want Shea to have a chance, a real chance at a good life."

"So do we, Louis." When he stood to leave, Jazz added, "I need to talk with you about something else, but I'll find you on my way out." Jazz slumped in her chair and looked at Bennett. "There has to be more we can do."

Bennett studied her for a few seconds and asked, "The cell phone you gave her, was it a burner?"

Jazz sat up straighter. "No. Why didn't I think of this sooner?"

"We need a warrant to track the phone, but given the circumstances, it shouldn't be hard to convince a judge. You might want to let me handle it though. You're too close." Bennett held up a hand when Jazz started to object. "Don't say it."

"What?"

"I know exactly what you're thinking." Jazz gave her a skeptical look. "Situations like these are the reason you bend the rules. I get that, sis. I really do."

"You don't want to hear this, but if breaking a rule gets even one child back home safely or keeps one from going through what I did, I'll break that rule every time."

Bennett's eyes shone with tears. "Leave this with me."

Jazz located Louis in the snack area and motioned him out the seldom-used front door so they wouldn't be overheard. "I need to ask you something and I need an honest answer."

"Always, Lieutenant." He straightened as if standing inspection in his former military squad and gazed down at her.

"Did Karen Patrick give you money to foster Shea?" The slightest twitch of Louis's right eyebrow was the only indication the question surprised him, but he remained completely still.

He focused straight ahead for several seconds, then parted his lips, and blew out a long breath. "I should've known because it didn't feel right, but she told me it was a standard payment for what she called hard-to-place children. Starter money, she said, for new foster parents who might need help. I didn't question her, but I put the money straight into a savings account for Shea's college education. So, it's not legit? Am I in trouble?"

"You haven't done anything wrong, Louis. I might need you to tell someone else about this later, but not right now. For the time being, please keep this between us."

"I will. If you need it, I have a picture of the check. I keep detailed records, thanks to my job as an army financial management technician, fancy title for an accountant."

Jazz clasped Louis's hand and shook vigorously. "You're a true gem, Louis. I'll get back to you about this." She glanced at her watch and headed toward her car. Emory would be leaving work soon. She shot her a text. *Ready when you are? Your place?*

❖

Emory jumped when her phone pinged with Jazz's text. Her desk looked like a disaster zone with CPS monthly reports and stats piled on one side and the USAA pages on the other. Her normally open door had remained closed all day while she compared the numbers, and her vision blurred from too much reading. She pulled a stack of papers toward her, stuffed them into a folder along with the notes she'd made, and returned Jazz's text. The ten-minute drive home wouldn't be enough to process what she'd confirmed today or how to explain it to Jazz.

When she pulled into the parking lot of her complex, Jazz was leaning against the side of her 280Z, feet crossed at the ankles like a roguish hero on the cover of a paperback. Emory's mouth dried, but she tamped down her desire. This meeting was about work and her career so she had to focus on that, not how delicious Jazz looked.

Jazz lifted a plastic bag from the hood of her car as Emory approached. "I brought Chinese." Emory's stomach growled. "And apparently a good thing too."

"Didn't take time for lunch," Emory said, unlocking the door and depositing the folder of papers on the kitchen counter. "Give me a second?"

"I'll get the food ready if that's okay. Wine?"

"Yes, please." She changed into a pair of tights and a thigh-length sweatshirt before downing two aspirin for her persistent headache. She returned to the kitchen where Jazz had set the small dining table with food and their drinks. The setting was intimate, the small light over the oven casting muted shadows through the room. "Nice."

Jazz offered her a glass of wine. "Looks like you could use this."

She took a sip and then another. "Mmm, you have no idea how much."

"Rough day?"

She nodded. "Do you mind if we eat first? I'd appreciate a few minutes to unwind before diving back into the mess I've uncovered."

"Your wish is my command." Jazz pulled out a chair and waited for her to sit. "I wasn't sure what you like, so I got a variety. Chicken, beef, and pork dishes, along with a tofu option, lots of vegetables, fried rice, and of course, fortune cookies."

"I like everything." She spooned some food onto her plate and asked, "So, what have you been up to since we slept together?" She blushed and the warmth spread when Jazz grinned. "I mean since Sunday night."

"Please don't let it get out that all we did was sleep. I have a rep to protect."

"I'm sure you do, darling."

"Which I'd gladly relinquish for you, Ms. Blake." Jazz squeezed her hand and told her about the trip to Atlanta and her reprimand.

"Sorry you got into trouble. Guess it was my fault."

"Well, you did draw quite a crowd at the ballgame, but I violated the rules, so I deserve the punishment. Wasn't as bad as it could've been."

"Any further word on Shea?"

"We put out a nationwide alert but nothing yet."

They ate quietly for a while, Jazz apparently content to allow her to decompress and enjoy her meal. When she pushed her plate away and emptied her second glass of wine, Emory was ready to get down to business. "I've done some number-crunching on Karen's proposal, but before I share what I think I've found, I'd like your opinion." She reached for the folder on the counter, removed her notes from the stack, and handed the rest to Jazz. "Why don't I get you another beer and clear the dishes while you read, and then we can talk?"

Jazz settled on the sofa with a beer in one hand and the folder in the other while Emory busied herself to keep from commenting. The minutes oozed past. Emory wiped the table and countertop for the second and then third time, glancing at Jazz and searching for some indication of what she was thinking, but her face was blank.

Finally, Jazz closed the folder, placed it on the coffee table, and drained her beer. "Can I get another, please?"

Emory twisted the top off the beer, handed it to Jazz, and joined her on the sofa. "Well?"

"I'd say Ms. Patrick's bookkeeping is suspect."

"You think?" Emory's voice was tight, her tone high and sharp.

"And it appears she's making quite a profit from USAA adoptions."

Emory pulled the notes she'd made from her pocket. "Considering the going rate for private adoptions is between ten and thirty thousand dollars, I'd say she's making a killing. Either USAA isn't aware she's jacking the prices up or they don't care as long as they get paid."

"The only way to prove she's done anything wrong is to check the company records and see if they match hers or if there's a discrepancy. If she's reporting the higher rates, and the company doesn't object, I'm not sure we have a case. The prospective parents aren't likely to file complaints. They're often willing to pay exorbitant rates for children, especially babies."

The knots in Emory's stomach from earlier in the day when she'd come to the same conclusion returned but twisted tighter. "The other part of the issue is the money she apparently pays foster parents to take kids on the hard-to-place list."

"I talked to Louis today, and he confirmed his payment. Karen sold it as standard practice. Is it possible she justifies that as an incentive condoned by the company?"

"Anything is possible. I've never been on the private side of things, so I'm not sure how they operate or what is within the acceptable range. From my perspective, her actions are at least ethically questionable if not criminal."

"So, she's paying folks to foster older children, which ups her stats and makes CPS look less efficient. She fast-tracks the newborn adoptions because she's overpaid and motivated, which again makes CPS look inept by comparison. It all comes down to money. What happens now, Em?"

"Without USAA's records to compare to Karen's, we're at a dead end, and—" Her throat tightened. The thought of anyone buying and selling children to the highest bidder made her nauseous. She'd worked her entire life for the best possible treatment and placement of children, and to see it reduced to dollars and cents was unacceptable. And with figures like these unchallenged, USAA could put CPS out of business entirely. "I could be out of a job shortly."

"Do you really think it'll come to that?"

"Private companies want their own personnel, people they can control. Outsiders cause problems and ask questions. I've already made it clear to Karen that I'm not a fan."

Jazz took a long pull of her beer and a strange look settled across her face. "All this sure puts a different spin on my experience." She seemed to be thinking aloud, her voice low, eyes distant and unfocused. "CPS handled my adoption." To Emory the statement sounded like an indictment. "Privatization wasn't even on the radar. No one paid to adopt me, and my foster parents certainly didn't receive any compensation to take care of me, except for the measly twenty-eight dollars a day, which was probably less back then. Maybe private companies could do a better job."

Emory stared open mouthed while disbelief and pain bolted through her. "What?"

"I don't mean the payment part, but if incentives help get children better homes, why—"

"I can't believe you right now, Jazz."

"I just meant I wouldn't have minded if money changed hands as long as I had a family who treated me well. I think any kid would feel the same."

Emory slowly placed her wine glass on the coffee table. "So, checks and balances are unnecessary, and an impartial government agency is outdated? We should turn the whole operation over to a for-profit agency whose only concern is their bottom line?"

"It might've saved me four years of hell." Jazz took another sip of beer and seemed to realize what she'd said. "Em, I didn't mean to insult you or your profession."

"But you've managed quite nicely." Emory stood and waved toward the door. "Thank you very much for your opinion. I'm sorry to have wasted your time. I'll be happy to reimburse you for the meal." Jazz's comments stung professionally and even more personally. She'd expected encouragement and support, not a recommendation for the opposition.

"Emory," Jazz said, moving toward her. "I'm just giving you another perspective. I didn't mean to upset you."

The revelations of the day had left her raw and unsettled. Jazz's defense of a system so obviously compromised was too much. "I'd like you to go, please. I might be overreacting, but I need time to think. If I'm to be unemployed soon, I have to plan. Good night, Jazz." Emory opened the door and waited until Jazz crossed the threshold before closing it behind her. The hope of Jazz as an ally, and possibly more, seemed further away than ever, and the absence hurt more deeply than she'd imagined it could.

Chapter Fourteen

Jazz was on her way home from work, still thinking about her disagreement with Emory yesterday, when her cell rang. She snatched the phone from the console, eager to explain one more time what she'd meant about the privatization issue, but hope vanished when she saw the Fairview Station number. "Lieutenant Perry."

"Loo, we've got a location on that phone we're tracking," the tactical sergeant said.

"Get your team together. I'll be back at the station in five minutes."

"We're assembled and waiting."

When she pulled up to the station, six tactical officers, three in uniform and three plainclothes, were near the loading dock checking their vehicles and equipment. She parked, pulled her vest over her head, and walked to the sergeant's car, waving the officers together. "Everybody seen the alert on this suspect?" The officers nodded. "We have warrants for failure to appear on a felony cocaine charge and assault. He has a violent history so let's be cautious. He should have an eleven-year-old girl with him, which means we need to be especially careful. Any questions?" When nobody spoke up, she added, "Let's move."

Jazz rode with the squad sergeant, a man of few words. "Where are we going?"

"Red Carpet Inn on Isler Street. I'll send one of the plainclothes to the desk to see if Spencer is registered once we're in position."

Jazz wiped her sweaty palms down her pants legs. The thought of Shea with her so-called father in this sleazy motel made her stomach roil. She checked the sergeant's tracking app, and Shea's phone was on, but she hadn't answered for days. To Jazz, that meant she couldn't. Another flash of discomfort burned through her.

"Do we need to stage before going in?" Jazz asked.

The sergeant glanced at her. "We've got this, Loo. The guys know where to be and what to do. If he's in there, he won't get past us."

She nodded. "Sorry, you know what you're doing." He was one of her best tactical supervisors, and she didn't need to second-guess his decisions. She was more personally involved than she should be, and it showed in how she felt and reacted. Never good in high-stress situations.

One of the undercover vehicles pulled into the Red Carpet lot while the marked vehicle continued out of sight. The sergeant stopped at a business across the street with a clear view of the front of the motel.

"I'm heading to the office," an officer said over their operational frequency.

A plainclothes officer approached the lobby. The radio was silent, and the minutes stretched. Jazz scanned the area trying to spot the undercover vehicles, but they blended nicely with the others on the lot. If she could pick them out, Spencer could as well. When the plainclothes officer walked out of the office and disappeared around the back of the building, Jazz blew out a long breath. Almost show time.

"He's registered in room fourteen, ground floor, no windows or doors on backside. The vehicle isn't in the lot. Standing by, Sarge."

"You get the pass key?"

"Roger."

"Use it if you can." The sergeant pulled across the street toward the motel. "All units move in."

Police swarmed the Red Carpet parking lot, and officers jumped out of vans, cars, and from behind buildings and rushed toward the room. One carried the heavy battering ram. As she ran to join them, she heard an officer yell, "Police. Warrant." And then a crash as the ram shattered the flimsy door.

"Police. Freeze. Police." A few seconds later, the shouting quieted and she heard only a very loud TV in the background.

The hairs on Jazz's neck stood up as she pushed her way into the room.

"We're clear," the sergeant said. "Turn that damn thing off."

"But where's—"

"There." He pointed to the cell phone she'd given Shea lying on the nightstand.

"Damn it." The room offered no signs of a struggle or any evidence Shea had been there. Now what? She scanned the parking lot and surroundings for Spencer's van. Maybe the prick was watching, laughing at them and his own cleverness. She stormed toward the office, her hands clenching and unclenching at her sides.

"Where is the man in fourteen?"

The greasy-haired attendant rose from his chair behind the desk, bringing a strong odor of cigarettes and fried food with him. "No idea. If you busted my door, you're going to fix it."

"And if you don't tell me everything you know about that man and the child he had with him, you're going to jail." Jazz reached across the counter to yank him closer, but stopped when the sergeant came in. "Tell me." She stared at him long enough to convince him she was serious.

"Okay." He raised his hands. "Hold on while I check the records." He shuffled through the papers strewn across his desk. "Here it is." He waved the registration form in the air, and Jazz snatched it.

"Checked in two days ago. Registration the same as we got from Atlanta PD." She dropped the paper back on the counter. "What about the girl?"

"What girl? I never saw no girl. He checked in alone as far as I know. Got change for the vending machines a couple of times and kept to himself. Never let us clean the room."

"You ever seen him before?" Jazz asked.

"What do you mean?" The man looked away.

"I mean has he been here before, alone or with anyone else?"

The sergeant leaned over the counter. "You better tell us the truth. If you lie, I'll have a marked police car in your lot every day until you're forced to close the doors. I don't think your clientele would like us monitoring their activities."

"You can't do that."

"Watch me."

Jazz crossed her arms and waited while the man pondered his options. A few seconds later, he nodded. "He used to be a regular with some other guys. They'd rent a room for a couple of days and then move on."

"What other guys?" Jazz asked.

"No idea who, but I know what they were."

"Don't make me drag this out of you," she said.

"Drug dealers. Paid in cash and threw in a nice bonus if I didn't make them sign in or give their vehicle registrations. Always took the last room on the end. I'd see people park on Isler Street and walk in. Steady flow of traffic. You know the drill."

The sergeant glanced at her. They were thinking the same thing. Definitely drug dealers. "Anything else?"

The manager shook his head.

"You sure?"

"I'd tell you."

The sergeant handed him a business card. "If any of those people come back, call me, and I mean immediately, not after they're gone." He followed Jazz out of the lobby into the parking lot. "Sorry, Loo."

"We follow the leads. At least we know they're in town. Keep your guys sharp. I'll have a little something for the officer who finds Spencer and the girl."

❖

Emory opened her apartment door to a smiling Diane holding two bottles of wine. "You're such a perfect dinner guest."

"Totes." She hugged Emory, pulled back, and gave her a slow appraisal. "What's wrong?"

"Nothing." Emory turned before Diane could ask more and headed for the kitchen. "Get comfy. Dinner is low-carb so we don't totally undo our spinning success, and because there must be wine." She stirred the pork browning in olive oil and pulled the vegetables she'd chopped earlier from the refrigerator. "You like stir-fry, right?"

"You know I do." Diane hefted the two bottles of wine in the air. "If it's pork, must be pinot. Could I interest you in a glass?" She flicked the rim of Emory's empty goblet with her finger. "Or in your case another glass."

"Please." Emory stirred the vegetables into the pork, added soy sauce, a pinch of brown sugar, fresh grated ginger, and red pepper flakes. "It's almost ready."

Diane poured herself a glass of wine and scooted up to the island. "I love you."

"Uh-oh. That usually means you're about to say something I won't like."

"Can't a girl tell her bestie that she loves her without being sus?"

"Out with it."

Diane took a long sip of wine. "Okay, I love you because you hooked me up with your friend Jane. TBH she's GOAT!" Emory flashed her a speak-English glance. "Sorry. To be honest, she's the greatest of all time. FR. For real."

"I thought you two would hit it off. Have you slept with her yet?"

Diane grabbed her face with both hands and opened her mouth in fake shock. "A lady never kisses and tells, but she is totally not the dick and dash type. She's special."

"So…"

"Not yet, but I have hopes for the weekend."

Emory dished food onto their plates and carried them to the table. "Grab my wine." She lit a candle, mostly to keep Diane from examining her too closely, and waved her to a seat. "Promise you'll be nice to her. She's a friend too."

"Of course." Diane raised her glass. "To delicious food cooked by a wonderful woman and to our lovers."

Emory started to clink her glass but stopped short. *"Our lovers?"*

"I came by late Sunday night to dish about my date with Jane, but you had company."

Emory stirred her food absently. "Company?"

Diane's stare didn't waver. "I *could* be wrong. One of your neighbors *could* have a copper-colored Datsun 280Z with a thin blue line sticker on the back bumper just like the one lieutenant Jazz Perry drives. Or the lieutenant *could* be seeing someone else in the complex."

Emory finally looked up and met Diane's gaze. "Okay. Fine. She spent the night Sunday, but it's not what you think."

"I really hope it is, because I think the two of you screwed like rabbits."

"We had business to discuss, Di. She'd had a hard day, and we fell asleep on the sofa. That's all." But Emory smiled as she remembered how perfect Jazz fitted against her and how content she'd been, hoping it never had to end. She'd thought about sex, but it was the intimacy that remained like a brand on her skin and in her mind.

Diane leaned closer. "When will you stop using business as an excuse to spend time with Jazz? It's more than that…or at least you want it to be."

Emory raised a forkful of food but returned it to her plate. "It's not that simple."

"Karen Patrick?"

Emory's stomach tightened at the name. "Ms. Patrick, our jobs, Jazz's family, and our opinions about how things should be done. She steps over a line, and I lash out. We apologize, make up, get closer, and the cycle repeats. Hot and cold. I don't know what to make of it really."

"You're passionate about each other, and your jobs, or things wouldn't be so explosive. Besides, the course of true love is never smooth."

"Oh no, don't go all wives' tale on me. Give me a snappy comeback so I can laugh."

"I think you should shoot her a CU46 text and just do it."

Emory grinned. "Dare I ask?"

"See you for sex."

Emory shook her head, but her body tingled. "Eat your dinner before it gets cold."

Diane forked some of the stir-fry into her mouth and chewed slowly. "Mmm, this is so good." She waved her fork in a circle. "Tell me how you left things Monday morning."

"Sunday night and Monday morning were great. We talked about some stuff and bonded, I think. She implied that she wanted to date me seriously. Yesterday was the problem."

Diane rolled her hand for more details as she chewed.

"Jazz said privatization of CPS services might not be such a bad idea."

"Ouch."

"Exactly. I might've overreacted and told her to leave. I thought we were on the same page." Emory grimaced. "When I say it aloud, I sound like an insensitive shrew."

"Did she tell you why she feels that way?" Diane asked.

"Her life before the Carlyles was bad, so the fact that she wants to find a better way than traditional placement and adoption shouldn't surprise me. Damn, I totally overreacted. Now I owe her another apology. See what I mean?"

"But you were close Sunday night."

"I've never felt such intimacy with anyone." The fear in Jazz's eyes flashed through her mind and then the relief as she allowed Emory to comfort her. "I feel like she sees me, the real me, and opens up herself. What am I going to do, Di?"

"You're going to grab her and hold on, no matter how rough the ride. Do you hear me?"

Emory nodded.

"I mean it, Em. Jazz makes you feel things you haven't felt before. If you don't try, the regrets will be fierce. Say the words."

"I'll try." Di gave her a hard stare. "I'll really try to hold on." The words left her lips, and Emory relaxed. Her path seemed obvious when someone else pointed it out, but could she follow through?

CHAPTER FIFTEEN

Jane had been off since Emory made the discovery about the USAA stats, but now she hurried down the hallway toward the emergency room to see her. She waited until Jane finished a chart at the nurses' station before approaching.

"Do you have a minute?"

Jane checked the large wall clock. "I'm due a break. Canteen?"

Emory nodded, and they walked to the elevator. Neither spoke until they were alone.

"What's wrong, Emory?" Jane took her hands and forced her to look at her.

"I don't want to put you in a compromising position. And you can totally say no." She hesitated, second-guessing her request. "I'm wondering if your source on the USAA contract can provide more information?"

"I'm not sure. What do you need?"

She explained what she'd discovered in Karen's files and her suspicions. "The official USAA adoption statistics for the past two years for comparison would be great. If the company is letting these inflated costs and backdoor payments slide, we need to know before the state turns everything over to them and puts good people out of jobs." She searched Jane's face, seeing the same concern that she felt. "I'm also looking into the number of abuse and neglect cases involving USAA adoptees."

"Is this about the case we had the other day?"

"It certainly got me thinking, but right now I'm just exploring everything and having to do it quickly."

The elevator door opened at the canteen, and they got drinks and headed for a table. Jane sipped and nodded at coworkers who waved or spoke in passing.

"If you'd rather not get more involved, or if this would compromise a friendship, I understand. I'll appeal to the state for the statistics. I'm sure USAA files periodic reports to maintain their certification. I just don't want to tip my hand before I have more details and those numbers will be too old to be useful."

"My source is a former CPS employee who now works at USAA headquarters. The reason she gave me the contract information in the first place is because she's questioning some of the company's practices. I don't think either of us would have a problem providing what you need, but I should check with her before I commit."

For the first time since Jazz left her condo three days ago, Emory felt hopeful. "That would be great, Jane. You'll let me know?"

"Of course, and before we go..." She checked her watch. "I just wanted to say thanks for giving Diane my number. We've been out a few times, and it feels good."

Emory scooted her chair closer. "And?"

"I really like her, but she's sort of out there. Should I be worried about getting hurt?"

"Di is different, but she's also one of the most loyal people I know. She's not a player. If she's into you, she's a keeper. Do you have chemistry?" Jane dipped her head. "I'll take the rosy color of your cheeks as a yes." She cupped Jane's hand. "I'm so happy for both of you."

Jane smiled. "May be too soon for congratulations, but I think we have potential."

"If I didn't think so, I wouldn't have given her your number. Keep me posted?"

"I'm sure you'll hear it from both sides." She glanced at her watch again. "I have to get back, but I'll check on your request as soon as I can."

"Thank you so much, Jane." Emory stared into her teacup letting her conflicted emotions settle. The information about USAA could put people out of work as easily as the privatization contract. It also had the potential to destroy an agency that provided a benefit to children. Were her motives pure or was she striking out at Karen for her interest in Jazz and because she reminded Emory so much of the woman Jean had dumped her for? Was she that shallow?

She pushed the cold tea aside and headed back to her office with another question niggling at the back of her mind. How had Karen gotten the most recent CPS statistics? Time was needed to compile, analyze, and publish data, and the publicly released results were usually a couple of years behind the time period being analyzed. Maybe she had an inside person as well. The most logical place to start was Sheri McGuire because she worked with Karen placing older children and seemed to be a big supporter of USAA. Had she already secured a position in the new regime in exchange for inside info?

Jazz stood in front of the last squad lineup and prepared to repeat the same spiel she'd already given three times today. "Check your alerts for the description of a van that brought drugs into the area from Georgia. Joshua Spencer, Caucasian male, is the driver, and he reportedly has an eleven-year-old child, Shea Spencer, with him. As of two days ago, he was still in Greensboro. Last known location was the Red Carpet Inn off Gate City Boulevard. Contact your informants about recent drug shipments. We need to locate this child ASAP, and a big drug arrest wouldn't be bad either. I have something for the officer who finds them."

"Bribing an officer is against the law, Loo," one of the officers said, and everyone laughed.

"Motivation isn't."

"Is this guy usually armed?" a younger officer asked.

"Unclear, but he's been violent in the past, and he's a drug dealer, so assume he is. But don't let an overabundance of caution make you reckless or too quick to act. The child's safety is paramount."

Jazz spoke with the squad sergeant and a few officers before heading toward the locker room for a quick shower. Third shift lineup ran long, and she'd been at work before dawn, so a hot shower and change into civvies before the ride home was perfect. As she toweled off and slid into her jeans, her cell vibrated on the bench. "Yeah?"

"Is this a bad time?" Emory asked. The background noise sounded like she was in a bar or restaurant.

Jazz's breath hitched, and she froze with her shirt unbuttoned. "Never for you." She'd wanted to call a hundred times since their disagreement on Tuesday but didn't know how to apologize for something she believed but regretting saying.

"Are you at home?"

"Just about to leave the station. It's been a long day." Emory hesitated, and Jazz heard a heavy sigh. "What's up, Em?"

"I guess you're too tired to meet for a drink...and a chat."

Jazz tucked the phone under her chin, buttoned her shirt, and maneuvered her arms into a pullover sweater. "Then you'd guess wrong. Where are you?"

"M'Coul's downtown, but I could meet you somewhere else."

"That's good. Are you upstairs or down?"

"Up in the back booth."

"See you in ten minutes." Jazz tugged on her boots, slid her cell in her back pocket, and pulled into the parking lot behind M'Coul's a few minutes later. Her heart pounded as she took the steps two at a time, dodging people coming down the narrow stairs. At the top, she paused and searched for Emory. When she spotted her, everything slowed, except an unexpected rush of arousal.

Emory lifted a wine glass to her lips, took a sip, and licked the rim. Jazz's knees trembled as blood rushed to her core. Everyone else in the room disappeared, but Emory came into sharp focus. Her ivory complexion crinkled between her eyes and across her forehead with a look Jazz had come to recognize as deep thought. Her hand cradled the wine glass, and the red-glossed nail of her forefinger absently tapped the side. She wore a pale turtleneck and forest green button-up sweater that highlighted the sparkle of her emerald eyes when she looked up and saw Jazz. How had she ever doubted that she wanted to be with Emory, only Emory?

"I said, *excuse me*."

Jazz turned, and a line of patrons had queued up behind her on the stairs. "Sorry." She quickly moved to the booth where Emory sat and slid in across from her. "Hi."

"Impeding traffic, darling?" Her wide smile erased the worry lines and warmed Jazz through and through.

"Guess so, but I was distracted."

"Were you? It's good to see you too." Emory shifted uncomfortably in her seat. "Before I lose my nerve, I want to apologize for the other night. You should be able to tell me anything without worrying I'll go ballistic. I'm sorry, and I won't try to justify my behavior."

"It's okay. We're both passionate about our work."

Emory glanced down into her wine glass. "I guess I'd hoped we'd be on the same side."

"We both want what's best for the children. Isn't that the same side?"

"Technically, but we don't agree if privatization is best. Do we?"

Jazz reached across the table and cupped Emory's hand. "Maybe. We're just coming at the issue from different directions. We have more work to do, and I get that you're concerned about your job, so I'll try to be more sensitive. You may be surprised in the end."

"That sounds a bit cryptic."

"A little faith, Em?" She squeezed Emory's hand.

"I'll try." Emory motioned toward the bar. "May I buy you a drink? It looks like I could use another as well, liquid courage."

Jazz glanced at their joined hands and swallowed hard. "Would you mind terribly if we left? I'd really like to be alone with you." She stood and offered her hand.

Emory blushed, slid to the edge of the booth, and took Jazz's hand. "I don't mind at all."

"Did you drive?" Emory shook her head, and Jazz threw some bills on the table and guided Emory outside to her car. Her body ached as she closed Emory's door and made her way to the driver's side. She sat down and gripped the steering wheel not trusting her empty hands with Emory so near. "Can we go to your place?"

"Yes, please." Emory reached over the emergency brake and placed her hand on Jazz's thigh as she drove, making the short distance feel much longer. "Is this all right?"

"If you mean is it distracting as hell, yes. If you mean do I like it, very much."

Emory grinned. "So, you're into sadism?"

"Apparently where you're concerned." She stopped in front of Emory's door, rushed to the other side of the car, and helped her out. When Emory stood, Jazz pulled her against her and kissed her lightly. "I've missed you."

"Uh-huh." Emory stepped back, her breathing fast and rough. "Let's take this inside." She unlocked the door and pushed Jazz back against it when it closed. "Kiss me again, Jazz." Emory's voice was husky with need. "I can't wait another second."

Jazz pulled Emory's hips against her and bent her head for the kiss. Emory grabbed the back of her neck, and what Jazz had intended to be a light, seductive kiss turned hungry and urgent. Her body heated so quickly that she felt dizzy. "Em...Emory."

"Shush." Emory rubbed against her, stroking Jazz's thighs. "You feel so good." She sucked Jazz's bottom lip and teased it with her teeth. "I want you, Jazz."

Jazz eased Emory back so she could check for the truth in her eyes. "Are you sure, because I want you to be sure. I'd never want you to—"

"I'm sure." The only thing Emory was sure about was that she had to have Jazz, everything else be damned. If all they ever had was this night of just sex, she'd settle for that, but she'd take it on her terms. Emory reached for the tail of Jazz's sweater, but she stopped her.

"And if this is only—"

"Then I'll have no regrets." She shucked Jazz's sweater over her head. "Can we stop talking now?" She tugged Jazz's shirt from her jeans and tore at the buttons, leaving the shirt open to expose her bare breasts. If she slowed down and thought about what she was doing, she'd lose her nerve. That wasn't happening tonight. She was going with Di's advice and her own feelings.

"Wouldn't you like to take this somewhere else, like the bedroom or a sofa at least?"

"I want to make you come. Right here. Right now." Emory unbuckled Jazz's belt and folded her jeans over just enough to slide her hand under the waistband of her briefs. "I'm going to touch you, Jazz. Is that okay?" She wasn't usually so brazen, but this was an opportunity to prove she wasn't all about rules and propriety.

"Uh-huh." She cupped Emory's head and brought them together in a kiss. "You taste so good, Em."

The softness and taste of Jazz's lips threatened to sidetrack Emory, but she withdrew long enough to draw a full breath and then slid her hand lower down Jazz's body. She captured Jazz's clit between two fingers and eased back and forth. "Will you let me have you, like this?"

"Is that a…trick question?" Jazz groaned and shoved her hips forward. "Do whatever you want. Just don't make me wait too long."

Emory quickened her strokes for several seconds but slowed when Jazz tried to match the pace. "Look at me. See *me*." She loved controlling the pace of Jazz's pleasure, bringing her close and pulling back, making Jazz want and need her over and over. Jazz looked into her eyes, and the connection pulsed through Emory, a bolt of adrenaline sparking energy and desire. "That's it, darling."

"Can I take these off?" Jazz pulled at Emory's clothes. "I want to see you, feel you."

"Not yet." Two things gave her the confidence to take Jazz like this—her absolute hunger for her and the fact that she was still clothed. Worrying about Jazz's reaction to her body and dealing with her own insecurity would kill the mood and her courage. She concentrated on Jazz's responses and increased the pace of her touch.

"Harder," Jazz pleaded. "Not easy…standing."

Emory stepped closer, hiked her skirt up, and slid her leg up Jazz's firm thigh. "See how hot you make me?" She guided Jazz's fingers between her legs. "Keep your hand there while I make you come." Emory squeezed Jazz's tender flesh again and pumped faster.

"Please, Em."

"Wait." Emory stepped back and stripped the remainder of Jazz's clothes off, her jeans and boots pooled around her ankles. "I want to see your body when you come." She again wedged her hand between Jazz's legs and watched her thrust to meet her, her head thrown back against the door.

"Ahhh." Jazz pumped faster, her hand cupping Emory's center.

"Don't you dare come until I'm inside you." Emory slid her center along Jazz's leg again, leaving a wet trail. "You're so hot, Jazz." Emory teased the tip and milked the base of Jazz's clit, and her breathing became raspier.

"I'm going to come."

"Stay with me just a…little longer, darling." Emory felt Jazz's legs tremble and pressed her tighter against the door to keep her from falling. "Soon. Very soon." Her fingers slid back and forth in Jazz's arousal. "So wet."

Jazz grabbed Emory's hand, trying to increase the pace. "Finish me, Em. Please."

Emory dropped to her knees and eased Jazz's legs farther apart. "Now, darling." She captured Jazz's clit between her lips and slid her fingers inside.

A couple of strokes later, Jazz surged to her tiptoes and then slumped across Emory's shoulders, her body shivering. "Oh my God." Jazz collapsed to the floor, pulling Emory across her lap as she fell. "That was…"

"What?"

"So not what I expected for our first time."

"Is that good or bad?" Emory couldn't believe she'd been so forward, so demanding—not her style at all after the confidence-bashing breakup with Jean, but Jazz made her want and need things she never had.

"Just different. You've been so uncertain about us. I wasn't sure this would ever happen or what to expect if it did, but no complaints. At all. You were awesome."

Emory couldn't meet Jazz's stare. "Well, if I'm totally honest, this isn't exactly what I envisioned either, but I couldn't wait any longer. And I wanted you like this, at my mercy. Guess I needed to be in charge after Jean. It's definitely a high." She buried her head in Jazz's shoulder. "I hope you didn't mind being fucked against a door. Such a cliché."

Jazz pulled her back and stared into her eyes. "You're kidding, right? You were so hot. I'm used to women waiting for me to make all the moves. The switch was nice." She kissed Emory gently, and heat blossomed between them again. "But I do have one request."

"Name it."

"I'd like to make love to you. In a bed. With both of us undressed." She glanced down at Emory's clothes. "Not that I don't like your outfit, but it has to go."

"You realize that could be the hardest part for me."

"Harder than a butch letting herself be totally dominated by a shy femme? Really?"

Emory laughed, and some of her uncertainty evaporated. "Well, you do have a point. What's a little body shyness compared to one's dignity and rep?"

"Exactly." Jazz eased Emory off her lap, stood, and offered her hand. "Shall we?" Her stomach twisted with a mixture of excitement and anxiety. She wanted to make Emory feel comfortable, beautiful, and special. If she rushed or was insensitive, it could be devastating. She took a step forward and stumbled.

Emory grabbed her arm to keep her from falling. "You might want to get out of your restraints first, darling."

She leaned against Emory, shucked her boots and jeans off, and followed Emory to the bedroom. Tossing her clothes into a side chair with one hand, Jazz reached for the delicate buttons of Emory's sweater with the other and tried to unfasten them, but her fingers shook too badly. She glanced down into Emory's smiling face.

"Relax. I'll do the heavy lifting since you're still in a weakened condition." Emory removed her sweater and stepped out of her panties but left on her skirt and turtleneck before leading Jazz to the side of the bed. "You're so handsome."

Jazz blushed from the comment and the way Emory was staring down at her.

"Surely that's not the first time you've heard that."

"It's the first time I've believed it."

Emory lay down beside Jazz and stroked the side of her face. "You better get used to it, because I plan to say it a lot."

Her insides tightened, and her sex pulsed from Emory's caress. Her attraction to Emory had followed a gentle path, but the last couple of times they'd been together she'd wanted more, needed more. "Kiss me, Em, please."

Emory slid a leg over Jazz's and kissed her, slowly at first, tracing her lips with the tip of her tongue before sliding inside. They both moaned, and Emory pressed herself along Jazz's side. "It feels so right to be this close to you."

Jazz pulled Emory on top of her, hands resting on her hips, and kissed her again. She tugged at the skirt Emory still wore that fanned out across her torso. "Can I take this off?"

"Not just yet."

"How about the top to start? You're so beautiful. I want all of you."

"You make me feel that way, Jazz."

She cupped Emory's breasts and teased her nipples with her thumbs before sliding down to her thighs. "I want to watch you tremble when I touch you. I want to see every muscle tense and release when I make you come."

"Keep talking like that and the coming will be too soon." She moved Jazz's hands from her hips back to her breasts. After a few seconds, she said, "Okay, the top can go."

Jazz slipped her hands under the hem of the turtleneck and smoothed her hands up Emory's sides, bringing the fabric with her. She stopped with the shirt around Emory's neck and buried her face in Emory's breasts. "I'm in heaven." Her breasts were perfect and smelled like she'd bathed in oranges and flowers. "So sweet."

"Let me out." Emory squirmed playfully, and Jazz pulled the shirt over her head, followed by the lacy bra.

"Your breasts are so beautiful. They fit my hands perfectly. And they're so suckable." Jazz rolled Emory over and kissed her again before lowering her mouth over a puckered nipple. She loved curving against a woman's body and feasting at her breast until her clit ached.

"Oh, yes." Emory held Jazz's head in place, surging with each pass of her tongue. "More of that."

Jazz alternated breasts, sucking one and massaging the other until she felt herself grow wet and hard again. She tried to spread Emory's legs to rub against her thigh, but only felt the long skirt underneath her. She gave a frustrated sigh. "This skirt is totally slowing my roll."

Emory laughed. "Slowing your roll? Seriously, Casanovette?"

Jazz propped up on her elbows and stared at Emory. "Yes. Take it off. I've imagined you undressed often enough. Please put me out of my misery."

"Fine," Emory said with feigned irritation. "Turn your back."

Jazz heard the skirt zipper, the fabric falling to the floor, and the shuffle of covers.

"Okay, come back to me," Emory said.

Jazz tugged the edge of the covers to pull them away from Emory, testing her readiness.

"No peeking yet." Emory held the sheet tight against her until Jazz slid in beside her and brought their bodies together. "Much better without clothes."

"So much better, Em, so soft and hot and perfect."

"Make love to me now, Jazz?"

She felt liquid inside from Emory's whispered question. No woman had ever asked her to make love to her. Things usually just happened, but Emory's request spoke to her insecurity about her body and to her desirability and broke Jazz's heart.

She worshiped Emory's mouth and breasts, losing herself in the rhythms of pain and pleasure. Jazz surrendered to Emory's warmth and eagerness while Emory responded to Jazz's touches with the enthusiasm of a woman too long deprived.

When she slid down Emory's body to the fork of her legs, the covers fell away and Jazz gazed up at her. Emory's Rubenesque body was beautifully flushed and responsive, and she'd never wanted anyone more. "I'm going to taste you, Em."

"Please."

When she covered Emory's center with her mouth and slid her fingers inside, Emory gasped and clung to her shoulders.

"Oh...ohhh." Emory dug her nails into Jazz's flesh and surged to meet her thrusts.

She couldn't take her eyes off Emory, mesmerized by her attempts to breathe normally followed by moans that seemed to rise from her soul as hungry growls. She pinched Emory's breast with her free hand, and Emory bowed off the bed, holding Jazz's head to her.

"Faster, Jazz. I'm close."

Emory's body grew hotter and her skin turned bright pink. When she opened her eyes and stared down at her, Jazz said, "Come for me, Em." A few seconds later, Emory stiffened and her thighs quivered until she made a low guttural sound and collapsed beneath her.

Jazz crawled up and curled against Emory's side. "Could you give me a hand for about two seconds while you recover?" She sucked Emory's breast into her mouth and nudged her hip with her pelvis.

Emory chuckled and tucked her hand between Jazz's legs.

Two strokes of Emory's fingers, and Jazz emptied into her hand. "Thank you...so much." She draped a leg over Emory's body and pressed against her until the aftershocks passed. Emory reached down for the covers, but Jazz stopped her. "Please don't. I love looking at you."

She tried to tug the sheet from Jazz's grasp. "You were good, but you didn't fuck me blind. I still know how I look."

"Apparently not. You're gorgeous, much better than I imagined, which is saying a lot. I've always preferred substantial women with feminine curves, softness. and a feisty attitude to carry it off. You're the whole package."

Emory turned toward her. "Exactly how many *substantial* women have been among your plethora of conquests, Lieutenant Perry?"

"Several." Emory gave her a skeptical look. "I'm serious, Em. And if I had a perfect type, it would be you, totally, but you're so much more than my type. I'm not kidding and it's not the orgasm talking."

Emory rolled on top of her again. "You're a smooth talker, Jazz Perry, but right now I'm more interested in your mouth for other purposes."

"Hold that thought, Ms. Blake. I need to make a quick call. Don't move." Jazz dialed the station. "This is Lieutenant Perry. Do we have an update on the Shea Spencer case?"

"Nothing yet, Lieutenant," the records clerk responded.

"Okay, thank you. Be sure to call if there's anything at all." She hung up and turned back to Emory. "She's still out there somewhere."

"And you feel guilty about being here with me, enjoying yourself?" Emory asked.

She pulled Emory close again. "I'll never feel guilty about being with you. I just want Shea to be safe and back with loving parents."

"I know. Would you feel better if you went out and looked for her? I'd understand."

"What can I do that two hundred other cops can't? Besides, I recall you saying something about needing my mouth."

Emory moaned as Jazz slid down her body.

Chapter Sixteen

O h...I can't...breathe." Emory gasped, her latest orgasm still pulsing through her. Jazz reached for her, but she waved her off. "A minute, please." She pulled for air as her heart rate slowed and her body regained strength. "We haven't been out of bed for more than ten minutes since we got in Friday night."

"Complaining?"

"Never. Just an observation."

Jazz stretched her arms toward her and wiggled her fingers. "Then get back here. I'm far from done with you, Ms. Blake."

She'd lost count of how many cute and adoring things made her want to tell Jazz she loved her since Friday. Emory added the playful way Jazz reached for her now to the list. Jazz had wooed and worshiped her physically, ravished her sexually, and won her emotionally over and over the past two days, and Emory couldn't have stopped her if she'd wanted to. The dream had come alive in her arms and accepted her cellulite and all. But there was still one more secret.

She pecked Jazz on the lips and settled against her chest. "I have something to tell you."

"I hope it's not serious. My brain cells are suffering from lack of oxygen because of increased blood supply to other areas of my body."

"It is...serious."

Jazz pulled back enough to look at her face. "Tell me, Em. It'll be fine. Whatever it is."

"When I start, please let me get through the whole thing before you ask questions. Promise?" Jazz nodded, and Emory's heart almost broke at the worried look in her eyes. She took a deep breath and began the explanation she'd practiced often since their first lunch at the Iron Hen.

"I can't have children." She searched Jazz's face for a reaction and saw only the same worried look as before. "I always had severe menstrual periods, which worsened with age. Heavy bleeding, intense pain, and cramps. I developed uterine fibroids, and some of them contained pre-cancerous cells. My doctor recommended a complete hysterectomy when I was thirty-two. I struggled with the decision to have surgery, but now it's a part of who I am." The words rolled off her tongue easily, but she'd had years to adapt. She'd accepted it, but would it change the way Jazz felt about her? "Jazz?"

Jazz pulled Emory back against her chest. "I'm so sorry you had to go through that. It must've been horrible."

Emory's insides twisted in a combination of relief at the show of compassion and uncertainty about what came next. She had to know. "What does this mean for us, if we become like a permanent thing?" She played with a strand of her hair, unable to look at Jazz.

"Even if you *could* have children, the health risks might've been too great. I guess I never thought you'd want to have kids because pregnancies become more unlikely and harder to sustain full term the older you get."

"It's a non-issue for me."

"All it means for us is that if we're together and want children, we adopt or I carry the child, but I'm not crazy about that idea." She lifted Emory's chin and made eye contact. "Em, did you think I'd be upset?"

"I wasn't sure. We've never really discussed a family." She kissed the spot between Jazz's breasts and breathed in the fragrance of their blended scents. "I thought my butch cop would want her little missus to carry their children."

Jazz chuckled. "Stereotype much? What kind of representative would I be for adoptees if I didn't recognize the value and necessity of adoption? For you, I just might consider the whole pregnancy thing. I thought I'd like a big family, but what you want is equally important."

"Honestly, I'm not sure I'd make a very good parent because of all my hang-ups."

"If that was the criteria for parenthood, none of us would be allowed to raise children."

"And you're sure you're okay with this?" Emory asked.

"Of course, I'm okay. Nothing can change the way I feel about you."

Emory kissed Jazz and tried to convey her appreciation for Jazz's understanding, along with the other feelings she hadn't voiced yet. "Thank you." She gave Jazz a final kiss and rolled out of bed, just escaping her grasp. "I need a shower, to stand up for more than five minutes, and food, possibly lots of food."

"Can I join you in the shower?"

She glanced over her shoulder at a naked Jazz kneeling on the bed with her palms raised in submission and said, "Only if you promise to keep your hands to yourself."

"I promise."

Emory adjusted the shower spray for heat, stepped under the jets, and hummed as warmth penetrated her aching but satisfied body. She poured shampoo into her hands and massaged her scalp, remembering Jazz finger-combing her long tresses last night. When was the last time she'd had sex with someone who looked at her with the desire and adoration Jazz had? Her body stirred again as she washed the suds from her hair. When she turned, Jazz stood behind her in the shower staring. "Hello."

"You are so gorgeous." She reached for Emory, her brown eyes hooded with desire.

Emory stepped back against the shower wall. "You promised to keep your hands to yourself." She squirted shower gel in her palms and rubbed the foamy soap over her breasts and down her torso slowly while Jazz watched every move. Emory was playing a dangerous game and didn't care who won.

"Seriously, Em?"

The hunger in Jazz's eyes heated Emory's body faster than the hot water. When Jazz looked at her, she felt attractive, desirable, and ready for her again. "Gel?" Without waiting for a response, she pumped dabs on Jazz's breasts and between her legs. "Wash." Emory lathered her own body and rubbed in slow circles.

Jazz spread the body wash around her breasts and licked her lips. "You're a wicked woman, Emory Blake."

"W—why?" She tried to sound innocent, but her voice broke from watching Jazz touch herself.

"You make me promise and then tease me unmercifully." Jazz shifted her legs apart, bent her knees, and scooped the frothy gel between her legs. "If I can't touch you, I'll have to—"

"Do it." Emory stared at Jazz's hand at the fork of her thighs, remembering how her fingers had initially soothed Emory's anxieties and then skillfully urged orgasm after orgasm from her. She cupped her own sex and kept time with Jazz. "Help me."

Jazz leaned against the opposite wall, looking from Emory's lips to her breasts and then lower until the cycle repeated. Jazz rolled and pinched a nipple with one hand while the other worked at her crotch. Her muscled legs flexed and released with each stroke of her fingers, and her chest heaved with labored breaths.

Emory mimicked Jazz's actions like a mirror reflecting her own desire. When Jazz stretched on tiptoes and groaned deep in her throat, Emory stroked faster.

Jazz reached for Emory but kept her distance. "Come with me, Em." They joined hands, and Jazz's moaned relief combined with Emory's cries and echoed off the tiled walls of the shower. They moved together, slumped to the floor, and curled into a ball under the warm water.

Emory trembled in Jazz's arms, her insides as raw as her sensitive flesh, but for the first time in her life, she was comfortable in her body and satisfied in her mind that there were no more secrets. "Thank you for this."

"For?"

"Everything since Friday night. Just thank you." She snuggled into Jazz's chest, and neither spoke again until the water turned tepid and eventually chilly.

"Come to brunch with me," Jazz said.

"Great. I'm starving. Give me ten minutes to get dressed."

Jazz laughed as she rose and pulled Emory to her feet, wrapping her in a thick towel. "In femme speak that's thirty minutes, right?"

"Possibly. Depends on where we're going and how dressed I have to be."

"Just my house." Jazz dried her hair as casually as if she'd suggested IHOP.

"*What?*" Emory shook her head. "No, no, no, no, no."

"It's only my family. You already know everybody, and they like you."

"Absolutely not." She shook her head harder. Jazz had to see what a bad idea this was.

Jazz tucked a towel around her waist, looking as comfortable naked as she did half-dressed or completely clothed. She placed her hands lightly on Emory's shoulders as if their full weight would scare her even more. "You might as well. I've already told them we're dating."

Emory's mouth fell open. "You what? When?"

"Brunch last Sunday. The secret is out, and I assume you haven't gotten any threatening phone calls or been stalked by the family."

Emory kept shaking her head, words failing.

"Em, it's time."

"No, it's not time. Not even close to time. I'm so not ready for this." Jazz pulled Emory into a hug, and she tried to keep her body from trembling, this time with fear instead of desire.

"When will you be ready?"

"For starters, when I haven't had sex with you for two days and don't have your scent in me and on me everywhere. When I can walk into a room without feeling pigeon-toed from having you between my legs for hours. Maybe when my breasts don't sting from the lace of my bra because you've sucked them raw. Or maybe when I stop wanting you every time I look at you." Jazz grinned wider the more Emory talked. "It's not funny."

"So, let me get this straight. You're afraid my family will know I've had sex?"

"I'm worried they'll know you've had sex with *me*, and they'll disapprove."

Jazz shook her head. "I'm still not following."

"I respect your family, but the truth is, they probably won't consider us a good match. I'm too old for you. I'm a social worker, and you were adopted. Plus, I can't have children, and your family is *big* on children."

"If the past two days are any indication, I'm the one who'll have trouble keeping up."

Emory tried to smother a smile and play-slapped Jazz's arm. "Don't distract me."

"As for the career stuff, who better to understand and appreciate an adoptee than someone who works with them every day? And don't worry about children. My family will love any child we love."

Emory adored that Jazz wanted to take her to the sacred Carlyle family brunch and shot down all her objections to make her feel better. "You're almost too good to be true, darling." She circled back to the fact that Jazz had told her family they were dating. "What did they say…when you told them we were going out?"

"Nothing, which I took as a really good sign."

"Or total shock and disbelief, which would be a really bad sign."

"You worry too much." Jazz kissed her again, and Emory's legs weakened.

"Stop that or we'll be late."

"Does that mean you'll come with me?"

Emory gave her a hard stare but softened at Jazz's smile. "Every. Single. Time." Emory squeezed Jazz's sex before spinning out of her arms and grabbing the hairdryer. "Now go so I can get ready. I need to look presentable not freshly fucked."

While Emory dressed, Jazz paced her small living space and called the station to check on Shea's case again, but got no good news. She'd also called G-ma to make sure it was okay to bring a guest, deciding not to share who in case Emory changed her mind. When Emory walked out of the bedroom, Jazz stopped and stared, her mouth dried, and the rest of her sweated and grew wet from wanting.

"Do I look okay?" She glanced at the outfit she'd chosen and swiped a nervous hand down her skirt. "I could change again. This is only number seven or maybe eight. I'm sure I have something more—"

"You're absolutely breathtaking. Possibly a tad overdressed. Family brunch is more a sweatshirt and jeans affair, often followed by tag football or baseball."

"I'll change again. Don't want to look like I'm trying too hard."

"Lose the skirt and sweater and add jeans and a T-shirt."

Emory returned a few minutes later, gave a tentative smile, and pushed at a lock of loose hair at her temple. "Better?"

"Perfect. Somehow you manage to make casual look dressy. And I love your hair in a French braid with stray bits hanging around your face."

"Very succinctly stated, darling." Emory grinned up at her, stood on her tiptoes, and said, "Kiss me. Lightly. Mind the lipstick."

Jazz tried to comply, but when their lips met, she couldn't stop the urge to grab Emory and pull her against her. "I want you so hard right now."

Emory kissed her as urgently but finally backed away. "Great, now we both smell like we're in heat…again."

"I would say serves you right for making me jerk off in the shower, but it was worth every second of the pain. Besides, I like the smell of you in heat." She offered her arm to Emory and ushered her to the car.

"Are you sure it's okay if I just show up?" Emory asked on the short drive.

"I checked with G-ma to make sure there was room, and she said—"

"There's always room for one more at our table," Emory finished for her.

"Exactly." She took Emory's hand and brought it to rest on her thigh. "Please relax and be the woman they already know and really like."

"I'll try."

❖

When Jazz pulled up to the Carlyle home, Emory saw Simon's twins playing with Dylan on the wide porch. She and Jazz approached, and Ryan yelled through the screen door before disappearing inside with his sister, "Jazz is here with a hottie. Can we eat now?"

Jazz grinned at her with an I-told-you-so look. "Even a twelve-year-old boy can see how gorgeous you are." She wiggled her brows suggestively. "Let's go straight up to my room."

"Stop it." Emory wasn't sure if she blushed from the child's comment or Jazz's but suspected a little of both. "And behave yourself. Here comes your little sister."

Dylan sprinted down the steps and pulled Emory into a hug. "It's good to see you outside of the hospital. You look fantastic, almost glowing." She glanced at Jazz. "What have you two been up to this morning?"

"Dylan," Jazz said in a warning tone.

Emory was certain Dylan could see *we've just had sex* written all over her face. "Thank you, Dylan. It's nice to see you when one of us isn't rushing down the hallway to some emergency. How's residency?"

"Almost finished. I'm looking for a job, but enough about me. I want to hear how you and Jazz connected. Details." She looped her arm through Emory's and led her up the steps.

"Dylan, you promised to behave." Jazz trailed behind, her voice almost pleading.

"Those words never crossed my lips, but I will allow Emory to wait and answer at brunch, otherwise she'll be repeating herself all day." She kissed Emory's cheek and added, "Besides, if you're going to be part of this family, you'd better get used to sharing everything. The Carlyles aren't good at keeping secrets from each—"

"But I—" Emory tried to object or at least clarify.

"I mean, really," Dylan inclined her head toward Jazz, "who'd want to keep her a secret anyway. She's totally hot and obviously into you."

Jazz jogged up beside Dylan and tried to pull her aside. "Can I talk to you?"

Dylan ushered Emory into the entry hall. "Sure, at brunch."

"Seriously, Dylan, can Emory and I have a minute before we go in? Please?" Jazz rocked back and forth on her heels, and Dylan finally released Emory's arm.

"Since you asked so nicely. See you in there."

When Dylan sauntered away, Jazz hugged Emory close. "How are you? My little sister can be a bit full-on."

She'd been to this house more times than she could count, but never as a girlfriend. The combination of possible receptions that awaited her with this family who shared everything sent her insides into another dive. "I'm not at all sure about this."

"Guess I'll have to be strong for both of us, because I'm certain."

"Brunch is served," G-ma called from the back of the house.

"There's just enough time to make it to the car." Jazz kissed her lightly.

The concern in Jazz's eyes bolstered Emory's courage just enough. "I can do this."

Cupping Emory's elbow, Jazz led her toward the dining room. "Just be yourself."

"Emory, welcome." Norma drew her into a warm hug as soon as they entered the dining space. "Jazz said she was bringing someone, but I had no idea it was you. A lovely surprise. Nice to have you at our table again." She waved toward two empty chairs. "I've made room for you beside Jazz."

"Thank you, Norma. I hope this wasn't inconvenient."

Gayle gave her a long hug when Norma released her. "Of course not. You're always welcome here." Her words sounded sincere, and her greeting just as authentic as the last time she'd been here. Gayle continued, "You remember the rest of the family?" She waved toward the others standing behind chairs around the table before motioning for everyone to sit.

"I think so, though I almost didn't recognize Riley and Ryan. They've grown so much since I saw them last."

Bennett moved toward her with Kerstin in tow. "And you remember my wife, Kerstin. So glad you're here, Emory."

"Thanks, Ben."

Kerstin hugged her tight and whispered, "Relax. They don't bite. I've got your back."

Emory almost burst into grateful laughter. Something about Kerstin's comment, as a former outsider, made her feel lighter and more prepared. "Thank you." She moved to the chair Jazz held for her while everyone watched. What were they thinking?

Jazz took a seat to Norma's left, and Emory settled between Jazz and Riley. Everybody took their places and the room suddenly quieted, except for a loud growl from Emory's stomach.

"Sounds like you're in the right place," Norma said. "Let's eat." She picked up a platter of bacon, sausage, and ham and forked some on her plate before passing it to Gayle, which seemed to be the starting buzzer.

Jazz spooned scrambled eggs on her plate while Emory thought about the times she'd sat at this table working on fundraising projects with the Carlyle matriarchs. The atmosphere had been easy and full of laughter, warmth wafting around them as evident as the aromas of bacon and freshly brewed coffee, just like today.

For the first several minutes, conversation consisted of asking for dishes and murmurs of appreciation. When everyone's plates were full, Kerstin said, "In honor of our special guest, why don't we go around the table and each person say whatever they like about their week, their life, what's happening or about to happen, whatever."

"That sounds perfect," Bennett said, giving her an appreciative nod. "Do you want to start, Kerst?"

"Love to. Ben and I are still moving stuff into my new office, which used to be our garage. The renovation turned out better than I could've imagined. Ben had this great idea to build a ledge near the ceiling for my old models. I even put my first Lego set on display. I can't wait to start working in the space next week." She looked at Emory, "You should come check it out sometime. We're right next door."

"I'd love to see it. Thank you."

Stephanie spoke next. "After last Sunday's discussion, Simon and I talked about my taking over Ma Rolls when G-ma and Mama retire. I think I want to give it a try if that's okay with everyone." She looked expectantly toward Norma and Gayle. "What do you say?"

"I love that plan," Norma said. "Keeps our hard work, and the business, in the family."

"So do I," Gayle agreed. "You can go out with us the final two weeks of the season, before we shut down for winter, and we'll introduce you to everybody."

Simon cupped Stephanie's hand. "I'm so proud of you. You'll be great."

Ryan stuffed a slice of bacon in his mouth and raised his hand. "I just got the new Monster Hunter World game, and it is *awesome*." He grabbed another piece of bacon and waved it toward Riley.

"My class visited the International Civil Rights Museum this week," she said.

Norma lowered her coffee cup and said, "That used to be a Woolworth's department store way back in the day. Your grandfather Garrett sat at that famous counter for breakfast almost every day when he walked a beat downtown."

"I know, G-ma." Riley grinned. "I listen."

"Of course you do, honey." Stephanie smiled lovingly at her.

Kerstin's suggestion broke the ice, and each member of the family contributed until it was finally Jazz's turn. She placed her fork and knife across her empty plate. "Well, I have a couple of things going on right now." She took Emory's hand and brought it to her lips. "One is this beautiful woman beside me."

"Jazz, please." Emory's face burned as she tried to pull her hand from Jazz's grasp, but she held firm.

"Seriously, Em. I'm grateful you finally agreed to go on a real date with me. I look forward to getting to know you better…and to whatever the future holds." Jazz stared into her eyes, and Emory forgot anyone else was in the room until Stephanie spoke.

"And the second thing?"

"Shea Spencer is still missing. We've followed up a few leads but nothing solid so far. I'm really worried because her dad is so unpredictable." The light in Jazz's eyes dimmed.

Emory clasped Jazz's hand under the table and whispered, "You'll find her, darling."

"If anyone can, it'll be our Jasmine," Norma said. "Now, I'm sure everybody wants to hear how the two of you…met isn't exactly the right word…how you…ended up here."

Norma Carlyle had never been uncomfortable or at a loss for words on any topic, and her awkwardness was endearing but also unsettling. "Maybe you should tell the story, Jazz."

Jazz rested her arm across the back of Emory's chair. "She threw money at me in the canteen like I was a stripper."

Norma cackled with laughter until she started coughing and needed a drink of water.

"*Jasmine Perry!*" Emory stared at her. "That's not what happened at all."

"Maybe you should tell it then."

"I was getting change out of my purse for a cup of tea, and when I saw you…" Her voice trailed off. She couldn't tell the Carlyle family that the sight of Jazz excited her so much she became a clumsy, uncommunicative bundle of nerves and dropped all her money.

Jazz grinned. "And did you or did you not spill your change at my feet?"

"Well…yes."

"And do you deny I had to make up work-related excuses to see you until you finally agreed to a real date."

"You what?" It never occurred to her Jazz had fabricated reasons to see her when they first reconnected, and the thought made her warm all over.

"You played hard to get."

Emory lost herself in the hunger in Jazz's eyes, remembering how she'd ached for her every time she was close and still did.

"Get a room, you two," Simon said. "How about dessert? Warm enough on the porch?"

"I believe it is, son," Gayle said. "Kerstin and Bennett, your turn to clear the table. Emory, would you help me and Norma with coffee and dessert in about five minutes?"

Emory's stomach twisted. She'd heard about the matriarchal summonses to the kitchen. She gave Jazz's hand a quick squeeze and whispered, "Wish me luck."

"I keep telling you to just be yourself. And answer any questions honestly. G-ma will know if you're holding back."

A few minutes later, Kerstin inclined her head toward the kitchen as she followed Bennett to the front porch. "You're up, Em."

Jazz took her hand and led her into the kitchen where Norma and Gayle stood at a center island laden with desserts. "Maybe I can help too?"

"We can manage, Jasmine," Norma said. "We'll be out shortly."

Emory swallowed hard. Should she say something first or wait for the inquisition? A few seconds ticked slowly by until she couldn't bear the silence. "These desserts look delicious. How do you know who wants what?"

"This family is as predictable about desserts as a dog at meal time. Simon and I always have a taste of everything. Bennett, Riley, and Ryan prefer chocolate pie. Gayle and Kerstin have a slice of red velvet cake. Dylan is strictly a key lime pie girl. Stephanie doesn't usually have dessert, just a hot chocolate with lots of whipped cream and mini marshmallows."

"And Jazz?" Emory felt shy asking. She knew Jazz's sexual tastes and every inch of her body after the past few days but practically nothing about her other preferences.

"What do you think?" Gayle asked.

Emory examined the three dishes for several seconds until a feeling washed through her. "I'd say Jazz likes chocolate and key lime pie."

Norma placed her hands on her wide hips and smiled. "Good guess."

"*Our* Jazz," Gayle's emphasis on our left no doubt she'd intended to sound possessive and protective, "is partial to sweet and tart, gooey filling and flakey crust, new recipes and old."

Was Gayle making a point with the old comment? Time to find out. Emory took a deep breath and said, "This is probably difficult, or at least awkward, having me here…with Jazz."

"Why would you say that?" Gayle asked as she scooped coffee into the machine and turned it on before facing Emory again.

"You, Norma, and I have always been honest with each other, and I love and respect you like family. I'm not sure what Ross and I would've done without you after Mother died. And we've always worked well together on volunteer projects."

"But?"

"I'm in a different role today." She wrung her hands and willed her courage not to desert her before she finished. "If you disapprove of me seeing Jazz, I'd like to know now. I am older, by quite a lot, and—"

"What?" Norma stared at her as if she were suddenly a stranger. "No, honey. Your age has nothing to do with anything. A more seasoned woman is probably exactly what Jazz needs."

Norma cast Gayle a pleading look, and she took over. "Jazz is still unsettled in some ways, not exactly sure where she belongs. I'm afraid I'm not saying this very well. What I mean is, Jasmine's dating life so far has been giving in when she tires of being chased. She's never cared enough to go after anyone."

"I'm not sure what you're saying, Gayle," Emory admitted. "I told Norma at the ballgame that I wouldn't compete for Jazz. She had to come to me."

Gayle nodded. "And apparently she has."

A flush of heat began in Emory's center and spread slowly through her. "Yes." The realization made Emory feel more loved and special than she ever had. Jazz *had* come to her, accepted her, and introduced her to her family as someone that mattered in her life.

Gayle moved to Emory's side and placed her hand on her forearm. "You'll always have a place at our table, whether you're with Jazz or not. I only have one piece of advice."

"Please." She welcomed any guidance Gayle might have because she wanted Jazz and wanted to be a part of this family.

Gayle hugged Emory for several seconds and then pulled back to look her in the eyes. "Always be honest with her. She's got enough questions about the past to last a lifetime. Don't make her question you."

Emory nodded as a knot formed in her throat and tears filled her eyes. How had she ever thought the Carlyles would be anything but the warm, welcoming, and loving people she'd known for years. She sent up a silent thank you that she'd had the guts to talk with Jazz earlier about her surgery and that Jazz had been so understanding. How could she have been anything else with role models like Norma and Gayle? "I have been and always will be honest with her."

"Then welcome to the family, Emory," Gayle said.

"Yes, welcome," Norma added and joined them in a group hug.

Chapter Seventeen

Emory dodged other hospital employees in the hallway to catch up with Karen and Sheri as they all left the Monday afternoon staff conference. Karen had officially pitched her privatization proposal to the group and received a mixed response. No surprise there, but the announcement made Emory's next move more urgent. "Sheri, hold up, please."

Sheri glanced back but kept walking toward the exit instead of their office. "I worked last night, and this damn meeting interrupted my sleep. Can't whatever this is wait?"

"Not really." She finally came alongside and guided Sheri into an unoccupied waiting room. Karen followed, her incredibly high heels tapping against the tile with each step. Emory bit back a snarky comment and addressed Sheri. "I just need a minute. Alone."

Karen cocked her hip against the wall and lifted her finger in the air as if she'd suddenly had an idea. "If this has anything to do with the meeting, I'd like to hear what you have to say." She scanned Emory's body head to toe and finally settled her gaze on Emory's lips. "You look different today. Exciting weekend?"

Emory debated telling her why but decided it wouldn't stop her from chasing Jazz and it was tacky to gloat. She hefted her briefcase on her shoulder and crossed her arms. "This is CPS business."

"Which I'm going to be a significant part of in the future if CPS still exists."

"Yeah," Sheri said. "Anything you need to say, Karen can hear too."

Maybe this was the perfect setup for her question. She'd see both their reactions at the same time and determine which one was telling the truth. "Fine. Sheri, did you give Karen CPS monthly reports?"

"Of course, I did." The matter-of-fact response brought a satisfied grin to Sheri's lips, and Karen's perfect expression didn't change.

"Why?"

"She asked for them to compare USAA and CPS operations. They become public eventually anyway. I just made them more readily available. Seriously, Emory, what's the problem? Everybody knows where this is heading. You'd be better off applying for a job with USAA instead of riding the CPS dead horse."

Karen grinned and added, "What she said. I could use a woman like you."

"You can't afford me," Emory said.

"You might be surprised what I can offer. Fringe benefits alone are worth the change." Karen looped her arm through Sheri's and started to leave but turned back to Emory. "Oh, would you have Jazz call me if she's not too preoccupied. We have unfinished business of a sort." She air-kissed Emory and sashayed down the hall on her perfectly long legs in her perfectly tight skirt with her perfectly shaped ass taunting Emory.

The only thing that kept Emory from chasing Karen down and telling her about her weekend with Jazz was her weekend with Jazz—having sex with her, going to brunch with the family, being accepted into the family, and returning to her apartment with Jazz and having sex until this morning. Jazz had made her feelings clear. Emory made a fist and then flicked her fingers at Karen. "Bye-bye." Not even Miss Perfect could totally dampen Emory's mood today.

She was almost back to her office when her phone pinged with a text message from Jane. *Meet me in the canteen?* She responded and made a U-turn. Jane smiled and raised two cups as Emory approached the table. "Guess I don't need to ask how things are going with you and Di."

"I can hardly walk." She gave Emory a quick once-over. "You look happy too."

"I have the similar symptoms, trouble walking or sitting, unable to stop smiling. How tawdry of us." Emory cupped a hand over the mouth to keep from laughing and then waved Jane closer. "We can compare notes later, but right now I need other information. I'm about to kill a blonde, and the consequences would seriously hamper my good mood."

"We wouldn't want that." Jane slid a thumb drive across the table. "My friend came through. I think you'll find everything you need. I heard the USAA rep made her pitch at the staff meeting. Is that the blonde on your kill list?"

"The woman rubs me raw, and not in an enjoyable way."

"Emory, I'm afraid the writing is on the wall with this privatization issue. Everything I'm hearing supports the hospital moving in that direction."

Her instincts had been telling her the same thing for months. "I know, but the least I can do is make sure we go with the best company. I'm just not convinced USAA is the right fit. And maybe this," she pointed to the thumb drive, "will help me prove it. Thanks for the info and the tea. We'll catch up properly soon." She gave Jane a hug and hurried to her office.

An hour later, Emory pushed back from her desk as the columns of figures on the computer screen blurred. She rubbed her tired eyes with a satisfied sigh. Jane's information had proven exactly what Emory feared—Karen was misrepresenting facts by manipulating the numbers. She was also making quite a personal profit by jacking up the USAA adoption and placement fees. Were the company administrators aware of the rate hikes or were they complicit in the matter, possibly receiving a percentage off the books?

The only way Emory would know for sure was if she presented the information to someone in management or the USAA board. Her mentor at CPS had been associated with USAA when they worked together, but that was years ago. She pulled up the website and scanned the list of board members, relieved to see Henrietta's picture. Emory scrolled through her contacts and punched Henrietta's number.

"Henrietta Goldstein."

"Henri, it's Emory Blake. How are you?"

Henrietta's signature chuckle rumbled into a full laugh. "I'm excellent. Yourself?"

"Very well, thanks."

"I'd like to think this is an invitation for a martini since I'm in Greensboro for a conference, but I hear that edge in your voice. What do you need, dear?"

Henri always had the knack for making Emory feel anything was possible if the two of them put their heads together. "If you're in town, martinis are on me. When and where?"

"Lobby of the Sheraton Four Seasons at five sharp. We'll go to the Club Lounge."

"Perfect. See you then." Henrietta had left CPS to take over the family accounting business when her father died, so she'd be the perfect person to recheck Emory's numbers, and she had a personal stake in USAA. If she'd thought of this sooner, she could've gone directly to Henrietta for the stats, but she'd been a tiny bit preoccupied.

Emory propped her feet on the edge of her desk and replaced the unpleasantness of the staff meeting with thoughts of Jazz kissing and touching her. She smoothed a hand up the inside of her thigh and moaned.

"That looks like fun."

Emory dropped her feet to the floor hard enough to jar her insides and edged her skirt down as she rose. Jazz leaned against the doorframe grinning. "You almost gave me a heart attack."

"Looked like I was giving you something else entirely, if the satisfied look on your face is any indication. Am I too late?"

"I was remembering this weekend. Lock the door and come here." Emory scooted onto her desk, hiked her skirt up to her waist, and spread her legs. She'd never been so forward or so needy with a lover, but Jazz made her feel sexy, special, and like nothing was off limits. "I need your hands on me."

"Why, Ms. Blake, I do believe this is unprofessional conduct and inappropriate use of hospital facilities." Jazz shoved the desk chair against the wall and stopped in front of Emory just out of reach. "So, you've missed me the past few hours?"

"Desperately." Emory reached for her, but Jazz backed away.

"How desperately?"

"So desperately that if you don't touch me right now, I'll do it myself." One look in Jazz's hungry eyes and Emory's challenge turned to a plea. "Please."

Jazz stepped between her legs and pulled Emory into a kiss so heated that Emory felt a gush of arousal. Jazz teased and tortured Emory with her tongue on Emory's mouth, her neck, and the rim of her ear.

"Quick, darling. Fingers."

Jazz ripped the lacy fabric covering Emory's center and slid into her slowly, too slowly.

"Jaaaaazzzz."

Jazz pulled Emory's hips closer to the edge of the desk with one hand while her other answered Emory's prayers.

"That's it. Harder. This...will be...quick." Jazz breathed erratically, increasing Emory's desire with each burst of air against the side of her neck. "Yes. Deeper. Yes. Coming." She pressed tighter into Jazz's hand when she climaxed and then collapsed against her chest gasping for air. "I needed that so much."

"I love to make you come." Jazz stared down at her, and Emory felt her body trembling. "You're the most beautiful woman I've ever seen and when you come, you're breathtaking."

Jazz's expression didn't waver, her stare holding Emory's and she felt her sincerity. "You have no idea how much that means to me." She reached for Jazz. "Now let me take care of you."

"Maybe we shouldn't. I'm fine." Jazz tried to back away, but Emory grabbed her belt and pulled her closer.

"You'll be even quicker." Emory unzipped Jazz's jeans and tucked her hand into her briefs. "You're almost there already. Fingers or lips?"

"Oh, Em..."

Jazz's throaty moan was the only answer Emory needed. She stripped the jeans down Jazz's legs and knelt in front of her. Cupping Jazz's tight ass in her hands, Emory buried her face in the fork of Jazz's thighs and feasted.

Jazz held Emory's head against her, rose up and down on her toes once, twice, and with a long sigh of relief, went slack. "I... need...to sit."

Emory knee-crawled with her to the chair, unwilling to relinquish her position between Jazz's legs. "I love the taste of you." When she looked up, Jazz was smiling at her. "Did you enjoy that, darling?"

"So much that I wouldn't mind if you did it again, but we probably shouldn't. What if somebody comes to the door?"

"They'll knock. I'll stop, and you'll pull your pants up. Simple." Emory teased Jazz's clit with the tip of her tongue, and Jazz rewarded her with another resigned moan. Emory edged closer but stopped when she felt a strange sensation against her knee. "Your jeans are vibrating."

"Sorry. Would you hand me my phone? I've been expecting another update on our search for Shea and her fugitive father."

Emory slid the cell from Jazz's pocket and glanced at the caller ID as she handed it over. "Karen Patrick."

"Damn. She can wait," Jazz said.

"You should probably get it." The mood was broken, so Emory stood, pulling Jazz's jeans up with her. "I dislike that woman so much more right now." She lowered her skirt and started to walk away, but Jazz grabbed her around the waist and held her close as she answered the phone.

"Lieutenant Perry."

"Jazz, it's Karen. How are you?"

Karen's tone was more than a little flirty, and Emory tucked her head against Jazz's shoulder to hear what she said.

"I'm good, a little busy," Jazz said, giving Emory a light kiss on the forehead.

"You're always busy. Anyone I know?" Karen's teasing tempted Emory to answer, but she nibbled Jazz's neck instead. "Any chance we can get together? I've been pitching the official proposal all day and would love to use you as a sounding board."

Jazz looked down at her questioningly, and Emory trailed her hand down Jazz's chest and cupped her sex, bringing Jazz to her toes. "I…guess that would be okay."

"My place at six?"

Emory shook her head emphatically, but Jazz shrugged and said, "Six," before dropping the phone. "You tease."

Breaking their contact, Emory backed away. "You're going to her condo, again? Have you forgotten what happened last time?"

"Nothing happened." Jazz grinned and tried to kiss her, but Emory turned her head.

"Not because she didn't try."

"Are you jealous, Ms. Blake?"

Emory shook her head but remembered Gayle's advice about honesty and nodded. "She's never been subtle about wanting you, and women like her are everything I'm not." She finally let Jazz pull her into a hug.

"And everything I don't want anymore. I'm with you for as long as you'll have me." She lifted Emory's chin to meet her gaze. "Because I'm in love with you, Emory Blake."

Everything around Emory disappeared, and her pulse pounded in her ears as she tried to process the words she'd waited all her life to hear from someone she loved so much. "What?"

Jazz grinned and repeated, "I'm in love with you. Surely you know that."

Emory shook her head, uncertain the words were true or this moment real. "I'd hoped, prayed for this. Jazz, are you sure?"

"Totally. And I want to spend the rest of my life with you…if you feel—"

"Yes. I mean, me too. The love and lifetime part." She waved her hands in frustration. "Restart. I'm in love with you too." She caressed the side of Jazz's face, stared into her eyes, searched for any flicker of doubt, and found none. "I love you so much it scares me."

"Nothing to be afraid of, Em. I'll always protect you. How about we continue this conversation at your place?" She chuckled. "Doesn't have the same ring as my place, but I don't have one yet."

Emory relaxed in Jazz's arms, letting this moment and Jazz's words dissolve her anxiety and fill her with hope and possibility. "I'd love nothing more, but I have to meet a colleague for drinks, and after what just happened, I need to freshen up before I go. It's an important meeting, about USAA. I'd never turn you down otherwise, especially not now. How about tomorrow night for sure?" Jazz nodded, and Emory kissed her again. "Jazz, I love you. Please be careful with Karen tonight. She's dangerous."

"I'll be fine, Em. Danger is my business." She grinned and walked Emory to her car.

Two hours later, Emory sat with Henrietta Goldstein in very plush leather chairs at the Club Lounge of the Sheraton Four Seasons. Henrietta hadn't changed since she left CPS—still elegantly outfitted, hair pulled into a tight bun at the nape of her neck, and her signature smile belying her seventy-five years.

"You look absolutely joyful, Emory, and we'll get to the reason for that later." Henrietta took a sip of her gin martini, dabbed the corners of her mouth, and said, "Now that we've dispensed with the pleasantries, what's really on your mind, dear?"

"Have I always been so transparent, Henri?"

"Only to me."

Emory fidgeted with her glass. "I miss having you nearby for our weekly martini chats."

Henrietta placed her hand over Emory's and held until she looked up. "I can tell whatever you have to say is hard. Just spit it out. I'm not getting any younger, and you deserve the benefit of my mind before this martini kicks in."

Emory laughed and recited the speech she'd practiced on the way over. Since Henrietta was on the USAA board, Emory had to tread lightly. "So, I'm not saying anything illegal is going on, but I do believe there's cause for concern with the proposal." She hesitated, but her mentor knew her too well.

"And what else, Emory?"

"I looked into the percentage of USAA adoptees who've been reported as neglected or abused, and I'm relieved those numbers don't seem extreme. But I'm afraid the operational stats are too high. I was wondering—"

"You were wondering if I'd utilize my vast accounting skills to check into the matter."

Emory nodded.

"Because you do in fact suspect something illegal but don't want to say so because I'm on the board and because we're friends."

"In a nutshell, yes."

"I not only will, but I must," Henrietta said. "I'm not sure if you know this, but my father was on the founding board of USAA. While I was working with CPS, he and I talked often about the system and how some clients received better service than others. He predicted privatization would be an issue in the future and wanted to assure it was handled properly by the company. Doesn't sound like that's happening. I assume you brought information for me?"

Emory pulled the flash drive from the side of her purse and handed it to Henrietta. "And before you ask, I received these documents legally."

"Good to know." She tucked the drive into the pocket of her suit jacket, picked up her martini, and asked, "So, who is she?"

The sip Emory had just taken of her drink almost spewed out her nose. "What?"

"The new woman in your life. The joyful comment from earlier. Do keep up, dear."

Emory wiped her mouth and eyes, stalling for words that described Jazz and their relationship adequately, but failed. "It's very new, so I'm not sure where it's going."

"But you're already in love with her," Henrietta said.

"I...yes, I am. I think I've been waiting for her a very long time without realizing it."

"Does she feel the same?"

"She told me she loves me for the first time today. Our lives are a little complicated, Henri, so I worry. She's a cop who was adopted very young, and I'm a social worker with a steady diet of abuse, neglect, and adoption. We have conflicting views on the privatization issue, and it's caused problems."

"What's her name?"

"Jasmine Perry." Emory couldn't suppress a smile as she said her name and remembered their romp in her office earlier and the words Jazz had spoken so convincingly. "Jazz."

Henrietta propped her elbow on the arm of the chair and stroked her chin. "Perry. Jasmine Perry." She snapped her fingers. "I was her caseworker."

"You're kidding. Do you remember anything about her?"

Henrietta chuckled. "It was a long time ago, and I was much younger."

"Of course. I'm sorry."

"You haven't read her file?"

"*No!*"

Henrietta patted her arm. "I'm very proud of you. I obviously taught you well. Have you been tempted?"

Emory considered her answer, wondering if Henrietta was still teaching or simply testing. "I'd be lying if I said I haven't thought about looking at her file, but it would feel like an invasion of privacy, and I can't do that to her. I want to know everything about her because she chooses to tell me. I want us to be honest with each other."

Henrietta studied her for several long seconds, and Emory swore she could almost see her next question forming. "So, you've been totally honest with her?"

"Yes. We talked about my surgery and what that means for our future if we decide to have a family. And she was wonderful. She is wonderful. I'm so happy, Henri."

"I like this woman already. She has my stamp of approval," Henrietta said. "I expect an invitation to become reacquainted with her sooner rather than later."

❖

Jazz stood outside Karen's condo door reliving her weekend in bed with Emory and the afternoon on her desk until the tender and passionate images filled her head and heart and there was no room for Karen to tempt or intrude. She and Emory were in love and wanted to spend their lives together. She'd never been happier. Her strategy backfired. The memories of Emory's insatiable need, her gentle touch, and the possibilities of a lifetime made her burn and ache all over again—not a good state to be in around Karen. The woman homed in on sexual arousal and frustration like a tracer round marked a target. She paced the hallway to calm down before finally knocking on the door.

Karen opened almost immediately and propped against the doorframe wearing a V-neck T-shirt that stopped mid-thigh. *Does she own anything that isn't revealing and sexy as fuck?* Jazz quickly glanced away from Karen's exposed cleavage and stepped into the room. "Hi."

"Hi, yourself. I'm so glad you could stop by." She kissed Jazz's cheek, closed the door behind them, and led her to the sofa. "Beer?"

"That would be great. Thanks." She wiped her sweaty hands down the legs of her jeans and focused on an upcoming community meeting Bennett had tasked her with organizing. They'd discussed a child-friendly event to include games, face painting, and music on the lawn behind Fairview Station. Jazz loved the idea and hoped Shea would be there with the Robinsons.

"A penny."

"Huh?" Jazz looked up, and Karen stood beside the sofa with a beer in one hand and a rocks glass in the other. "Guess I spaced out."

"Why the serious expression?" She clinked the glass against Jazz's bottle.

"Sorry. Shea is still missing. I got an update on our search on the way over. We've checked and double-checked all her father's contacts in the city with no luck. We found the van he drove from Atlanta abandoned, so he's probably got another vehicle. Who knows what this guy is into or how much danger Shea is in? You haven't heard from her, have you?" Jazz downed several gulps of beer.

"Why would you ask that?" Karen rolled her glass between her palms.

"I just thought maybe, since you've been dealing with her for so long, she might've reached out if she had a chance. She'd probably remember your number easier than mine."

"You'll find her. Don't give up." Karen joined her on the sofa, so close that Jazz slid toward the edge.

Had Karen always made her this uncomfortable or had being intimate with Emory and realizing she loved her made her more aware of other feelings as well?

"Okay, work it is," Karen said. "As I mentioned on the phone, I spent all day Friday and today pitching my proposal to the state board and various stakeholders who work with CPS and USAA. I think it went well. Of course, there were some dissenters..." Karen's voice trailed off as if she expected Jazz to fill in a missing piece, but she didn't take the bait. "Emory was the most vocal. She had quite a lot to say at the hospital meeting. Any idea why she's so opposed to my proposition?"

Jazz took another sip of beer and chose her words carefully before answering. "Nothing I haven't already told you. She's a career CPS employee, knows the system inside and out, and is convinced they are the best option for helping children in all areas, not just adoption."

"And she doesn't like me."

What was the point of denying the obvious? "That's not really a secret." She tipped her bottle toward Karen. "And the feeling is mutual."

"Mine is purely a professional distinction, but I think Emory feels personally threatened by me. Doesn't she?"

Jazz wasn't about to discuss Emory's insecurities with anyone, especially not Karen. "You'd have to ask Emory about that."

Karen took a delicate sip of her drink and placed the glass on the coffee table. "I admire your loyalty, Jazz, but let's consider the facts." She waved her hand down her body. "I'd put this package against Emory any day, but looks aren't everything. I'm a successful business manager who commands an impressive six-figure salary plus bonuses. I have contacts all over the world who make their vacation homes available whenever I ask. My *appetites* range from the traditional to the exotic in food, travel, wardrobe, and pleasure."

Jazz reached for the coarse hair at her ear but stopped, unwilling to let Karen see her discomfort. Emory's words rang in her head, *"Karen Patrick is dangerous."* Unlike her previous encounters with Karen, Jazz now sensed that danger more acutely and not as simple flirting.

"I love competition and challenges, physically, emotionally, and sexually. And let's not forget, I'm a *whole* woman."

Jazz choked on a swallow of beer that went down the wrong way. "A what?"

Karen tried to look shocked, but her expression came off as predatory. "Oh, she hasn't told you, has she?"

A sick feeling settled in Jazz's stomach as she rose from the sofa. "Who hasn't told me what? If this is a trick to get my help with your proposal, you should stop. I won't hear anything derogatory about Emory."

"You've grown fond of her. Possibly more than fond. I see it in your eyes, and the way you shy away from me now. I promise you, Jazz, this is no trick. Please listen. There are things you need to know."

Jazz crossed her arms over her chest. "Then tell me." Karen paused as if she were struggling with what she wanted to say, but Jazz suspected the tactic was for dramatic effect.

"Emory can't have children."

How dare Karen invade Emory's privacy in such an egregious manner and then try to use something so personal to her own advantage. Jazz fought her anger, forced herself to remain calm and figure out Karen's game. "How do you know that?"

"Part of my job is finding out personal information."

"For what purpose?" Jazz returned to her original thought. This was a ploy, Karen's way of manipulating her and turning her against Emory and CPS. Everything about Karen was flashy, extravagant, and available for the right amount of money. She'd made the right decision not to get personally involved with her.

Karen rose and clasped Jazz's hands. "Jazz, look at me. Look at me." When Jazz made eye contact, Karen continued. "I'm sorry, but if you have any interest in having a family of your own, you deserve to know."

Jazz wanted to gloat and tell Karen the truth—that Emory had already told her she couldn't have children and it hadn't changed anything between them—but decided to play along and see just how far Karen would go. "Why are you telling me this?" For a moment, Jazz thought Karen wasn't going to answer, but when she lifted her head again, her eyes had a triumphant twinkle.

"Because I'm in love with you."

CHAPTER EIGHTEEN

K aren attempted to move closer, but Jazz shook her head. "Don't." The declaration of love sounded hollow and false and left Jazz feeling the same.

Karen took another step.

"I said *don't*." Another wildfire of disbelief coursed through Jazz, and she clenched her fists and focused the pain into her hands. First Karen tried to manipulate her by invading Emory's privacy and now this. Jazz slowed her breathing, and as the anger leeched from her, she yielded to curiosity. "Do you really think I can't see through you, that I don't know what you're trying to do with this sudden love proposal?"

"I know it sounds sudden, but life got complicated…something I usually try to avoid. Will you stay with me, let me explain?"

"I've heard all I need to from you, Karen. And if you spread Emory's business to another person, you'll answer to me." Jazz finished her beer and dropped the bottle in the trash on her way out. When the door closed behind her, Jazz heard something crash against the wall. More of Karen's true colors coming through.

She left her car in the parking lot and walked. Misty rain clung to her face and brought everything into sharper focus. Karen would use anything to get her way. Jazz wasn't sure what she expected to find out tonight, but this certainly wasn't it. Now that Karen's agenda and her tricks were exposed, Jazz felt relieved. She could deal with any problem if she knew what it was.

The next time she looked up, she was staring at Emory's condo door. She should go home because it was late, but Emory would be worried about her seeing Karen. She'd just reassure her and be on her way. She'd told Emory she loved her, and she deserved to know everything. She knocked, got no answer, and knocked harder.

Emory opened the door in pajamas, her hair an auburn tangle, and her eyes heavy with sleep. "Jazz? What're you doing here...at this hour?"

She looked so gorgeously tousled and innocent that Jazz couldn't stop staring. Of course, she'd come to Emory. She loved her and wanted to share her life with her. Where else would she go? "Can I come in? There's something I have to tell you."

"Of course, darling. Are you okay?"

Jazz nodded.

"Is it Shea?"

"Nothing new. She's still out there."

"And I'm sure you've been spending every spare minute looking for her." Emory guided Jazz inside. "You're soaking wet and shivering. Have a seat while I get a towel." Without waiting for a response, Emory hurried to the bathroom. Damn you, Karen Patrick. If she'd hurt Jazz in any way, Emory would make her life's mission to repay the debt. She grabbed a towel and returned to the kitchen where Jazz sat at the small table. "Are you cold?"

Jazz shook her head but didn't look up. "Sorry I woke you."

Emory dried some of the moisture from Jazz's hair and then draped the towel around her shoulders. "You're upset, so I'm glad you came to me." She pulled a chair closer and rested her hands on Jazz's knees. "What happened, darling? Talk to me."

"Karen tried to use your hysterectomy to get me on her side." She clenched and unclenched her fists as she spoke.

Emory took a deep breath, struggling to contain her anger. "How could she possibly know about that? I've told only three people, Diane, Henrietta, and you. Definitely *not* Karen."

"She has ways of finding out what she wants to know. I thought you needed to be prepared. If she'll use something that personal, you're probably in for an ugly fight on the privatization contract."

"I don't care about that right now. We should probably tell the rest of your family about my surgery. It won't matter to them any more than it did to you, but who knows what Karen will try to do with the information if we treat it like some big scary secret that we're ashamed of." She rubbed her hands up and down Jazz's legs and felt her muscles relax. "What else? You're upset about something else. What other weapons did she trot out of her arsenal?"

"Just one."

Jazz's voice was so low that Emory leaned closer to hear. "Which one, darling? About you? Me? Us? Please tell me so I can help."

"Crap really." Jazz shook her head, and Emory thought she wasn't going to explain. When she finally did, her words were cold and harsh. "She said she loves me."

"What?" Was there no end to Karen's manipulation? Emory felt a momentary flash of full-blown insecurity and panic. This was her worst nightmare. She slowed her breath and remembered what she and Jazz had shared and the words they'd spoken to each other. No need for panic. She and Jazz were in love.

"Yeah, can you believe that?"

"Of course, I can. She'd say anything to get what she wants." Emory cupped Jazz's hands and forced the next question out. "And how did you feel when Karen said she loves you?"

"Angry. Sick. Because I finally see her the way you do, as a manipulating liar with no moral compass. I'm even more worried about the children she's supposed to help."

"What do we do now?"

"Wait for her to make her next move, I guess. She was pretty pissed off when I turned her down. In the meantime, we live our lives," Jazz said.

Emory hugged Jazz and kissed her lightly. "Do you want to spend the night...I mean since you're already here?"

"I should go, but I'll see you tomorrow night." She stood and pulled Emory with her to the door. "I'm glad I stopped by. I needed to tell you what happened, and to say again that I love you, Emory Blake."

"That's very good news indeed, Lieutenant. Remember, be careful out there." Emory kissed her and nudged her toward the door before the urge to drag her upstairs won out.

"Trust me, Em."

❖

Jazz ran, barely registering the rain that pelted her face like tiny needles. She retrieved her car from Karen's, drove home, and ran next door. She texted Bennett from outside, hoping not to wake Kerstin. Jazz wanted to tell Bennett the good news and couldn't wait a second longer. How would her family handle the news about Emory, declaring their love so soon, and about her inability to have children?

A light came on inside the house and Bennett opened the door. "Jazz, are you okay? Is it G-ma? Mama?"

"I guess they're fine. I haven't been home in a while. Can we talk?" She seldom cried but felt on the verge as Bennett pulled her inside.

"Whatever you need, which looks like a change of clothes. You're drenched." Bennett disappeared in the direction of the laundry room and returned with a towel and a pair of sweats. "Put these on before you catch pneumonia."

"But I have to tell you—"

"Get out of these things first." Bennett hugged her and started peeling off the wet clothes.

"I can do this." She reached for the sweat pants Bennett held and quickly pulled them on.

"Let's sit." Bennett guided Jazz to the sofa in front of the huge fireplace. "Okay, talk."

"I'm sorry about the time, but I couldn't wait—" She stopped at the sound of footsteps behind them.

"Is everything all right, Ben?" Kerstin asked from the foot of the stairs.

"Family powwow. Join us."

"That's okay. I'll leave you to it."

Kerstin turned to go back upstairs, but Jazz said, "You're part of the family too. Stay."

Kerstin pulled a blanket from an ottoman, flipped on the gas logs, and covered their legs as she settled on the other side of Jazz and fingered her wet hair. "Whatever's going on, Jazz, we've got you. We love you very much."

"Thanks." Kerstin's words caused a surge of emotions, but Jazz choked it down.

"The last time I saw you, you and Emory were leaving brunch headed toward another night of horizontal dancing, unless I'm mistaken," Bennett said.

"That seems like a while ago."

"So, this is about Emory?" Kerstin asked, her tone oozing kindness and concern.

"Some of it."

"There's more?" Bennett's expression turned serious.

"Yes, and don't give me that Jazz-has-stepped-in-it look." She repeated what Karen had told her about Emory and about Emory looking into the finances of USAA, and then waited.

Kerstin toyed with the edge of the blanket before asking, "And you believe Karen?"

"It's true. Emory and I talked about her surgery before brunch on Sunday. She's fine with me telling the family."

"Wow," Kerstin said, "I'm even more impressed with Emory now. You haven't been dating long, and she's already sharing something that significant with your entire family."

"She is pretty special. And I told her I'm in love with her."

"Seriously?" Bennett asked, staring at her as if waiting for the punch line.

"Oh my." Kerstin's comment was practically a whisper.

Bennett turned sideways to face Jazz. "And…"

"And she said she loves me and wants to spend the rest of our lives together."

"This is huge," Bennett said. "You've never said those words to anyone before. Now I get why you couldn't wait to share the news."

"I know, right? And the children thing is not a big deal. She's had years to adjust to the idea and isn't sure she wants kids right now."

"And you? You've always talked about a big family," Bennett said.

Jazz nudged Bennett. "Guess I'll have to settle for playing with all of yours, which might change my mind about kids entirely. Or Emory could change her mind. And there are so many children without homes. We can always adopt or I could carry a child. It's early days. I just know I love her and she loves me. I never thought I'd get this far. If this is my happily ever after, I'm good with it."

"I like your attitude, sis," Bennett said.

"I'm happy for both of you, Jazz," Kerstin said. "Coffee anyone?"

"Please," Jazz said. "A triple shot of espresso would be good. I've got a long day ahead and not much sleep to back it up."

Kerstin headed toward the kitchen. "Coffee in five."

Bennett followed Kerstin, and Jazz stopped by the half bath and pressed a cold cloth to her forehead. Her hair looked like she'd slept upside down. She finger-combed the mess and tried to make it look deliberate. What a wild few days. She couldn't wait for the privatization business to be over so she and Emory could start living their lives together. When she joined Bennett and Kerstin, they sat at the kitchen table nursing coffee cups and a third waited for her.

Bennett rolled her hand and asked, "Issue number two?"

"Karen Patrick told me she's in love with me."

Bennett and Kerstin exchanged a glance before Kerstin said, "I love you, my adorable sister-in-law, but you're sometimes naïve about women."

"Oh, don't get me wrong, I didn't fall for it, but it does make me wonder what she hopes to gain beyond an ally on the privatization issue."

"I can think of several reasons she'd reveal Emory's condition and declare her love," Kerstin said.

Jazz raised her palms in a don't-keep-me-waiting gesture.

"First, she's obviously trying to get you on her side. It's not a slam dunk, and law enforcement support would be helpful. Second, she wants to drive a wedge between you and Emory. She's gambling that the fact Emory can't have children, will bring the two of you closer. Is she aware that you already knew about Emory?"

Jazz shook her head.

"Good. Keep it that way. We might be able to use it later. I've only been around Karen once, but it was obvious she has the hots for you. And it sounds like she's not quite as sure as she likes to appear that the contract will be approved."

Bennett looked like a bobble head. "What my wife said. If Emory's search of the stats and finances pans out, Karen could be in real trouble. Just be careful, Jazz."

Kerstin reached across the table and took Jazz's hand. "This is a lot to process all at once. Declaring your love for Emory, and her admitting she's in love with you is one thing, but all this other stuff can be distracting when the two of you should be spending time, bonding, and planning your next steps together. Don't let the other stuff discourage you."

Bennett kissed Kerstin on the cheek. "I married a very smart woman."

"Why, yes, yes, you did, Captain," Kerstin replied.

Bennett stood, gave Kerstin and Jazz a quick hug, and headed toward the stairs. "I need to shower for work."

Kerstin squeezed Jazz's hand and said, "We love you and we're always here." She wiggled her eyebrows and shouted at Bennett, "Hold on, Captain. We need to conserve water."

"Thanks, guys. I knew you'd understand. And I'm sorry again for waking you up." Jazz placed the dirty dishes in the dishwasher and started toward the front door. Twenty-four hours ago, she'd been happily making love with Emory. She should've never gone to Karen's. An old saying about a tube of toothpaste came to mind. Once you squeezed the filling out, it wasn't going back in, just like Karen's lies and deception.

Chapter Nineteen

Emory stuffed the file she'd tried to read three times back into a drawer and prepared to leave work. Before she could lock the door, her cell rang. "Emory Blake."

"It's Henri. You were right about the USAA figures."

"You can tell already?" She wasn't imagining the discrepancies in Karen's stats. What else was she hiding from her company and the board?

"I was up half the night, not good for a seventy-five-year-old, but I had to be sure. I'll see this woman fired and prosecuted if possible. I sent you a document outlining the inconsistencies and a formal statement from the board on our position. Can you do something for me now?"

"Of course, Henri, anything."

"Be at the corporate office on Elm Street tomorrow at two. You've saved the company a ton of embarrassment by letting us get in front of this issue. More later."

"Wait. What do you want me to do?"

"We might not need you at all, but if the board wants to hear from you, tell the truth. Explain your suspicions about USAA operations, and I'll do the rest. The numbers tell the real story. Have to go."

The line went dead, and she did a jig all the way to her car. "Take that, Karen Patrick." Emory was working her own plan to get

Karen out of their lives, just like Jazz had rebuffed her love proposal last night. She couldn't help feeling happy and confident.

She recalled Jazz's words last night and smiled. *"Trust me."* Jazz had taught her trust slowly—drinks in the canteen, meals disguised as work, stories about her life and family, sexual restraint, no secrets, and finally love and acceptance of her body—slowly, so Emory could feel her intent and sincerity and not panic. *Jazz loves me, and we have a future.*

After dinner, Jazz helped with the dishes and excused herself for the evening. If she sat around with G-ma and Mama like usual watching TV or reading, they'd know she was withholding something important. They always knew. She wanted to share the good news about her and Emory, but they should do that together, like a couple.

Closing the bedroom door behind her, she continued to the window overlooking the back yard. The sky was dark, exposing stars and soft light from the cottage Dylan now called home. Had Jazz made a mistake by passing her turn in the carriage house? Dylan had wanted the privacy, and Jazz's need to be around family had seemed like a good idea at the time. She could've had a place to be alone with Emory, explore their love, and plan their future.

Their relationship was new, and there were so many things to learn and accept about each other, including Emory's inability to have children. Jazz learned from the Carlyles that love transcended blood. Her lesbian family of choice reinforced the same truth. Children were important to her, but not as important as the woman she loved. She turned from the window and opened the drawer containing her mother's Celtic love knot necklace, stretched it between her hands, and slipped it over her head. *Two hearts united are stronger than steel.* She wanted and needed Emory to challenge and complement her, and the sooner they got on with their lives, the better she'd liked it.

Jazz pulled the pillow under her head, closed her eyes, and summoned an image of Emory whispering, "*I love you, Jasmine Perry,*" just before she fell asleep.

❖

Jazz headed to the shower next morning to the comforting sounds of the family stirring around her. G-Ma slammed her bathroom door at the end of the hall and muttered an apology loud enough to wake anyone trying to sleep. Mama rattled pots in the kitchen and hummed softly to herself. No point trying to sleep after the sun came up, so a cold shower and strong coffee would have to get her through the day.

She couldn't wait to have a home like this, full of familiar sounds and smells, and the security of total acceptance and unconditional love. She'd doubted it would happen most of her life, but Emory had given her hope for so many wonderful things. She was pulling on her boots when her cell buzzed. "Jazz Perry."

"Jazz?" a whispered voice asked.

"Yes."

"It's me, Shea."

"Shea? Are you all right?" Jazz slid her Walther into the holster inside her jeans waistband and ran down the stairs. "Where are you? I'll come get you."

"Red Carpet Inn I think, near the highway."

"Is your father there?"

"No. He left in the middle of the night and now the manager wants money. I don't have any money, Jazz. I don't have anything. I'm scared."

"Let me talk to the manager. Hand him the phone." Jazz heard a door open, street noise, and a muffled exchange before a man's voice came on the line.

"Yeah?"

"This is Lieutenant Jazz Perry with GPD. Keep that child safe in the office with you until I get there and I might not put your ass in jail for harboring a fugitive, again." She hung up and reached for the front doorknob.

"Stop." Jazz turned, and Mama stood wiping her hands on a dish-cloth with a stern look on her face. "I haven't seen you for more than a few minutes at dinner last night for the past two days and now you're running out to some emergency. I need to know you're okay. What's going on, Jasmine?" Mama stepped closer and opened her arms.

Jazz started to leave, but the pained look in her mother's eyes stopped her and she leaned into the hug. "I'm okay. There are things I want to tell you, but not right now. Shea just called, and she needs my help. We'll talk soon. I promise."

"I love you, Jazz." She kissed her forehead and nudged her toward the door. "Go."

Jazz activated her blue lights and siren, though the run wasn't technically an emergency. She'd gladly take the reprimand if challenged. Her only concern was getting to Shea as quickly as possible and making sure she was unhurt. Worse-case scenarios of what Shea might've endured the past several days flashed through her mind until she skidded to a stop in front of the hotel office.

Shea burst through the office door and ran toward her car. Her eyes were as wide and scared as they'd been the first time Jazz had seen her. Shea's blond hair was greasy, and her long bangs brushed the end of her nose. Jazz flung the car door open and lifted her into a hug. Her clothes stunk of stale cigarette smoke and days of wear. "Are you okay?"

"Good now. Thanks for coming to get me." She clung to Jazz, and tears dampened the side of Jazz's neck.

"You're going to be fine." Jazz pointed to the manager who'd followed Shea outside. "I'll deal with you later."

"But I'm owed money."

"You're owed a trip to jail." She helped Shea into her police car and pulled out of the lot. "What would you like? Anything at all. Name it, and it's yours."

Shea twisted a lock of her long bangs like Jazz did sometimes and grinned. "I'd really like a bath and maybe some food that didn't come out of a bag or a can."

"I know just the place." Jazz called Mama and put her on speaker. "Hey, Mama, I've got Shea in the car, and she's hungry for some good home cooked food."

"And lucky for her, I'm making breakfast."

"Would you call Emory and see if she'll come over?" Jazz could shoot the breeze, be a buddy, or ask police questions, but Emory was trained to get to the difficult issues. Shea had been missing for days, and Jazz wanted to know she hadn't been mistreated or worse and needed medical attention or special care. "My grandmother and mother, we call them G-ma and Mama, make the world's best breakfast. You can take a long bath in my room, and we'll eat together when you're clean again. Deal?"

"You rock, Jazz. I've missed you."

"Me too, pal." She guided Shea into the house, made introductions to G-ma and Mama, and then escorted her upstairs to the bathroom.

As the claw foot tub filled with water, Shea tugged at the hem of her T-shirt and looked around the large room. "What if I splash water?"

"We'll wipe it up." She stamped her foot on the floor. "Tile, practically indestructible. Don't worry about anything. Just relax while I find you something to wear. I'm sure G-ma kept every piece of clothes we ever had."

"As a matter of fact, I did." G-ma laid a stack of clothes on the hamper and said, "Something here should fit. Now, scram, Jazz, and let the girl bathe."

Jazz placed a washcloth and towel on the toilet top and backed toward the door. "If you need anything, yell. I'll be downstairs helping Mama cook up a pound of bacon for you." She started to close the door but stopped. "I'm so glad you're back, Shea."

"Me too. Will you call Mr. and Mrs. Robinson? Will I be able to go back to them?"

"Of course, you will. I'll call right away." Jazz headed toward the kitchen wondering how to cancel the alert for Shea and notify the Robinsons she'd returned without contacting Karen. She tapped out a quick text to Bennett. *See me at Mama's before work.*

A few minutes later, Bennett and Kerstin entered through the back door. "What's up?" Ben asked, and Jazz filled them in on Shea's return and her dilemma.

"I'll take care of Ms. Patrick," Bennett said. "A quick call to USAA will seem routine after the alert is canceled. You don't have to deal with her."

Mama gave them both a sideways glance. "What else is going on? I sense more tension about this Patrick woman. Is she causing problems again?"

Jazz exchanged a look with Bennett and sighed before filling Mama and G-ma in on Karen's attempt to use Emory's hysterectomy as leverage and her recent declaration of love.

"Humph," G-ma huffed. "Don't sound like love to me."

"I wanted us to tell you this together, but things ramped up this morning," Jazz said. "Did you get hold of her?"

"She's on her way," Mama said. "I can't believe this."

G-ma slapped a pack of bacon down on the counter. "Never trust a woman that looks like Karen Patrick. Always got an agenda. Well, she's messing with the wrong family."

"Anything else?" Mama asked. She studied Jazz the way only a mother could.

"I was going to call Emory and see if we could talk about the files she found, but Shea called. Ben, could you—" Jazz stopped when she heard footsteps on the stairs, and Bennett nodded. Shea appeared around the corner a few seconds later.

"Am I in trouble?"

"Why would you ask that?" Jazz asked.

"My dad stopped talking every time I walked into a room. And I was always in trouble."

Mama knelt in front of Shea and hugged her. "The only trouble you have is eating that big plate of bacon and eggs. It's time for the adults to take care of you now."

"Is Ms. Patrick mad with me?"

"Why would she be?" Jazz asked.

"I called her a few times when I was with my dad and told her where I was. She told me to sit tight. I lost your number but kept trying the parts I remembered until I got you."

Jazz grabbed the back of a chair and squeezed. Karen had something else to answer for. She'd lied when Jazz asked specifically if she'd heard from Shea. She'd crossed a hard line this time, and it was enough to get her fired and thrown in jail. She knew the police were desperately searching for Shea, knew her life was in danger, and she'd done nothing, denied knowing where she was. "Don't worry, Shea. I'll take care of Ms. Patrick."

Shea let Mama guide her to a seat at the table, looked across at G-ma, and said, "Thanks for the clothes. They fit good and they're soft. I like 'em."

"Thought you might. They belonged to Jazz when she came to us. Jeans and plaid shirts were always her favorites."

"Not much has changed," Jazz said as she sat next to Shea. "Would it be okay if Ben took you to the Robinsons after breakfast? They're anxious to see you again. I have some work to do, but I'll check on you."

Shea nodded and piled bacon and eggs on her plate. She bit a slice of bacon, groaned, and scooped up a spoonful of eggs. "Mmm, good. Thanks."

Bennett followed Jazz to the front door and said, "I'll ask Shea about her dad on the way to the Robinsons. We need to locate him on the outstanding warrants. And I'll have the tact guys visit the hotel manager. He was told to contact us if Spencer or his drug buddies returned."

"Thanks, Ben." She hugged her sister and her eyes clouded. "I'll call Louis and tell him about Shea and then send him home for the day. He and Denise will be over the moon." She started toward her car, but saw Emory pull up. She walked toward her, debating if she should touch her, afraid she'd never let go.

Emory grabbed her in a hug and held on. "Are you all right, darling?"

She let out a long sigh. "Better now. I wondered if you'd talk to Shea. I'm not taking her back to that Sheri person or Karen, especially after what I just heard. I want somebody I trust to make sure she's...she hasn't been—"

"I know." Emory lowered her arm around Jazz's waist, and they walked toward the house.

"A couple of things you need to know before we go in." Jazz kissed Emory and pulled back breathless. "I told G-ma and Mama about your surgery. It just came out with everything else going on this morning. I wanted us to tell them together, but—"

"It's all right, darling, as long as they know."

"And they're fine with it, with us."

"I never doubted they would be." Emory stroked the side of her face. "What else?"

Jazz told her what Shea said about calling Karen, and her intention to file criminal charges if she could prove it through phone records.

"Unbelievable, just when I thought I couldn't dislike that woman anymore." Emory opened the door and waited for Jazz. "Are you going to sit in while I talk to Shea?"

Jazz nodded. "Not long."

Emory hugged G-ma, Mama, Bennett, and Kerstin, joined them at the table, and struck up a casual conversation with Shea. In a few minutes, they were laughing and talking easily while Jazz marveled at the exchange. Emory thought she wouldn't make a good parent. If she could see herself through Jazz's eyes, she'd know the truth.

"I have to go," Jazz said and gave Shea a fist bump and Emory a quick kiss. "I'll check in later." Emory followed her to the front door and kissed her so deeply Jazz didn't want to leave.

"Shea seems fine on the surface, but I'll dig deeper. Don't worry about her."

"I trust you. I'd never seen you interact with a child before." She cupped Emory's cheek and stared into her beautiful green eyes. "You were great with her."

"Maybe I'm not such awful mother material after all?" Emory gave her a play shove. "Remember that I love you."

"And I love you. Can we get together later? I need to track down some phone calls first." Jazz felt a tangible connection between her and Emory pulling taut as she walked away. She wanted to stay, to start their life together now, but she needed to tie up some loose ends.

"Won't you be at the USAA board meeting this afternoon?"

"Of course. See you there with enough ammunition to bury Karen Patrick."

Chapter Twenty

E mory clenched the straps of her briefcase and refused to make eye contact with Karen sitting on the opposite side of the USAA reception area in a designer suit. Emory unconsciously tugged her sweater tighter and noticed it didn't feel quite as snug as usual. Those spin classes must be paying off. She straightened in her seat and flashed Karen a faux smile. She wanted to confront Karen about so many things—trying to seduce Jazz, accessing her medical files, selling children to the highest bidder, ignoring Shea's cries for help—but Emory's agenda could wait until Henrietta finished with her.

Karen returned a blazing smile, apparently unconcerned by what awaited her behind the conference room doors, but she didn't know Henrietta Goldstein the way Emory did. Henri didn't take prisoners when it came to business or ethics, especially when her family name was involved. Emory could warn Karen what was coming, but before the idea took hold, Karen walked toward her and stood several feet away as if Emory's off-the-rack style might rub off.

"Do you have any idea why I've been summoned to an emergency board meeting and why *you're* here?"

For the first time, Karen looked ruffled, and Emory took more than a little pleasure in her discomfort. "I might."

"Care to share?"

"The way you shared my personal medical information?" Karen's eyes sparked with heat but when she blinked, it dissolved into icy blue. "Some things deserve to unfold in the moment."

"One day very soon, Ms. Blake, you're going to wish—"

The waiting room door opened and Jazz walked in looking gorgeously official in her uniform. She stopped between Emory and Karen. "Am I late?"

"I'm so glad you're here, babe," Karen said, rushing to Jazz's side. She glanced between Jazz and Emory. "Can we have a minute in private before this circus starts?"

Before Jazz could answer, the conference room door opened and Henrietta announced, "We're ready for you." She waved Emory in with a smile and addressed Karen. "All of you." Henrietta preceded Karen in but didn't wait for her to sit. "Come with me, Ms. Patrick."

Karen's gait lacked some of its usual swagger as she followed Henrietta to the front of the room. "What's the purpose of this meeting, Henri?"

"It's Ms. Goldstein, and you're about to find out." She handed Karen a document. "Is this the privatization proposal you presented to the state?"

Karen glanced through the stack of papers. "It is."

From her seat at the back, Emory felt the tension swell in the room. It was like watching a tornado gain strength and she couldn't look away. She wasn't a vengeful person, but Karen deserved whatever Henrietta was about to dish out and more. She waved Jazz over, but she shook her head and remained by the door.

"We've found discrepancies between the figures you cited in the proposal and the ones you presented in your monthly reports to USAA. Can you explain the differences?"

"What's going on here?" Karen asked, giving each member of the board a scathing stare. "I have a right to know if I'm suspected of some wrongdoing."

"You're more than suspected," Henrietta said, "I submit that you've falsified documents, taken unauthorized payments for the placement of children in foster and adoptive homes, and bypassed privacy laws, all in violation of your contract with the US Adoption Agency…and human decency."

"Don't be ridiculous."

"I'm prepared to offer evidence to support every allegation." Henrietta glanced at Emory for confirmation and then did the same to Jazz. When Karen didn't immediately respond, Henrietta continued. "Very well, I call Lieutenant Jazz Perry to address the board on possible criminal charges."

"Stop." Karen's face blanched and she grabbed her throat. "No."

"Or should I start with your HIPPA violation for accessing another person's medical records without permission or legal authority?"

Emory searched Henrietta's face for any indication she was bluffing but saw none. How could she possibly know about that?

"What do you want?" Karen asked through clenched teeth.

The corners of Henrietta's mouth twitched slightly, an involuntary response Emory associated with victory. She'd won without showing her hand.

"I want your signature on this statement of allegations, the return of funds that exceed the set company fees, and your immediate resignation. If you need an account of how much you bilked from our clients, I have the figure down to the last cent."

Karen seemed to consider her options. Her gaze settled on Jazz, and her expression hardened before she asked Henrietta, "Do you intend to pursue criminal charges?"

"I have no such intention as it pertains to the USAA records," Henrietta said.

"And will there be a public announcement or can we handle my resignation discreetly?"

"The agency will issue a media blast, but the content will be contingent on how amicably we settle things here. And before you ask, I've been in touch with the state administrators, and you'll be permanently banned from working with children in North Carolina."

"But it's my liveli—"

"Take it or leave it. I have two press releases." She waved the pages in the air. "You choose which one goes public."

"Fine. I'll resign and leave this backwoods town with pleasure. But trust me, you will all regret the way you treated me today. I'll see to it." She signed the papers Henrietta shoved in her direction and started toward the exit with Jazz right behind her.

"A moment, Ms. Patrick," Jazz said. "I have a warrant for your arrest for child endangerment and falsifying documents." Jazz waved the paper in front of Karen, and she seemed to wilt.

"*What?*"

"Remember Shea Spencer, the young girl who called you begging for help when her drug-dealing father kidnapped her?"

"You can't believe that lying little brat," Karen said.

"I have phone records to support her allegations. Turn around. I need to handcuff you."

Karen turned toward Henrietta. "But you promised no criminal charges."

"About the USAA files, not this. You're a disgrace to the profession."

Jazz handcuffed Karen and escorted her out. The quiet room erupted in cheers and applause, and Henrietta slumped in a chair. Emory was torn between following Jazz or checking on Henrietta. She forced herself to stand, still unsure which way she'd go, but finally decided to help Henrietta. She knelt beside her chair. "Are you okay, Henri?"

"Yes, my dear, just very glad Ms. Patrick didn't make a bigger scene."

"You handled her beautifully, but how did you know about the medical records?"

"You have quite the champion in your corner with Jazz Perry."

Emory squeezed Henrietta's hand and said, "I have two."

Henrietta motioned for quiet and accepted a folder from another board member. "There is one more issue to address before we adjourn." She turned back to Emory. "The board has authorized me to offer you the position as director of the US Adoption Agency. The privatization proposal will pass in a revised form within the year, and we'd like an experienced person we trust at the helm. Your tenacity uncovering this situation and bringing it to our attention has proven you're the right person for the job. I think you'll find our terms more than generous. What do you say?"

"I…really?" She looked around for Jazz. She wanted to consult her partner before deciding an issue that would affect their lives.

"You can take a couple of days to consider the offer if you'd like. Meeting adjourned."

Emory nodded. "Thanks, Henri." She turned to leave, desperate to find Jazz, and bumped into someone. "Sorry."

"Didn't we start out like this, except money was involved," Jazz's teasing sent shivers through Emory.

"Oh, you." She placed her palms against Jazz's chest, connected with the steady beating of her heart, and then gently pushed her away.

"Em? Are you crying?"

"No, of course not. I've just had the best job offer of my life, and you missed it."

Henrietta had been watching them and moved closer. "Why don't you two discuss the offer and let me know in a couple of days." She offered Jazz her hand. "I'm very sorry I didn't do better by you at the time, Ms. Perry. I had to work within a flawed system, but hopefully we're making progress."

"You've more than made up for it," Jazz said. "Thank you for everything."

Emory waited until Henrietta left before taking Jazz's hand and pulling her toward the door. "What happened to Karen?"

"I handed her over to a couple of officers I had on stand-by."

"Good," Emory said. "So, you're free to come with me?"

"Always."

"Good, let's go. And I hope you have civilian clothes in your car."

"I love it when you take charge, Ms. Blake."

"You just wait. If you think I'm being bossy now, you're in for a surprise."

Jazz tried to kiss her, but Emory walked faster. "Will you at least tell me where we're going, Em?"

"My place."

"Perfect."

❖

"I'm sorry—" They said together as soon as Emory's condo door closed behind them.

"You go," Emory said and motioned Jazz to the sofa. "If you want. It's been an emotional day for both of us. Maybe we should—" Jazz kissed her lightly and then deeper, sparking desire.

She waited until Jazz settled on one end of the sofa, and she sat on the other. If she was too close, they'd never talk, just more kissing, and touching, and eventually sex. Maybe not such a bad idea. *Stop it.* Things needed to be said now before the physical made everything seem rosy.

Jazz licked her lips and looked at Emory. "Would you mind if I came a little closer? I talk better when I'm touching you." She held out her hand and waited for Emory's permission.

"All right, just no…fondling until we talk. Okay?"

Jazz 's mouth quirked into a tempting grin, and her eyes twinkled with mischief. "I promise." She scooted over and brought Emory's hand onto her lap. "Do you want me to start?"

Emory nodded.

"I'm sorry I rushed off this morning, but I wanted to get the phone records and the warrant before the board meeting. I feel like it's been hours since we talked or touched." She rubbed her thumbs across Emory's knuckles. "How did the talk with Shea go?"

"Good, she's fine. Nothing serious happened, just little food or sleep for days."

Jazz released a long breath. "Thank God." She inched closer. "I was so proud of you today, Em. You didn't let Karen rattle you and you stood up to her. The evidence you found in the stats got the ball rolling."

"And the criminal charges you filed sealed the deal. My shero." She grinned and gave Jazz an encouraging kiss.

Jazz pulled back just enough to look Emory in the eyes. "Now can we move on to the fun stuff? And maybe talk about us?"

Emory's heart pounded hard, and she fought back tears, unable to fully comprehend that she and Jazz could be together at last. "Are you sure I'll be enough for you?"

"You've always been perfect for me, just the way you are. I just needed a triple tap to get the big picture."

"A what?"

"Triple tap. It's a close-quarters shooting technique. The shooter fires twice into the torso of a target and follows up with a head shot," Jazz said.

"I'm afraid I don't get the rather graphic analogy, darling."

"It's about family. The Carlyles and my family of choice have never been about blood, genes, or DNA, only love and loyalty. But when I met Shea and was reminded of my past and how my life changed, that was the head shot. It finally came together. What I'd known in my heart, suddenly made sense. We make our own family. We chose each other, now we can *choose* if we want children and then *choose* our child." Jazz stared down at their joined hands for a few long seconds and brushed at her eyes.

"That was beautiful and so perfect for us," Emory said.

Jazz kissed Emory lightly, and then reached around her neck and pulled off her necklace. "I want you to have this. It belonged to my mother. She left a note with it that said, 'Two hearts united are stronger than steel.' I believe we are, Em." She placed the necklace on Emory.

She touched the love knot and felt the heat from Jazz's body at her throat. "It's beautiful, Jazz. I'll cherish it always."

"And I'll cherish you, Em. My happily ever after is really happening with the woman of my dreams."

"I love you, Jasmine Perry." Emory stood and reached for Jazz's hand. "I think it's time for the fun stuff now. Take me to bed, darling."

"With pleasure."

THE END

About the Author

A thirty-year veteran of a midsized police department, VK was a police officer by necessity and a writer by desire. Her career spanned numerous positions including beat officer, homicide detective, vice/narcotics lieutenant, captain, and assistant chief of police. Now retired, she devotes her time to writing, traveling, and volunteering.

VK can be reached on Facebook at @vk.powell.12 and Twitter @VKPowell.

Books Available from Bold Strokes Books

A Wish Upon a Star by Jeannie Levig. Erica Cooper has learned to depend on only herself, but when her new neighbor, Leslie Raymond, befriends Erica's special needs daughter, the walls protecting her heart threaten to crumble. (978-1-163555-274-4)

Answering the Call by Ali Vali. Detective Sept Savoie returns to the streets of New Orleans, as do the dead bodies from ritualistic killings, and she does everything in her power to bring them to justice while trying to keep her partner, Keegan Blanchard, safe. (978-1-163555-050-4)

Breaking Down Her Walls by Erin Zak. Could a love worth staying for be the key to breaking down Julia Finch's walls? (978-1-63555-369-7)

Exit Plans for Teenage Freaks by 'Nathan Burgoine. Cole always has a plan—especially for escaping his small-town reputation as "that kid who was kidnapped when he was four"—but when he teleports to a museum, it's time to face facts: it's possible he's a total freak after all. (978-1-163555-098-6)

Friends Without Benefits by Dena Blake. When Dex Putman gets the woman she thought she always wanted, she soon wonders if it's really love after all. (978-1-163555-349-9)

Invalid Evidence by Stevie Mikayne. Private Investigator Jil Kidd is called away to investigate a possible killer whale, just when her partner Jess needs her most. (978-1-163555-307-9)

Pursuit of Happiness by Carsen Taite. When attorney Stevie Palmer's client reveals a scandal that could derail Senator Meredith Mitchell's presidential bid, their chance at love may be collateral damage. (978-1-163555-044-3)

Seascape by Karis Walsh. Marine biologist Tess Hansen returns to Washington's isolated northern coast where she struggles to adjust to small-town living while courting an endowment for her orca research center from Brittany James. (978-1-163555-079-5)

Second in Command by VK Powell. Jazz Perry's life is disrupted and her career jeopardized when she becomes personally involved with the case of an abandoned child and the child's competent but strict social worker, Emory Blake. (978-1-163555-185-3)

Taking Chances by Erin McKenzie. When Valerie Cruz and Paige Wellington clash over what's in the best interest of the children in Valerie's care, the children may be the ones who teach them it's worth taking chances for love. (978-1-163555-209-6)

All of Me by Emily Smith. When chief surgical resident Galen Burgess meets her new intern, Rowan Duncan, she may finally discover that doing what you've always done will only give you what you've always had. (978-1-163555-321-5)

As the Crow Flies by Karen F. Williams. Romance seems to be blooming all around, but problems arise when a restless ghost emerges from the ether to roam the dark corners of this haunting tale. (978-1-163555-285-0)

Both Ways by Ileandra Young. SPEAR agent Danika Karson races to protect the city from a supernatural threat and must rely on the woman she's trained to despise: Rayne, an achingly beautiful vampire. (978-1-163555-298-0)

Calendar Girl by Georgia Beers. Forced to work together, Addison Fairchild and Kate Cooper discover that opposites really do attract. (978-1-163555-333-8)

Lovebirds by Lisa Moreau. Two women from different worlds collide in a small California mountain town, each with a mission that doesn't include falling in love. (978-1-163555-213-3)

Media Darling by Fiona Riley. Can Hollywood bad girl Emerson and reluctant celebrity gossip reporter Hayley work together to make each other's dreams come true? Or will Emerson's secrets ruin not one career, but two? (978-1-163555-278-2)

Stroke of Fate by Renee Roman. Can Sean Moore live up to her reputation and save Jade Rivers from the stalker determined to end Jade's career and, ultimately, her life? (978-1-163555-162-4)

The Rise of the Resistance by Jackie D. The soul of America has been lost for almost a century. A few people may be the difference between a phoenix rising to save the masses or permanent destruction. (978-1-163555-259-1)

The Sex Therapist Next Door by Meghan O'Brien. At the intersection of sex and intimacy, anything is possible. Even love. (978-1-163555-296-6)

Unexpected Lightning by Cass Sellars. Lightning strikes once more when Sydney and Parker fight a dangerous stranger who threatens the peace they both desperately want. (978-1-163555-276-8)

Unforgettable by Elle Spencer. When one night changes a lifetime… Two romance novellas from best-selling author Elle Spencer. (978-1-63555-429-8)

Against All Odds by Kris Bryant, Maggie Cummings, M. Ullrich. Peyton and Tory escaped death once, but will they survive when Bradley's determined to make his kill rate one hundred percent? (978-1-163555-193-8)

Autumn's Light by Aurora Rey. Casual hookups aren't supposed to include romantic dinners and meeting the family. Can Mat Pero see beyond the heartbreak that led her to keep her worlds so separate, and will Graham Connor be waiting if she does? (978-1-163555-272-0)

Breaking the Rules by Larkin Rose. When Virginia and Carmen are thrown together by an embarrassing mistake they find out their stubborn determination isn't so heroic after all. (978-1-163555-261-4)

Broad Awakening by Mickey Brent. In the sequel to *Underwater Vibes*, Hélène and Sylvie find ruts in their road to eternal bliss. (978-1-163555-270-6)

Broken Vows by MJ Williamz. Sister Mary Margaret must reconcile her divided heart or risk losing a love that just might be heaven sent. (978-1-163555-022-1)

Flesh and Gold by Ann Aptaker. Havana, 1952, where art thief and smuggler Cantor Gold dodges gangland bullets and mobsters' schemes while she searches Havana's steamy Red Light district for her kidnapped love. (978-1-163555-153-2)

Isle of Broken Years by Jane Fletcher. Spanish noblewoman Catalina de Valasco is in peril, even before the pirates holding her for ransom sail into seas destined to become known as the Bermuda Triangle. (978-1-163555-175-4)

Love Like This by Melissa Brayden. Hadley Cooper and Spencer Adair set out to take the fashion world by storm. If only they knew their hearts were about to be taken. (978-1-163555-018-4)

Secrets On the Clock by Nicole Disney. Jenna and Danielle love their jobs helping endangered children, but that might not be enough to stop them from breaking the rules by falling in love. (978-1-163555-292-8)

Unexpected Partners by Michelle Larkin. Dr. Chloe Maddox tries desperately to deny her attraction for Detective Dana Blake as they flee from a serial killer who's hunting them both. (978-1-163555-203-4)

A Fighting Chance by T. L. Hayes. Will Lou be able to come to terms with her past to give love a fighting chance? (978-1-163555-257-7)

Chosen by Brey Willows. When the choice is adapt or die, can love save us all? (978-1-163555-110-5)

Death Checks In by David S. Pederson. Despite Heath's promises to Alan to not get involved, Heath can't resist investigating a shopkeeper's murder in Chicago, which dashes their plans for a romantic weekend getaway. (978-1-163555-329-1)

Gnarled Hollow by Charlotte Greene. After they are invited to study a secluded nineteenth-century estate, a former English professor and a group of historians discover that they will have to fight against the unknown if they have any hope of staying alive. (978-1-163555-235-5)

Jacob's Grace by C.P. Rowlands. Captain Tag Becket wants to keep her head down and her past behind her, but her feelings for AJ's second-in-command, Grace Fields, makes keeping secrets next to impossible. (978-1-163555-187-7)

On the Fly by PJ Trebelhorn. Hockey player Courtney Abbott is content with her solitary life until visiting concert violinist Lana Caruso makes her second-guess everything she always thought she wanted. (978-1-163555-255-3)

Passionate Rivals by Radclyffe. Professional rivalry and long-simmering passions create a combustible combination when Emmett McCabe and Sydney Stevens are forced to work together, especially when past attractions won't stay buried. (978-1-163555-231-7)

Proxima Five by Missouri Vaun. When geologist Leah Warren crash-lands on a preindustrial planet and is claimed by its tyrant, Tiago, will clan warrior Keegan's love for Leah give her the strength to defeat him? (978-1-163555-122-8)

Racing Hearts by Dena Blake. When you cross a hot-tempered race car mechanic with a reckless cop, the result can only be spontaneous combustion. (978-1-163555-251-5)

Shadowboxer by Jessica L. Webb. Jordan McAddie is prepared to keep her street kids safe from a dangerous underground protest group, but she isn't prepared for her first love to walk back into her life. (978-1-163555-267-6)

The Tattered Lands by Barbara Ann Wright. As Vandra and Lilani strive to make peace, they slowly fall in love. With mistrust and murder surrounding them, only their faith in each other can keep their plan to save the world from falling apart. (978-1-163555-108-2)

Captive by Donna K. Ford. To escape a human trafficking ring, Greyson Cooper and Olivia Danner become players in a game of deceit and violence. Will their love stand a chance? (978-1-63555-215-7)

Crossing the Line by CF Frizzell. The Mob discovers a nemesis within its ranks, and in the ultimate retaliation, draws Stick McLaughlin from anonymity by threatening everything she holds dear. (978-1-63555-161-7)

Love's Verdict by Carsen Taite. Attorneys Landon Holt and Carly Pachett want the exact same thing: the only open partnership spot at their prestigious criminal defense firm. But will they compromise their careers for love? (978-1-63555-042-9)

Precipice of Doubt by Mardi Alexander & Laurie Eichler. Can Cole Jameson resist her attraction to her boss, veterinarian Jodi Bowman, or will she risk a workplace romance and her heart? (978-1-63555-128-0)

Savage Horizons by CJ Birch. Captain Jordan Kellow's feelings for Lt. Ali Ash have her past and future colliding, setting in motion a series of events that strands her crew in an unknown galaxy thousands of light years from home. (978-1-63555-250-8)

Secrets of the Last Castle by A. Rose Mathieu. When Elizabeth Campbell represents a young man accused of murdering an elderly woman, her investigation leads to an abandoned plantation that reveals many dark Southern secrets. (978-1-63555-240-9)

Take Your Time by VK Powell. A neurotic parrot brings police officer Grace Booker and temporary veterinarian Dr. Dani Wingate together in the tiny town of Pine Cone, but their unexpected attraction keeps the sparks flying. (978-1-63555-130-3)

The Last Seduction by Ronica Black. When you allow true love to elude you once and you desperately regret it, are you brave enough to grab it when it comes around again? (978-1-63555-211-9)

The Shape of You by Georgia Beers. Rebecca McCall doesn't play it safe, but when sexy Spencer Thompson joins her workout class, their non-stop sparring forces her to face her ultimate challenge—a chance at love. (978-1-63555-217-1)